D0165379

Published by:
Grand Mal Press
Forestdale, MA
www.grandmalpress.com

ISBN 13 digit: 978-1-937727-25-3
ISBN 10 digit: 1-937727-25-4

Library of Congress Cataloging-in-Publication Data
Grand Mal Press/Johns, Clifford Royal

p. cm

Cover art by Stephen Bryant
www.srbproductions.net

FIRST EDITION

PRAISE FOR *WALKING SHADOW*

"In WALKING SHADOW, his accomplished first novel, Clifford Royal Johns spins the amnesia plot like a top. As the mysteries twirl, hit men, cops, reporters, and a variety of low-lifes and no-lifes haunt Benjamin Khan, an unlikely hero with enough secrets to fill a trilogy. With a sly sense of humor and a flair for oddball characterization, Johns has crafted a cross-genre debut that will please fans of both science fiction and crime fiction."
—- James Patrick Kelly, winner of the Hugo, Nebula and Locus awards.

"Here's a fascinating twist on the murder mystery. Benny is addicted to forgets, but now his life depends on remembering what he forgot about the judge's killing. In a warped future Chicago, he has to thread his way though a maze of double and triple-crosses, with crooked cops and underground criminals all out to get him. What really makes it memorable is Benny's unique voice, a wry and witty tone of noir".
— Lois Tilton, short fiction reviewer for *Locus Magazine*

"Johns' novel entertains while asking big questions—how much can you forget and still be you? And how much would you be willing to forget to be someone else? Fun and full of ideas."
— Maureen F. McHugh, Hugo Award-winning author of *After the Apocalypse.*

"In a cross between Raymond Chandler and Philip K Dick, Johns expertly explores themes of identity and morality. He has built a splendid dystopian Chicago—not quite what we know— in this thrilling noir speculation. As his protagonist weaves his way through his own past and an askew future Chicago, the reader must untangle this wicked and intricate plot."
— Paulo Melko, author of *The Walls of the Universe* and *Broken Universe*

WALKING SHADOW

a novel

by Clifford Royal Johns

Chapter 1

I knew I'd had some memories removed. I could tell because the removal company sent me payment-overdue notices every week.

I had just received another such bill, and this one was especially demanding, implying some unspecified action would be taken to recover their funds if I didn't pay immediately.

I wondered what memories I'd had removed. Had I killed someone? Had I seen some grisly death, or had an astoundingly bad breakup? Had a doctor told me I had only three months left to live? Forgetting was a drastic response to a dramatic event. What was my dramatic event? I lay in bed in my tiny apartment, staring at the ceiling and reviewing my history, trying to find the holes. It was sort of like trying to discover the hiding place of a needle in a haystack after I'd paid to have the needle removed.

When my PAL said, "Hey, it's eleven-thirty," I shook off speculation about my past, rolled out of bed and dressed to go meet my brother Arno at Socko's restaurant. I had lunch with him every Wednesday at noon.

I didn't have a car and the buses just didn't go that way. My brother did have a car, but refused to drive over to my part of town. He worried that the neighborhood kids who would promise to protect his brand new Moto-400 for a little pocket change, would instead strip it of everything and leave just the trackerID chip and the front axle lying in the parking space. I walked.

On the way out of my apartment building, I said hello to the doorman, a crusty, gray bum wearing two overcoats and three hats piled on top of each other. That day the hat on top was a once-white knit with a pompom dangling from one thread. He sat huddled against the entry way, out of the wind. It was his real estate. No one else ever sat there. He looked back at me, but didn't move. I wasn't one of his patrons.

It was a cold, gritty day in Chicago, much like the day before. Dark-bellied clouds lumbered past overhead, threatening a numbing fall rain. I shuffled south on LaSally Street, my jacket collar turned up to the wind, my thoughts turned inward to my memories.

As I walked along Diversity, dodging the land traffic, and closing my eyes against the dirt storm whenever a buzzcar lurched by overhead, I thought again about the bill I'd received the evening before. Forget What had sent me bills every week for the last month. According to them, I'd payed two thousand in bad money to "remove a memory or series of related memories," but I couldn't remember.

Of course, I hadn't seen money like that in years, and if I had, I sure wouldn't have wasted it on a forget. I would have spent it on something tangible; something that would have been repossessed if I left a bad money trail. Forget What couldn't reinstall a forgotten memory. Service had already been rendered.

The letters referred to me as Sir, but the computer that generated the impersonal mail really meant deadbeat; I could tell. I could feel the smirk embedded in each one.

OK, so I blinked them. I blinked lots of people. Most didn't bother to complain because they didn't want to admit they'd been taken, or because their accounting was so bad, they didn't even realize they were out any money. Forget What didn't seem to be willing to forgive or forget. They actually wanted their money. But if I'd paid in real money, they wouldn't have bothered me, and I would never have known I'd had any memories removed.

I crossed Hacker Drive and ducked into the Sliver Building. The real name of the building was The Silver Exchange, but no one called anything by its right name anymore. The Sliver looked like a Bowie knife sticking up out of the ground, as though someone inside the earth was trying to cut his way out. I went in through the 4G delivery entrance in the hilt, where the couriers delivered packages. Going immediately through a door to the left into the dock area avoided the security guard. I said, "Hey," to a flat-faced blonde girl as though I knew her and strode through the piles of pallets and boxes, scanning for a small box I could take with me. I didn't see anything sufficiently portable, so I slipped through into the catering area, then into the atrium and out onto Crackson. It was a useful shortcut and the more I used it, the less likely anyone was to notice I wasn't supposed to be there. I also avoided the overhead transit stop where police tended to loiter.

People pay to forget stuff that traumatizes them; memories that haunt them, that pull at their lives and bend the flow; memories they don't want to deal with in an honest way. Like Wilde said, "No man is rich enough to buy back his past," but now, at least, people who had the money could pay to forget what they had done. Walk in an emotional wreck. Walk out a new person. Consciences cleaned while you wait. If you were rich, you could be happy. You could steal, cheat and bribe your way to wealth, then forget everything you did to get your money, forget everyone you ruined, forget everyone you took advantage of. Forgetting is better than a priest giving you some penance and telling you everything is forgiven. Forgetting is true absolution; the guilt is surgically removed.

Socko's was one of those small, steamy, mostly takeout places that has astonishingly good food served on flimsy plastic. The padded vinyl seats were as old as the building and just as hard. The people there treated you like they were doing you a favor by allowing you to eat there. I ate there a lot.

Arno was at a corner table facing the entrance. He waved as I pushed through the revolving door, but then went back to reading the paper he had tucked above his plate. I stood in line behind a woman with no hair and two kids, then ordered a beandog, asparagus sticks and a citrus from a thin man with no eyebrows who wore a magenta plastic hat. I hadn't seen him there before. He had a tattoo of a beard on his chin and wore a Socko's shirt. "Say," I said, "do you have hair tattooed under that hat?"

He tipped his hat to me. There was another hat tattooed on his head. It looked like a bowler. It was blue. "One for every occasion," he said. His blue tattoo turned orange then violet as he turned to get my order.

When his head turned blue again I took my beandog and joined Arno.

"You're late."

"Hello, Arno."

"What were you doing this morning?"

Arno was like that. He seemed to think that just because I was late, I must have had something better to do, but the walk was twenty-five minutes, and it usually varied by five or so. I ignored his question.

"I got a bill from a forget company," I said, thinking to change the subject as quickly as I could. "They say I owe them for a forget."

"And you blinked them, right?"

"I guess so. I honestly don't remember. Do you know what I forgot? I must have talked to you about it before I had the memories removed. What was my pain?"

"I dunno," he said. "You don't talk to me about that stuff." He quickly went back to reading his paper, but I had the feeling he knew and wouldn't tell me.

My brother was tall, with thick black hair, and he worked out, though at his house I'd only ever seen him sitting on the machines, not pushing or pulling or lifting, but that's enough for guys like him. He looked fit and healthy, well fed, but not loose. His hands were steady and muscular. We didn't look at all alike. I was just a little shorter, but had sandy hair and a thin wiry build. The only reason I was physically fit was that I had to walk everywhere.

"But didn't I talk to you about it at all?"

"Don't think so."

"Would you remember if I had?"

He stopped eating and stared at me for a moment. Doubtless this was the very look he gave his employees that would make them work overtime without pay. "Probably not," he said. "You so seldom say anything of interest."

That's all I could get out of him. He folded his paper and started talking about what kind of job I should be looking for, and how I should think about my future and not my past. While he talked, I considered Forget What and decided I should go to the removal place and talk them into telling me what I'd forgotten. I think I said, "Uh huh," a few times and I kept my eyes trained on his right eye, so he'd think I was taking him seriously. Meanwhile, I chewed on my asparagus sticks and my thoughts.

The forget companies were secretive about how they did forgets. It wasn't something that had been exposed by the press, but there were a lot of rumors about it. I'd heard that to remove a memory, they evoke the memory, which is usually so terrible that it gets you all worked up, then they scan your brain looking for spots of high activity other than the places that were active in similar memory recalls. When they find the spots that are unique to this memory, they insert a long thin wire with a small loop on the end, then they spin it, scrambling up your brain at those spots, and you forget. That's how they used to do lobotomies: they would insert the wire up under your eyelid and mush your frontal lobe. The more expensive forget companies used lasers or crossing sonic beams or something, but I have to admit I was too cheap for that, even when I used fake accounts.

When Arno finished eating he said, "I've never understood why you would pay to forget a part of your life. It's like paying to become someone else. It's pretty close to death if you ask me. It's not as though you get to go back and try the forgotten event over again. Part of you is just gone. You just come out a different person." He looked at me hard, like he expected me to say something.

I swallowed the last bit of beandog and leaned back. "I really don't remember doing it, Arno."

"Benny, maybe this is your chance to change yourself. Obviously you did something so abhorrent you couldn't stand yourself and you had to change your past to reflect your own self-image, but you're really not that nice a person. You've got no job, no woman, no friends. You live by the dole, Benny. Bums live by the dole. Idiots and nuts. You're not stupid, and you're not fundamentally lazy. I know jobs are hard to get, but you could at least try." He sat back, apparently exasperated, yet I sensed an inside joke. I had a feeling he'd given this exact speech to me before, but I wasn't sure of it. Somehow, he found me amusing and that irritated me more than his boring lectures.

In any case, I couldn't figure out why my lack of a job bothered him so much. I never asked to stay with him and his wife. I didn't ask him for money. I wasn't a mooch. I thought he viewed me as a tarnished spot on his shiny public image, a pit in his chrome, but I couldn't see how I was holding him back. And, anyway, I considered myself retired. I really didn't want to work. I'd just waste the money on a few gadgets or some real food.

"Maybe I could be a car thief," I said.

"Maybe you could be a little more serious." Arno was a real brass pipe.

"All right, maybe I could be a buzzcar thief."

Arno was annoyed, but he smiled anyway.

"OK," I said, "who would give me a job, Arno? Like you say, I don't know anyone important, and certainly not anyone important enough to have control over hiring. I know a few people who could get me a job stealing stuff or selling stolen stuff, but real business types? Suits? If I came to you and you were a hiring manager, would you hire me?"

"I've hired you before, Benny," Arno said, looking at his watch. "I've got to meet somebody in ten minutes, but think about what I said and try to remember what you're good at. When you do, come see me."

I couldn't remember being especially good at anything in particular, and I couldn't remember working for Arno. It seemed like a bad idea to work for family. They would think they were doing you a favor and they would expect something in return; something more than just a day's work. And you couldn't quit because they had spent this effort on you, and they would think you had quit them, not the work. I didn't think Arno would take kindly to me quitting on him.

When Arno stood, I noticed he had a bit of green chili sauce on his white shirt. I didn't mention it. I ate my last stick and left.

When I returned home I looked at the bill again. The removal company had included a netdeposit address, but no street address, and, of course, I couldn't remember which Forget What clinic I'd gone to. There were over a hundred facilities in Chicago, seven or eight within easy walking distance. I probably went to one of the closer ones, but there was no way to know, and none of the people at the clinics would be willing to admit to being the source of my problem.

I sat down at my table and wondered if I'd actually had any memories removed at all. How would I know? I didn't remember having any memories removed, but the letter that came with the bill said I wasn't supposed to remember anything about the removal session, that's why they could guarantee it. They give you careful instructions on how to pay them, so you don't notice the debit later. They short-circuit your short-term memory and put you out on the street. You don't even remember having the procedure, so you don't go looking to find out what it was you forgot. But, apparently I'd given them a false netdeposit path and the money was later removed from their account. You're supposed to pay in advance for obvious reasons, but they claimed I'd cheated them.

Which I could believe. I could see myself doing that. I'd figure, hey, what could they do? It's not like I actually had that much money, or even the likelihood of getting that much money. I was on the dole and likely to stay that way. I was retired at thirty-one. I was a free man.

The forget still nagged at me, though, and I realized I just couldn't stand it. It was a tickle, and I knew it would soon be a ferocious itch.

So why be so stupid as to go looking to remember something I'd worked so hard to forget? Because I'd felt empty of late, passionless and listless. I went to the dole every week, had lunch with my brother, bought groceries, slept, pilfered when I needed to, worked odd jobs once in a while. I was walking along through my life without really thinking about it because I'd thought my life had always been that dull.

But Forget What kept reminding me that before September there had been something more, and I'd purposefully removed it. Whatever I'd forgotten had left a bigger hole than I must have expected it to. I stared at the wall, trying to remember, though I knew I wouldn't be able to.

I heard the vator doors open and close. The PAL in the next apartment played old Russian piano music. A pigeon landed on my windowsill high above my bed. I wrote "Dust me" on the wall with my finger.

I decided to let the issue slip for a while, figuring that if, back in September, I'd wanted to forget, I should trust my own decision. So, I tried to avoid thinking about it. I tried to imagine the forget never happened; that Forget What was actually blinking me; that I was the victim.

I watched some avatar fighting. The sport wasn't what it used to be. The teams were allowed to put too much artificial intelligence into the avatars, so the people controlling them were no longer hired for their ability to fight in the virtual world, but more and more as entertainment for the audience before and after the match. They were sharp, pretty people instead of the tough, real fighters who had competed before. The whole sport had turned slick.

The forget-the-forget strategy wasn't working. While I was in the bathroom trying to review my past and spot the hole in my memories, my PAL beeped at me. I yelled to it to read the mail out loud.

The message came from Forget What. They said they had completed a review of my account and decided that if I didn't pay up within three days, they would inform the police about the memory they'd deleted for me.

The police? My heart stopped while a list of hiding places shot through my mind. What kind of memory had I had removed that would interest the police?

Chapter 2

The police are OK if you're clean and working. But, for the rest of us, the legal system is quick to use the memory lasers based on a psychologist's recommendation about which childhood memories caused your current criminal schtick. They can wipe your whole childhood, wipe your memories of committing crimes and wipe your memories of friends and associates they believe might be harmful to your future. It saved them a lot of money they would have had to spend on jails. Since I couldn't remember what schtick I forgot, I expected that, if they caught me and convicted me of something, they might turn all my memories into pâté just to make the public safe.

I hunted down the first bill Forget What had sent me, looked at its date, subtracted a day, maybe two, for them to figure out I'd blinked them and decided that whatever I'd done, I probably did it before September tenth. Thinking back, I couldn't remember much from that time even though it was only a month or so earlier. Late summer, early fall tended to merge into one continuous highway. A few events stuck out; the eight-day rain, the day the fire melted Jummy's, the day I spent with Jolie. But, for the most part, there weren't many lumps in the pavement.

I printed a copy of the last bill, put it in my pocket and went to Reborn Street to see Chen. I remembered being on Quacker Street with Chen on the eighth. I knew it was the eighth because I'd had to go to a gov clinic and get my finger bandaged that night.

Chen was the only person I knew who I thought might do something while I was with him that I'd want to forget all about. He's an ass-thatcher for fun. He comes up behind a guy and lasers his ass with a preprogrammed laser etcher. He just pops it out of his pocket, focuses the targeting beam on the middle of the crack of the guy's ass and ticks it. The laser flashes around the guy's ass for about a tenth of a second, and then there's a lot of screaming and hopping up and down. I laughed thinking about it, then realized I would never purposely forget something as funny as that. I felt a pulse of guilt about the thatching, but Chen was good at picking out the most pretentious and pompous men from the crowd. Then I imagined the hospital write up, "Removed intricate drawing of Tweezy the Bumblebee from guy's ass." Tweezy. Chen was a whirl.

Reborn Street is near the Rocky Roads Expressway, right where it enters the new Chicago Automated Transit switching tunnel; about a fifteen-minute walk. The noise from the CAT trains there was thunderous, but the rents were low. Chen had a flat in the old United Nations World Police building, now called the Unapartments. It was all concrete with high narrow windows, and two large restaurants flanking the entrance like a pair of brown shoes poking out from under a ground-length, concrete trench coat. They had painted the building blue in hopes of making it look less institutional and less military. It helped a little. A painting of a twenty foot, twirling, kick-boxing bear in boxer shorts and sunglasses worked better, but the owners had painted over that not long after the artist created it. I still missed the bear. He'd always made me smile.

You never walked straight to Chen's. He had some odd rules. I took the vator up to seven and over to cross thirty-two. Side slide vators make me woozy, but it only lasted a minute. I walked slowly back down two flights of stairs to Chen's door.

Chen wasn't there, but Paulo let me in. "He'll be back in a tick," Paulo said. He winked at me, just like Chen always did, but I didn't wink back. "How 'bout you come in and sit? Wait for him. Like a derpal?"

"No, thanks," I said and took a chair in the music room.

Paulo was a small, no-fat guy who moved in short staccato bursts like a helper bot, but without a bot's focus or clear intent. My name for him was Brownian Motion. He wore an apron, presumably with something else on underneath, though that wasn't obvious. The apron showed two bibbed lobsters holding skewers and grinning. Grinning lobsters. Grinning lunch. Might as well have a smiling cow flipping real-beef hamburgers.

I sat in the music room and stared at the painting of Lena Horn which Chen had paid an out-of-work artist to paint on his carsicord. He never learned to play the thing, but he liked Lena, so he kept the instrument pushed backward up against the wall to display the painting. Chen liked to listen to her old recordings, and I'd acquired a taste for them as well.

Paulo was in the kitchen making dinner and noise. The apartment smelled like ginger and tomato sauce.

"Hey Paulo, you got any beer?" I yelled.

"Nah, just derpal."

I didn't drink derpal. I hadn't acquired the taste, and since it's illegal, I didn't want to. In any case, I didn't want that much bliss from a bottle.

Paulo stuck his head around the corner. "What brings you over here?"

"I got this bill from Forget What, and I wanted to talk to Chen about it. They're getting cranky."

"Oh!" Paulo ducked back into the kitchen. I heard some frantic stirring, metal on metal, then he yelled, "He should be back soon."

Beside the carsicord, I noticed a new decoration. It appeared to be a regular aquarium at first, but the fish turned out to be engineered to look like tiny people swimming around in the flow from the water pump. Their little faces looked frantic, as though they needed air, though of course they didn't. They came up to the glass begging me for something, but I didn't know what.

Chen came home then. He stopped by the kitchen to kiss Paulo and get a derpal, then walked into the music room. "What are you doing here, Benny?" Chen said warily.

Chen was a little shorter than me, and just as thin, usually. He had straight dark hair that day and a wide belligerent nose, which didn't match his close-set eyes. He must have been wearing padding around his waist, because he looked a bit chunkier than usual. He walked with a swagger that was so dramatic it looked a bit silly.

"Yeah, it's good to see you too," I said. "Maybe I should just go." I stood up, but didn't start walking.

"Oh relax, Benny. Why are you so touchy? You got so many new friends now, you can afford to walk out on your old ones?"

"What did we do the last time I was with you?" I asked, sitting down again.

"I'd prefer to forget all that. At least I will if you will. I bought a new gun. Want to see it?" He pulled what looked like a kid's spaceblaster out of his coat pocket, handed it to me, then went to hang up his coat.

The gun was real enough. I'd expected a slap gun, one that shot what amounted to a slapfaint which made the victim faint and stay out for an hour or so. I popped the clip. It had room for fifteen bullets, but contained only three.

Chen came back. "What do you think? Doesn't it look famous? Just like a toy. I could walk down the street with that in my hand and no one would take notice. You want a derpal?"

"No, thanks, and they would notice, Chen. The police know about these, although they're usually green rather than yellow. Green's a bit more subtle"

He looked around the room thoughtfully. "Where should I keep it?"

I told him that if he was worried about intruders, he should hide it in the bedroom somewhere. If he was worried about guests, he should put it at hand next to where he usually sat.

He sat down, then slid the gun into the drawer of his side table. Bright yellow, goofy looking plastic body wrapped around a businesslike gun. Very Chen.

"So, what did we do the last time I was with you?" I asked again. "I mean other than the fist fight. After that. Did I leave right after that?"

Chen was still looking at the drawer smiling. He liked his new toy. He sighed and looked at Lena as though for guidance. "Yeah. Fist fight. Beating you mean. You were pretty mad about me thatching part of your finger. It wasn't my fault. You moved."

"I know, but did we do anything together after that?"

"No. You ran off saying you had to go to the hospital. I haven't seen you since. It was just a nick." Chen stood, paused for a moment, then walked over and put on some low music; Lena singing, "I Gotta Right to Sing the Blues".

I pulled the Forget What bill out of my pocket and showed it to him. "I've been getting these letters from Forget What. They say I had a memory removed, but I don't remember it. They say if I don't deposit the money, they're going to tell the police about the contents of the memory I had removed." I watched him for a reaction.

"I wouldn't worry," said Chen, looking a bit worried. "Maybe you never had a memory removed. Maybe they're just blinking you. Could be they always do this when they're low on trade. Gov isn't real happy about the commercial forgetters anyway. The Senate is trying to pass a law that would require the police to attend every forget and have the forgetter pay for their time and expenses. And anyway, the fact that you've had something forgotten isn't admissible evidence. There's no telling what you forgot. Of course, it might be admissible if the forgetters kept records, maybe even video, of the whole thing."

"Can they do that? I thought it was confidential, like talking to a priest or something." I watched a little fish person get temporarily sucked down against the gravel bottom of the tank where the pump intake was.

"I don't remember hearing about the use of forget information at a trial before, but they probably keep that kind of thing quiet. What did the contract you signed say?"

"Contract?" I couldn't remember my session, so of course I couldn't remember a contract.

"I bet they record all the sessions." Chen said, sighing back into his chair. "They replay the removal session in court, then what?"

"Yeah," I said. "Then what?" I looked at my feet. Chen wasn't helping at all.

Chen yelled, "Hey, Paulo?"

Paulo danced into the room waving a large spoon. "Doesn't Carla work for Forget What?" Chen said, with an odd leer. "She could probably get a transcript of Benny's last forget session, right?"

Paulo glared at Chen like he had said something tactless. He lowered his spoon. "Yes, yes she does," said Paulo stiffly, "but I don't think she can help with that. She's a busy person."

Chen winked at him. "Sure she can." He turned to me and added, "Paulo will give her a call later."

Paulo wasn't happy with the idea, and I can't say I was overwhelmed either. Chen's friends generally weren't reliable, but I couldn't pass up the angle. Especially since friends usually work for free.

Paulo abruptly retreated to the kitchen. Chen smiled at me and took a long swig of his derpal. "Hey, you want to go over to Quacker tonight? Jon Tam built me a new thatcher. It cuts a picture of a rabbit diving down the victim's asshole."

Chen started laughing and couldn't stop. That started me laughing.

I couldn't even imagine what that hospital write-up would say. "Sure," I said, "just keep that thing pointed away from me."

Chen laughed hard enough to snort and started wheezing. He had to rip off his fat fake nose to get more air. He held it in his fist with the tip jutting out between his index finger and his middle finger. "I've got your nose," he said, then rolled onto the floor with tears in his eyes unable to speak.

Whatever Chen did for money, I figured it must be stressful.

Chapter 3

Paulo's friend Carla from Forget What wanted dinner. Not all friends work for free, but the cost of a dinner would be close enough. She chose an expensive restaurant.

I was to meet her at Beef Tucuman, which was once an Argentinian style restaurant, but now they specialized in any cuisine that contained real beef. The restaurant took up the right half of the first floor of a marble faced office building on Bigbash just north of the Coop, the old business district in Chicago. The front facade was simple and deceptive with a short blue awning and a doorman who wore a long red coat and a sneer. A small brass plaque bolted to the marble just to the right of the door was the only indication that this was the entrance to a restaurant. If you were just wandering down the street hungry and looking for a place to eat, they didn't want your business.

I strode purposefully past an end-of-the-earth guy who was hauling a huge wooden cross strapped to his back. Even if the wooden beams were hollow, it had to be heavy. He looked haggard and cold, wearing only carefully tattered pants and a tee shirt with a hole ripped in the side. He was handing out red fliers to anyone who would approach close enough to take one, "What You Need to Know About the Apocalypse!" I didn't think I really needed to know any more.

The doorman glared at the spectacle with intense concentration, apparently hoping he could will him away. He glanced briefly at me as I ducked past him and through the door. Had I moved more slowly, or had he not been distracted by the cross, I felt sure he would have turned me away. I wasn't dressed for the place.

Inside, I saw a woman who I assumed to be Carla posing in a large wing-back chair. Her slender wrists draped with apparent ease over the arms of the chair, fingers dangling and her long legs crossed under a navy dress that had a cream collar and belt. She wore her short dark hair as though she were looking into the wind, back and curled away from her face, which displayed her small perfect ears and clear gray eyes. Her expression conveyed displeasure, perhaps at my being late, but I thought rather it was to show the restaurant personnel that she meant to stay there without being badgered.

All this would have given the impression of money and the expected servitude of others, except that, as her crossed-over foot jumped up and down with impatience, I saw that her shoe was so worn through, it displayed part of her big toe.

I liked her immediately, which was odd because I didn't think she was my type. I usually preferred smiling, carefree women who didn't much care what others thought, but Carla was an odd combination, and her type wasn't especially obvious on first glance.

She noticed me, finally.

"Hello," I said, "I guess you must be Carla. I'm Benny. I hope you haven't been waiting long."

She gave me an appraising look, a brief smile, then stood, not saying anything.

I snagged the maître d's attention and held up two fingers. He glared, and sighed, then strutted into the dining area. I followed Carla, who followed the maître d'. She appeared to be fancifully imitating the maître d's walk, shoulders back and head held high in dramatic disapproval. She was fun to watch.

He led us past a field of empty tables all the way to the back near the station where they fill the water glasses and make the coffee. I could hear the clatter of dishes in the kitchen, but I wasn't there to talk.

"So, do you have my transcript?" I said as soon as we'd sat down.

"Yes, but that will wait till after dinner, I think." She had a smooth low voice, not husky, but mellow. It was clear she didn't trust me, which I could understand. She only knew me as a friend of Chen's, and that was no character recommendation.

"Sure," I said as I took the menu the waiter handed me.

The tables were covered with starched white tablecloths reaching most of the way to the floor and the maroon napkins had been folded into the shape of a bird. The pats of butter on each table were formed into tiny fish and set in a bowl of ice. The silverware, three forks, two knives, and two spoons, one set sideways above the plate, were set in exactly the same position around each plate. The plate would never be used for actual eating. It would be taken away and replaced with other dishes. Each table was set exactly the same. It sat a uniform distance from the next table, in a carefully arranged display of perfection. I imagined the head waiter going around like a drill sergeant after beds were made up, "You! Those two spoons are touching. Drop and give me twenty."

I said, "I haven't been here before. It looks pretty nice in an institutional sort of way."

She smiled a tight-lipped smile. She was more nervous than I'd thought she'd be. Something bothered her. I guessed it was the fact that she was stealing and reselling her employer's property, albeit for just a good dinner. "You seem familiar to me," she said. "Do you use the grocery at Quacker and Morph?"

"No, I live too far from there. I might have stopped in for a bottle of citrus or something. I think I would remember if I saw you there, though." I believe I grinned at her like some kind of letch, but she didn't take it that way. She had a smile that went on like a light bulb, bright and instant.

Regrettably, her smile went off like a light too. I missed it as soon as it was gone. Her voice, her hair, her very presence, seemed familiar to me as well, though I couldn't place why. It was just a feeling I got. I felt comfortable with her.

I quit grinning when the waiter stepped up beside the table, and I ordered a broiled butt steak, well done, aloo gobi, and a glass of real orange juice. Another waiter hustled by with a tray, leaving a trail of steam. I tilted my head back slightly, closed my eyes for a moment and drew in a breath slowly through my nose. Restaurants like this one were to be enjoyed at many levels.

Carla stared at the waiter with a—why didn't you take my order first—look. "What kind of beef cattle is your prime rib?"

"I wouldn't know," the waiter replied with a sigh and a look down at her still bouncing foot, which was picking up the drape of the table cloth and tossing it up and down.

"Well, you can stand there and wait for an inspiration."

"Yes, ma'am." He stalked off and began talking to the maître d'.

Carla gave me a knowing look and raised her left eyebrow. Her expression jarred me with an intense sense of déjà vu. I thought that someone I'd seen before had that same cast of countenance; perhaps an actress or a previous girlfriend.

The waiter stepped back up to the table. "The prime rib is from Japanese Wagyu cattle, ma'am."

"Oh, fine," she said in such a way as to strongly imply that the waiter could find a more appropriate job at a beandog emporium, and that Wagyu beef was well below her usual standard, but that it would have to do. She paused for a moment, looking at the ceiling, apparently praying for the strength to order food from such an amateur. "I'll have the prime rib, lightly peppered, rare to medium rare, a baked potato with sour cream, green beans with freshly cooked bacon, crumbled, and pearl onions, but I'd like the onions on the side. I'd like your house dressing, but mixed half with ranch. I like my dressings with a red tint. Oh, and a King Louis cognac." It was an old-fashioned dinner, but conservative choices seemed to fit the Beef Tucuman. I avoided running a tab in my head. I would have run out of fingers and toes just counting up my own part of the bill.

The waiter, who didn't have any apparent way to record our requests, began to squint halfway through her order and had his mouth hanging open in concentration by the end. He walked off, still concentrating, into the kitchen where I was sure he promptly wrote the whole thing down. It wasn't that complicated of an order, but I figured he must be new or he'd have known the breed of cattle.

"I thought cognac was an after-dinner drink," I said.

"Oh, well then I'll have to have one after dinner as well. With my dessert, perhaps."

"Perhaps," I said, resisting the urge to pull out my swipe cards to make sure I had enough fake money in them to cover Carla's tastes. My cards didn't have the amount displayed on the outside anyway. How much was really on them was a mystery even to me. It had taken months of careful experimentation, but I'd figured out how to modify the amount by some random quantity by putting them in the oven with a magnet on top and the temperature set at a hundred C, but it destroyed the display. I hoped that the three empty cards I had found and baked that morning would cover the meal.

I tried not to look nervous while I glanced around to find the emergency exit, just in case the cards wouldn't cover the bill. "How long have you worked for Forget What?"

"Three years," she said too quickly. "What do you do?"

"Retired."

She leaned back in her chair so the waiter could place the cognac in front of her. When he was gone, she said, "You're a little young to be retired, aren't you? Or are you just well-preserved? I've heard they can do that now." She was teasing me. I assumed Paulo told her enough about me for her to know I was on the dole.

"No more preserved than a beer now and then will make you," I said. "Were you in on my session? Did you watch?"

"I'm in marketing. I don't know anything about the actual forgetting stuff. I just know a few of the people who do it."

She tilted her head to the right, leaned forward, and clasped her hands together on the table. "If you're retired," she said, "what do you do in your spare time? Or, I guess it's all spare, isn't it?"

She wasn't really interested. Leaning forward and acting attentive was a ruse. When people are actually listening and interested they aren't that obvious about it. You can always tell when someone is faking by how perfectly they portray the part. A drunk will act so elaborately normal that his drunkenness is obvious to everyone.

I could take a hint. I said, "Maybe all my time is spare time, but that doesn't make it any less valuable."

Carla didn't want the conversation to be about her. I figured she just wanted to get her meal, so I waited quietly for the food while I looked around the restaurant. The walls were adorned with paintings of bowls of fruit, vases of flowers and somber gold-shaded portraits of frowning people staring down at us under the tasteful pink-cast light—still-lifes and lifeless stills. The two people at the next table over were having some kind of Mongolian beef dish that contained big lumps of fat. They were both enormous men in dark suits. They were sharing a bottle of vodka and were talking loudly in some language that seemed to be composed entirely of "s" and "sh" sounds.

Carla kept glancing at me. She seemed to expect me to say more, but I'd decided I wasn't going to blab on about inconsequential things. I didn't want to become inconsequential by association.

I found Carla's attitude a little annoying, but in a pleasant, familiar sort of way, like an old friend whose customary habits irritate you more and more as your friendship grows. It's interesting that those very same habits are what you miss about the person when they're gone.

"I'm sorry," she said. "I didn't mean to ridicule. I'm just a little anxious—and hungry. Can we try again?"

"Sure," I said. I looked over the edge of the table and down at her foot which was still waving the tablecloth up and down. I could feel the breeze on my legs. "Are those your dancing shoes?"

She looked down. Her foot stopped kicking. "Okay, I deserved that."

"I like your earrings. They accent your ears," I said.

"Oh, that's so much better. And I think your forehead makes you look smart. It's just the right size. It goes all the way down to your eyebrows."

The waiter brought the salads. Carla found a smudge on the salad fork and made him take it back. "He'll probably lick off the dirt and hand the same one back in a minute," she said, leaning forward and observing him carefully. We watched him together as he stared at the fork for a moment, presumably not believing there could actually be a smudge on it, then he dropped it in a plastic bus tray and picked up another. As he turned to come back to the table, Carla and I looked at each other and shrugged in unison, then laughed as co-conspirators.

She pointed behind me to a portrait of a gray haired man in a brown suit whose pinched visage regarded us disdainfully. "We shouldn't be having fun in front of him, should we? I think he might not have had any fun in his entire life." She pushed out her lower lip a little and tilted her head down and to the left, then she slowly lifted her gaze up to look at me; pouting, bashful, and repentant all at the same time.

"If you keep that act up any longer, I think he'll be out of that portrait and inside your dress."

She kept up the act. "Would you be jealous?"

"Of a two-dimensional old man wearing a scowl? Yes."

She batted her lashes and smiled, then tilted her head back and laughed a loud honest laugh that made people turn in their chairs and stare. Their expressions matched the expression on the portrait.

Carla surveyed the room. "Why do you think the people in the portraits all have such sour expressions?"

"Because all they can do is watch others eat?"

Carla thought about that for a moment as though the question were important. "Maybe. It makes you wonder what their pasts were like that made them so unhappy."

"Look not mournfully into the past. It comes not back again," I said, quoting Longfellow, who was quoting someone else.

OK, it sounds like a dreary aphorism, but I'd always thought of it as an enlightened view of what's important, the future. Carla's eyes widened then she scrunched her face in consternation. She seemed to have discovered something hidden in that quote that quieted her.

It took Carla twenty minutes to eat a real prime rib that looked bigger than her head. When she sat back, apparently satisfied and back to her flirtatious self, I asked her again for my transcript. She pulled from her purse a crumpled copy of the red end-of-the-earth flier the urban Jesus had been distributing and handed it to me. "Maybe you should read this instead."

I took the flier. "Are you concerned for my salvation?"

"I don't know. Do you need saving?"

"I'm hoping God has a sense of humor."

"What about after He stops laughing?"

I pictured myself standing at the gate with God, Him bent over, hands on knees, incapacitated with laughter at the idea of me getting into heaven.

Looking at Carla, I somehow knew she was imagining the same scene. I could see it in her eyes. She smiled her bright light smile, and I gave her a goofy smile back. We sat there for a moment, lost in a mutual awareness of how easy and relaxed we were together.

Someone took our plates away. Carla ordered flan and another cognac for dessert. I passed; my stomach felt tight.

Carla reached in her purse and came out with a sealed envelope. "Well, I guess I can give you this now."

It was the transcript for my forget session. I took the envelope and held it in front of me, but I suddenly dreaded reading it. I hesitated. I wasn't sure I wanted to know what I saw, heard, or did that forced me to such a drastic measure. "Thanks," I said, but I didn't really mean it.

Before I had the transcript, I'd thought getting a copy and reading it would answer all my nagging questions and the issue would be resolved. Now that I had the transcript in my hand, I worried that nothing would be resolved and all I'd get by reading it would be more information about myself than I really wanted to know. Maybe Longfellow was right.

I realized I had been gazing at Carla's eyes while I was thinking. She stared back at me, waiting. She expected a reaction. Her eyes felt good on my face. I smiled. "I think I'll read this later."

The waiter delivered the flan. I settled back and watched while Carla ate it and took sips from her second cognac. "I appreciate you going to all this trouble for me," I said.

"Don't worry about it. That was a nice dinner. I can't remember the last time I had a prime rib of that quality and that perfectly prepared. It was almost creamy."

"Maybe next time I feel like going out to dinner someplace nice, maybe I'll give you a call."

"If you do, maybe I'll go with you." She looked at her wrist. "But right now I'm afraid I have to go."

Carla stood, so I stood. She said good-bye and wove her way through the now crowded tables toward the foyer. I sat back down and wondered if she was aware of me watching her as she walked. I told myself again she was not my type. I liked her anyway. At the door, she glanced over her shoulder at me and smiled. I couldn't help but grin back. OK, maybe she was my type. I couldn't really remember what my type was anyway.

When no one was looking, I swiped my first pay card at the table reader. It didn't register at all. Sometimes that happened. The second one paid a quarter of the bill. I ate the after dinner mint then tried the last card which luckily had enough for the rest of dinner including a generous tip. It would take the restaurant a couple days to figure out I hadn't paid them in real money. I wouldn't be able to come back, but there were other good restaurants.

I walked out the door of Beef Tucuman and into a Chicago slanting mist. The transcript burned in my pocket, hot as an unopened love letter.

Chapter 4

There are some things I just don't want to know. For instance, I don't want to know when I will die, but I'm sure, if someone wrote it on a piece of paper and laid it face down on the table in front of me, I couldn't resist looking. I also know I would regret knowing as soon as I looked.

I didn't really want to know what was in the transcript either, but I felt like I had a gun in my pocket, and it was about to go off.

I'd planned to go home and read the transcript there, but my curiosity overcame my need for privacy. I stopped in the lobby of the Cuban Hotel. Only the rich could travel now that air travel was mostly gone, so the Cuban was one of the few hotels left in Chicago. They built their reputation on luxury and a sense of insulation from the real world.

I sat down in one of their big stuffed chairs and pulled out the envelope. I stared at it. Opening it was like opening my front door: It might be a friend just stopping by, it might be someone selling their religion, it might be the police, or it might be a big guy with a knife who wants your PAL to sell for parts and all your food and toilet paper and who gets mad when you only have half a tube of peanut butter and ten sheets of toilet paper and tells you that you should get a job.

I looked up at the mural on the ceiling, a few cherubs and a rosebush, steeled myself against the worst possibilities the transcript might reveal, and finally peeled the flap and pulled the transcript out of the envelope.

The transcript was of me talking about the memory I wanted forgotten so they could get a good fix on the brain locations. The transcript had details because the memory had to be focused for erasure to be accurate, complete, and not destroy too many unrelated memories.

It seems I went back to Quaker Street where Chen liked to thatch people. It's brightly lit, so it's easy to get good video of the victim. I'd looked for him, finally finding him in a darker alley where he liked to wait for the right prey. He was dead on the ground. I said I checked his neck for a pulse, but saw an ivory sliver of bone from his broken head sticking out above his left ear. The moment in my life I had chosen to forget was when I found Chen dead, his head bashed in, but his face recognizable.

I had repeatedly told them I wanted everything about the alley erased from my mind. Apparently seeing Chen dead was quite traumatic for me.

I carefully refolded the paper and put it back in the envelope. I slouched down in my chair. So I'd seen Chen dead, but of course, he wasn't. I'd just gone thatching with him the night before, and the forget was done back in early September. Still I had to review this fact to convince myself of something I already knew because I'd been so immersed in imagining the forgotten scene.

There were two possibilities. Someone might have faked the transcript, but I couldn't think who would misdirect me like that or why. Or, I'd described a fake memory, and why would I describe a fake memory in such detail? The picture created by the transcript of Chen's broken head was firmly set in my brain, and even though it was a created memory, it felt real.

The Cuban was a polished place. The brass trash cans reflected the grain from the waxed wood floor and the chandelier's lights left no shadows. A swarthy, sweaty man in a blue linen suit and white shoes stood talking to a woman behind the desk. He pointed at me and asked her a question. She squinted at me, tapping a cardkey on the mahogany surface.

They didn't want me there. I wasn't dressed in proper attire. They couldn't let just anyone sit in their chairs. Could they just throw me out, or was I meeting a guest? Someone important might come in or go out, and I would be a distraction. The woman fidgeted and whispered to the man. I stood, briefly bowed and left. I didn't want any trouble at that particular moment, though I noted to myself that some fun could be had at the Cuban if I ever felt like teasing the staff.

As I walked down Bigbash, head bowed to the gritty wind, I imagined the dead Chen going up to the front desk at a forget place and asking them to make him forget he was dead. The idea amused me. Once he forgot, he could then go back to his regular life, only slightly the worse for having died, but having to wear a hat because of the bone sticking out of his head.

I looked up into the wind to make sure I wasn't about to walk into any posts or people and saw a woman approaching who wore a hat which looked remarkably like a headless duck. It was a bulb on top of her head covered with white feathers and red feathers on either side. She stumbled along with one hand on top of her bird to hold it down. Dead Chen would look dapper in a hat like that. I stopped and laughed out loud. She stopped and stared at me. I imagine she hoped to intimidate me into thinking she wasn't goofy looking. I stared back, and she waddled off.

It crossed my mind at this point that the police might have figured out I knew Chen. Chen was apparently always in trouble with the police, or at least he was always hiding from them. The police might have mocked this transcript, intending to force me to reveal his address to get myself out of trouble for not reporting a murder, or perhaps for murder itself. But the strategy was too complicated for the police. They were more blunt and tactless. If they wanted Chen, and knew I knew where he was, they'd shove a gun barrel in my ear and make me tell them. They'd probably enjoy it, seeing that I was on the dole and all. No, it wasn't the police.

A buzzcar gunned its turbo just as it passed overhead and blew a pebble up my nose. I shuddered at that gritty scrape getting the stone back out. It happened to me twice before and both times, I wished I could afford a buzzcar buzzer. Just press the button and the car dropped to the ground like the pebble that had been up my nose. They were special police gear, but you could buy buzzers Under The River if you knew who to ask, and if you had a pot of money.

Perhaps Chen had tampered with the transcript. It would amuse him to put himself into my transcript as a dead guy. Chen's sense of humor was a bit zapped. He liked to talk loudly in public about losing his penis in a badminton accident. Yet I couldn't see why he would bother to falsify my transcript if he didn't get to see me as I read it. He wouldn't think it was fun unless he could watch. For a moment, I thought he might have been in disguise as one of the big Mongolian men at the next table, but he wouldn't have let the whole charade go by without revealing himself.

It was also possible that the entire transcript was a fabrication. Either way, someone had to have enough interest in my memory to bother to fake it, and I was worried it wasn't Chen. Chen's reasons would be simple. He would want to get back at me for poking him in the nose after he thatched me, or he would be playing a little joke on me. If it wasn't Chen, then the transcript might represent a shot across my bow. It could mean someone wanted my memory wiped for a reason I didn't know.

I decided to go back to Chen's and ask him about it. This time I approached his apartment by going in the E'Clair Street entrance, through the service corridors, and walking up three flights. I was thinking about Carla's ears and upswept hair and walked five or six steps down the hall before I looked up and saw police at the far end of the hall, outside Chen's apartment. There were three of them, and two were looking at me. One was a uniform and the other was a suit wearing a hundred year old fedora and a blond goatee. Chen's apartment door was open. A few of the other residents peered out their doorways down the hall, and one round man in a white undershirt, boxers and flip-flops talked animatedly to the third cop.

I turned to the first apartment and knocked, trying to appear indifferent, but aware of the goatee man's watchful eye. A woman opened the door. She had a bottle of derpal in her hand, obviously unaware of the police investigation underway just down the hall. I asked her if she'd found Jesus and handed her the end-of-the-earth flier Carla had given me. It was hard to resist glancing at the cops.

"Look mister, if you're selling something, I'm not buying, and if you're trying to convert me, I'm already converted." She slammed the door. I winced at the sound, trying to imagine what the cops were thinking. I turned back to the stairs without looking at the police again and walked home on the wide empty sidewalks of Fate Street.

Chen was always moving. He usually only touched down for a month or perhaps two before he relocated. He'd been at the Unapartments for almost four months. I figured it was Paulo's influence. He was the homemaker type. But staying in one place had apparently gotten Chen caught. If gov could prove Chen had committed any significant crimes, they would perform a series of forgets on him. I wondered what Chen would be like after a forget and what memories they would wipe.

I didn't know exactly why he might be arrested, but I figured Chen was probably guilty of lots of offenses against the public trust, not only some innocent thatching. Still, having the police overflowing out of Chen's apartment alarmed me. It made me feel a bit like they were closing in on me. But the gov knew where I lived. Cops didn't need to find Chen to find me. It was an irrational reaction, but I still felt boxed in.

I knew Chen hadn't been dead when I had my memory forgotten. Forget What could send the transcript to the police, as they had threatened, who would, no doubt, be interested and would talk to me for a couple days, but I thought they would let me go if I told them all I knew about Chen, which was just about nothing. Mostly, we just went thatching. All I knew of interest was where he lived, and they obviously knew that already. I doubted they would be able to make any more sense out of my Forget What transcript than I could.

So I had no reason to feel scared. I felt scared anyway. I also worried about Carla. She'd given me a copy of the transcript, and if the police received their copy and figured out during questioning that I had already seen a copy, they might want to know more about whoever gave me mine. They might see an arrest in it.

I tried to slough off my concerns about myself and about Carla by telling myself I was overreacting, but I just couldn't get them all off my mind.

I walked for a while, pushing into the wind, then turning back on another street when it got too cold on my face. I worked on picturing that moment when Carla smiled her genuine smile. I tried to force it into a permanent picture in my mind. It frustrated me though. I could get it for just a moment, then it would disappear, like the remnants of a dream when you wake up; vivid for a second, then gone. All I could remember were her ears and her hair. Her smile eluded me. Even so, the effort distracted me from my worries for a while.

Later, back at my apartment, the transcript still buzzed around in my head and I couldn't resist swatting at it. Why would I forget a memory I never actually had? I had to have known the forget company would come after me when the money disappeared from their account. I had to have done this on purpose, but figuring out why was beyond me that late at night. I read my mail and went to bed.

Three, maybe four in the morning, I was awakened by a gun barrel covering the end of my nose.

Chapter 5

I'd been dreaming about hitting Chen over the head with a length of angle iron. I was just telling him we could still be friends even though he was dead, when the gun barrel showed up. I almost incorporated it into my dream, which would have upset the huge policeman who held the gun, and probably would have made it easier for the dead Chen and me to be friends. The cop took a step back from my bed.

The lights were on. I sat up and pushed the blankets aside, blinking my eyes.

He gaped at me. "Gad, buddy, haven't you heard of pajamas?"

"I like the freedom," I said. "If you'd made a fist and hit your knuckles on the door, I would have put something on before I opened it."

There was another cop, a woman, not in uniform, but wearing her credentials in a holster under her left arm, wandering around my apartment looking into drawers and leafing through papers. I didn't have anything to hide, but I found the casual perusal of my limited possessions insulting and demeaning, like someone walking up to you and looking for nits in your hair.

"You Benny Khan?" said the enormous man with the gun pointed at me.

"Yeah, that's why I'm in his apartment, sleeping in his bed and not wearing his pajamas."

"Look, buddy, we can do this nice. Why don't you put on some clothes, and we'll go to the station without any antagonism."

I nodded my head over toward the woman. "Would you mind pointing out to her that she needs a court order to snoop through my stuff? And how did you get in here anyway?" The palm lock was supposedly proof against any illegal entrance, but I guessed the cops had their ways. Probably the landlord let them in. He lived in the building and, I suspected, did his own share of snooping around.

The woman put down my rent receipt. "You got two minutes, friend. Make good use of them."

Waking up to find someone in your apartment is a jarring experience. Waking up to find a policeman with his gun out in your apartment is scary. The uniformed guy, the one who pointed the gun at me, was as big as a doorway. The gun looked like a little plastic toy in his hands, but he didn't seem to be trying to intimidate me. The big ones never have to. He was probably in his mid thirties, which meant he wasn't going to make detective. He had a light complexion and thick red hair. The woman was tall, but thin, and wore a navy blue or black suit that had seen many arrests. Her shoes may have originally been black, but were now so scuffed and worn that they might have started life almost any color. She had straight, short hair, cut to stay out of her eyes. She was probably thirty, and she'd already made detective.

My clothes were lying on the floor. As soon as I looked at them, the woman stomped all over them to make sure there weren't any weapons in the pockets. "OK," she said.

They were the clothes I'd worn the day before. I figured if they were going to question me, I didn't want it to be any easier on them than it was on me. "Mind if I go to the bathroom?"

The woman went into my bathroom first and, by the sound of it, rummaged around a bit, then came out. "Sure, no problem. Just make it quick."

I grabbed my clothes off the floor. The bathroom didn't have any windows and the vent was too small to crawl through. I sat down and thought for a moment about why they were there. What could I tell them about my forget they wouldn't already know from the transcript? I was trying to think of something to add so they would feel successful, but I didn't know what it would be.

My copy of the transcript, which was in my pants pocket, was a problem. I didn't want the police to know I had it, since it had to have been acquired illegally, and they would want to know who gave it to me. I could have torn it up and flushed it, but I wanted to read it a few more times, so I punched a hole through a corner with the prong on my belt buckle and hung it on the hook on the back of the bathroom door under a towel. They wouldn't find it unless they closed the door after they came in, and they would still have to move something they probably wouldn't want to touch at all. I pulled on my clothes.

When I walked back into the main room of my apartment,

Doorway grabbed me and put cuffs on me. "This is just so we don't have to worry about you. Mistakes happen when we worry." He smiled broadly at me like I should appreciate his consideration for my safety.

"Thanks," I said, "Steel goes with everything."

The woman in the suit led the way, I came next, and Doorway followed with one hand on my cuffs. He closed the apartment door behind us, and, just like a child's toy, the door to the apartment next to mine popped open as though tied somehow to my door. The neighbors, the ones who always listened to Russian piano music, stuck their heads out like The Stooges, the man's head above the woman's, and tisked at me. "I knew he would get arrested eventually," she said. He just nodded like he knew it all along too and wondered what had taken so long.

I said, "They're coming for you next. They know why you play that piano music so loud." They looked startled and shut the door.

Doorway laughed, the detective just kept walking.

A quick car ride brought us to the local precinct which was housed in the east half of a factory that made ceramic good-fortune cats. One side of the building supported a huge cat on its roof. The cat had no tail and was waving a paw at passersby. The sign at the other end of the building was a large once-white sign with black lettering proclaiming, "POLICE".

The painted brick building covered half a city block and attracted dirt like a town gossip. It had small windows, more like holes in the deep walls, which acted as spotlights shining into the night fog. The factory and the cops were running multiple shifts.

On the way in, the detectors and sniffers went over me like bloodhounds with electronic noses. The machines didn't say anything, but I figured the monitor on the other side of the blast-proof wall probably said, "No weapons, but could use a bath."

Doorway and the detective hustled me past the front desk and straight down a long hallway to the back of the building. They put me in a small room, took off my bracelets, sat me at a steel table, which was bolted to the floor, and left. The room was painted a mustard shade of yellow and had stains where coffee had been splashed on the walls. The floor was hard industrial tile printed with splotches that looked like dirt, so they could hide the real dirt. The interior walls were foot-thick brick. There were no windows, and I didn't know how thick the exterior walls were, but it was quiet in that room. More quiet than I'd heard in a long time.

I waited awhile. Maybe they figured to intimidate me a little by letting me sit and worry. I put my head on my forearms and fell asleep. Actually I'd intended to just act like I'd fallen asleep, but I guess I was tired and they took a long time.

Police have always bored me a little. They seem to think what they do is so important—as though their time is more valuable than everyone else's. They can bring you in to the station whenever they want to, even at four in the morning, but are unwilling to take the time when you need their help to track down your stolen peanut butter. It always seemed one sided to me.

I woke up when the door opened. An older police guard came in. He had gray hair and a holstered gun. He didn't smile, but he didn't scowl either. He might have been bored too. A detective strutted in after him and pounded the table. It must have hurt, but he didn't show it. Maybe punching the steel table was the tip of the month in the detectives' newsletter: "How to intimidate your guests." He had a yellow goatee and no gun. He was one of the policemen I'd seen outside Chen's. His short brown hair lay flat and lifeless over his large ears. He had a long, Roman nose and eyes that didn't seem to be able to settle on anything. He dressed nice, though, wearing a gray coat and black pants with a white shirt that brightly reflected the fluorescent ceiling lights. His shoes were shiny and they made a gritty, sandy sound when he walked around the room as though they were even polished on the bottom.

"Where were you yesterday at four-thirty?" He didn't yell. That surprised me. He knew I was at Chen's. That was obvious. They probably had recorders at the entrances to the Unapartments from which they could pull an image and scan the databases to find likely matches. Then he shouted, "Answer me!"

"I went to the old UN building to see a friend," I said. I tried to look at him, but his eyes were wild, or perhaps mine were. I looked at the guard who looked at the ceiling.

"Who was the friend you went to see?" The detective was smiling now as though he thought he had intimidated me. He rubbed the fist he'd beaten on the table.

"I went to see Che Chen." What was the point of lying? The more I said now, the less likely they were to pick out the lie if I needed to use one later.

He stood straight. "Good. Good." His shoes made that sandy sound again as he walked once more around the room, then he leaned back against the brick wall and crossed his arms. "If you were going to see Chen, why did you stop at the apartment down the hall and give Ms. Montoya an apocalypse flier?"

My ploy hadn't worked. Not that I was surprised by that. This guy had been watching for anyone to show up. "I saw the police at Chen's door, and I didn't want to get involved."

"Why didn't you just leave instead of bothering that lady?"

"I don't know. It seemed like a good idea at the time."

"And why were you going to see Che Chen, Benny?"

I thought about saying I was just going to see a friend, but this guy wanted something. He would keep asking questions until he could justify the effort he'd expended sending a beat cop and a junior detective out for me at four in the morning. I wasn't sure if they knew about the forget yet, but I thought I'd play his card for him if he did know, and get some trump if he didn't. I spilled it slowly, doing my best to make it seem like a difficult admission.

"Well, I—uh. Well." I looked at him and swallowed. "I wanted to make sure he wasn't dead."

He took a step forward. I continued, talking faster. "I got a bill from Forget What. They said I'd had a memory forgotten and they wanted to be paid. They said I blinked them on the money I'd sent up front. The memory I'd paid to have forgotten was of Chen dead in an alley with his head smashed in, but that was a month ago and a mutual friend said Chen wasn't dead. That didn't make any sense, so I went to see him. When I saw the police at his door I got worried, so I turned to the first apartment and knocked. After the woman answered the door, I just gave her the pamphlet to make it look convincing, then left."

"Who was the mutual friend who told you Chen was alive?"

"Jon Tam." I picked someone who they would already know knew Chen. Jon was Chen's closest friend. He'd built Chen's ass thatchers. He was known to the police, who liked to arrest him once in a while just to keep him on his toes. They could never make anything stick well enough to do a forget on him. I didn't like Jon much, so I didn't mind using his name in this context.

"You said you saw Chen dead in the alley. Which alley?"

I couldn't tell whether he already knew about the memory or not. "Near Morph and Quacker."

"Use the real names."

"Near North and Quaker. Just south of there, in an alley on the east side of Quack, uh, Quaker. I don't know the alley name."

In a fit of civic pride the city had gone around and named all the alleys after former politicians. I knew this one had to have a name, but I didn't know what it was, or I couldn't remember. He would know all this anyway if the forget company had contacted the police.

"Mr. Khan, you've been very forthcoming, and I appreciate that, but you're not telling me the whole truth are you?" He was smiling now. His gums above his upper teeth showed pink and healthy. He put his hands on the table and leaned in, his face close to mine. He'd eaten something with a plum sauce. "What else do you have to tell us?"

I thought about that and realized I had told him everything. Damn. "I don't know what else you want to know. Perhaps if you told me what you wanted me to say I could be more helpful." I smiled politely, but he didn't like the inference.

He wrinkled his nose and stood back. "Perhaps you would like to explain why you killed Che Chen yesterday morning?" He stood up, smiled and crossed his arms. He might have said, 'checkmate,' but he didn't.

I looked at the detective. I had the feeling now that he was just fishing for reactions or admissions, but I wasn't sure. "I didn't know," I said. "I thought he was dead a month ago." I dropped the lie right there in the moment of my shock, hoping the mixture would fool any voice analysis machines they had rolling in the next room.

Chen was actually dead. It jolted me, but after that initial reaction, it didn't surprise me that much. He irritated almost everyone. Even me at times. Paulo would be out of his head, but I couldn't think of anyone else who would be broken up about it. I wondered briefly who ended up with his ass thatchers. I couldn't see Paulo using them.

Chen dead. I almost convinced myself that I'd found a time machine and seen Chen's death in the future, but you can only die once. The more I thought about it, the more Chen's death made me unhappy.

"How long have you known Chen?"

"Years. We met at a Glowball party." That was a lie too. I couldn't remember meeting Chen the first time, but I wanted the detective to believe I was answering with facts. It would have been a long time ago.

"Do you know anyone who would want him dead?

"No. At least no one in particular."

"What about his mate, Paulo?" He grinned at that. He seemed to think the question was funny, but I couldn't tell why.

"He and Paulo had their tiffs, but they were together for years. They always made up. They were in love. You could see that anytime you looked."

"Don't you think it's a pretty strong coincidence that you have a forget that includes Chen's death and then he turns up dead?" He momentarily turned to the guard. "Marley, don't you think that's strange?"

Marley didn't express an opinion. The goatee guy looked back at me with a curious expression. He seemed to think I could explain everything away if I wanted to, either by admitting I'd killed Chen, or by telling him who had. I couldn't do that, of course, so I just looked back at him, lifted my eyebrows and shrugged.

He groaned and sat down in the other chair. "Look, Benny," he said, all chummy, like he'd known me for years and we were good friends, "I don't think you murdered Chen, but you were in the area and you knew him. You're a lead, you see, and I have to follow up on all the leads. Who were Chen's other friends?"

"I don't know. Paulo and Jon were the only ones I knew about. When he could get hold of his other friends, he didn't call me, I guess." I tried to sound sad, but I don't think he bought it. The guard grunted out a little laugh. I kept from smiling though.

The detective sighed with disgust. "Do you have anything else to add?"

"I can't think of anything that would help you convict me of killing Chen, if that's what you mean."

"Look, Benny, you don't seem to understand the trouble you're in. I could keep you here for a full day if I wanted to. Heck, I could keep you here on suspicion for a week. You're acting all smug, but I could wipe that smirk away quick enough." He thought for a moment. "I could ask Marley here to leave for a few minutes if you had something confidential to tell me, something you wouldn't want on the record. I'm sure Marley wouldn't mind."

"I'd just as soon he stayed. I wouldn't want you to remember our conversation inaccurately."

He abruptly stood up and opened the door to leave. "Marley is going to get some pictures taken of you and get your contact information. Stick close to your apartment and check your messages. If we call, we want you down here within two hours."

If they wanted me, I doubted they would call and ask me to come down to the cat house to have coffee. They knew where to find me, at least at four in the morning.

I walked out of the police station and into the sunshine of Saturday morning without the handcuffs, but I knew I wasn't a free man. I was worried. Chen was dead. An immediate concern was that whoever had killed Chen might soon come after me. I was beginning to think I might end up either dead or in jail waiting to have my whole life wiped if I didn't figure out what I had actually been forgetting during that session. Chen dead in an alley wasn't exactly it.

It again crossed my mind that during my session I might have been thinking about one memory and talking about a different one, a nonexistent one, so no one would know the details of the actual memory I was forgetting. Maybe I'd talked about Chen's face instead of some real dead person's face I'd seen. Or the real memory might have been about something completely different. Either way, I had to unearth the memory I'd so carefully interred.

Chapter 6

On my way home from the police station, I stopped by the dole banana place and picked up my pay for doing nothing. I cashed the chit into a swipe card at Alphonzo's grocery and bought three apples, some soy milk and a squeeze tube of peanut butter.

At home, my PAL said there were three messages. One was from Carbide, a guy who did odd moving jobs and deliveries and who was almost as big as Doorway, but whose parents couldn't afford to fix his face when he was young. He looked dangerous, but was actually quite amiable. He wanted to know if I was interested in helping him move an apartment worth of possessions from North Instead to the Warrens. He needed two other guys to get the job, and he'd happily do most of the work, but I wasn't in need of cash. The second call was from a woman with a childlike voice who wanted to clean my carpets, three rooms for forty. I didn't have three rooms.

The third call was from my brother. He wanted to know if I could come over for dinner Sunday night. He said he'd found me a woman.

Maybe nine's a charm, or maybe he thought if I hooked up I might suddenly become a contributing member of society. Not likely, yet I'd gotten some from three of the eight so far, so I called him back and said I would. I asked him if I should bring the wine. He said, "No!" with a note of fear in his voice. I went to bed.

On Sunday morning I received a final letter on my PAL from Forget What saying they had given the transcripts of my forgotten memory to the police and that I should expect a visit based on the content of the memory. I wouldn't get one. The police already knew. It made me feel like I'd won, but Chen was still dead, I still didn't know why I'd paid to forget a memory I didn't have, and the police were still considerably too interested in me.

I pulled the transcript out from under the towel behind the bathroom door and reread it. It was surreal reading about Chen's death as though I'd seen the body and was trying to forget all about it. Chen actually being dead added a macabre bent. My imagination is pretty good, and I'd invented all sorts of details about the scene that weren't on the paper. My mind kept running the movie that I pieced together from the descriptions in the transcript and from my imagination.

On my walk to Arno's I found myself wishing I had someone to talk to. That wasn't a problem I usually had, but then, I was starting to have lots of problems I didn't usually have.

One thing that bothered me was my reaction to Chen's death. I guess he had been my best friend, yet I felt distanced from his murder. It felt like I was watching a movie, an intense movie, but not one where I would resist going to the bathroom if I needed to. Shouldn't I be more upset about him and maybe a little less focused on myself?

As I walked, the trees grew taller and closer together. The grass thickened and cars disappeared behind garage doors. Arno's house was set back from the street, obscured even in winter by a line of spruce he'd planted a few years back. He had about two acres of bushes and low trees with a single story, prairie style house and a detached two-story garage. The second story addition on his garage held his new Milwaukee buzzcar. There wasn't a gate at the driveway, but the home next door had one, iron with a bald eagle hanging on bars.

As I walked up his curving cobblestone driveway, the street noise drifted away behind me. The curtains were drawn closed as usual. I rang the bell.

Arno met me at the door, all backslaps and howdys. We went into the living room where a young woman perched on a wooden side chair, leaving the couch and two stuffed chairs free.

Arno did the formal introductions. Rela smiled shyly. She had shoulder length wavy blonde hair and light blue lipstick that made her look cold. Her clothes were carefully chosen to portray a no nonsense, yet youthful image. Her shoes matched her lipstick. I smiled back and sat down in the recliner closest to her.

"So, Benny, what do you do? Your brother was rather vague about your occupation." Her voice was high, a little strained.

"Oh," I said, "I do various and sundry."

"What exactly is 'various and sundry,' Mr. Khan?" She said while squinting and frowning in either concentration or disapproval, I couldn't tell which.

"Well, more various than sundry, actually."

Arno didn't like the way the conversation was going and decided to go in the kitchen and yell at his wife, so we'd both feel uncomfortable and stay quiet. He usually didn't yell at Denise. Rather, he usually bullied her with a low menacing voice, or just a look. She would sometimes glance at me when he did that, as though to say, he's not always like that, but somehow I knew he was always like that. They came out of the kitchen smiling, carrying drinks. A beer for me and green wine for Rela. Arno had something in a beer glass, but it wasn't beer. I wasn't sure what it was. Denise had some ice water in a wine glass. She looked like she was going to say hello, but instead, she fondled a hydrangea that stood blooming in a huge Chinese pot on an end table and examined a leaf with exaggerated interest.

I stood up and hugged her and said, "How's my favorite sister-in-law?" OK, it was a sappy thing to do, but she smiled at me and seemed to relax a bit. Arno kept her awfully taut.

We talked about the City's plan to convert the deep tunnel into a shopping mall, which Arno was enthusiastic about. Rela seemed to think the federal government should find a way to raise the level of the lake back up to where the deep tunnel's original use as a giant, underground storm overflow container would be needed again.

Denise interjected agreement with Arno when the opportunity allowed.

"Maybe we should convert it to a huge swimming pool," I said, "so if there was a surge in the lake level, it could still be used as a reservoir."

"Oh, that's a good idea," said Rela, but I think she was humoring me. I was patronizing her, so I guess that was fair.

Arno was annoyed with me for being flippant and not agreeing with him. He glared at me and gave a small shake no of his head. I smiled as though I didn't understand, but he knew I did, and that irritated him more.

The girl was too young and cute for me, but she was all right to talk to, kind of deep and philosophical like inexperienced people often are.

Arno ushered us into the dining room for dinner. The food smelled sweet and steamy. Denise had made Szechwan broccoli, vegetable pakoras, basmati rice with red beans, and grilled zucchini. She laid out the dishes on the table, waited for Arno to begin eating, then watched him for a moment before she dished up any for herself.

Arno sat at the head of the table and Denise sat to his right, so she would be nearer the kitchen. I sat at the other end and Rela sat across from Denise. Arno held a broccoli up with his chop sticks. "Denise is a wonderful cook, don't you think?"

I looked at Denise. "Yes, Denise, this is very good. Would you pass me the pakoras?"

I glanced at Arno who was scowling. He seemed to think the compliment should be his, perhaps for having married such a good cook. Arno could get enough compliments from his employees. He didn't need any from me.

I figured Rela worked for Arno and was somehow coerced into coming to dinner. She might have been worried about what she would have to do to keep her job. She picked and jabbed at her food. She ate a bit here and there, but mostly she just pushed the rice around and nibbled the leaves off a few broccoli trees. "I appreciate you making an all vegetarian dinner for me," she said. "I know you would usually have meat."

The girl was a vegetarian on purpose. I had wondered what the deal was with all the vegetables. I figured it was a new fad or something. Having meat at dinner showed how prosperous a person was and Arno normally wouldn't pass up an opportunity.

After dinner, Denise took the dishes to the kitchen and Rela, Arno and I moved back into the living room. Rela still seemed nervous and sipped at another wine while Arno and I talked about the train that had derailed off a bridge that morning and how close it came to killing the mayor who'd been on a field trip to examine the condition of the city's rail bridges. Arno seemed to think the whole thing was pretty funny, very ironic, but he didn't have to ride the train home.

After a while and a few changes in conversation topic directed by me to keep Arno and Rela from arguing, Denise came in to join us. "Does anyone want anything else to drink?" She hovered by the doorway.

She got a round of nos, then settled into the straight-backed chair nearest the kitchen.

I tried to bring her into the conversation. "We were talking about fish, saving them that is. Rela is a member of the Wildlife Protection League. She was just saying that just because fish aren't warm and fuzzy that's no reason to treat them badly."

"Oh, do you think fish are smart?" Denise said, smiling.

"What has smart got to do with it?" Rela shot back, now on her own ground. "Does an animal have to be smart to be important, to feel pain? And anyway, there's more in the oceans than fish. There are dolphins and whales, you know, mammals, just like us."

Denise sat back in her chair and clasped her hands on her lap. She looked at the wall. She'd tried to be pleasant and contribute. Now she would be quiet. I'd never sat and talked to Denise by herself. Arno was always there, larger in conversation than both of us put together. Even with Rela, Denise was quickly made small.

"Yes," I said. "Save the whales. Collect the whole set." OK, it was an old joke, but I'd always liked it, and I felt like biting Rela back a little.

Rela stared at me as though I'd choked the life out of a beluga with my bare hands. "Jokes like that undermine and belittle our whole life's effort," she said, but it sounded rehearsed, like she was told to say that whenever anyone tried to lighten up the conversation.

I looked at my brother and said, "You don't use bait for whales."

We laughed hard for at least a minute, tears coming to our eyes. "You don't use bait for whales," he repeated, and we laughed some more. It was a private joke, and it was unfair of us to laugh so hard and long without letting the women in on it, but that quote brought up a whole scene in our minds of a scam I'd set up, hoping to impress my brother's friends, that had failed so hopelessly and miserably that it had become the stuff of legend among the crowd we'd hung out with at the time. It was not the sort of thing you could explain. If you weren't there, it just wouldn't be funny.

Arno and I had some good memories in common. At the time, swimming in the muck that is the Chicago river, desperately trying to reach a pylon to hold on to, I'd hated him, but in retrospect I had to admit the whole thing was hilarious. Finally, Arno and I could stop laughing and look at each other without starting again.

Rela stood. "I think it's time for me to go home. I have to work early in the morning. It's been a nice evening."

Denise went off to get our coats. I followed Rela into the front hall. "Are you taking the train to Hackson?"

"Yes."

"So am I. It's kind of late to be walking around there. I'll go with you if that's all right."

She looked at me, seemingly for the first time that evening. She seemed to be trying to determine if I would be of any use if someone accosted her or if she'd have to protect me, or, worse, protect herself from me. Her appraising look gave me the odd feeling she could take me if she had to. "Thank you," she said.

She turned to Denise. "And thank you for the dinner."

Arno told us he hoped to see us again soon, but I think he knew Rela and I weren't a match, I couldn't imagine what had made him think we would be in the first place.

I rode home with her on the train. She said she worked for Arno as an expediter, but I assured her subtly that I wasn't going to take anything that wasn't earned. We walked quietly to her apartment building, but I didn't go in.

I strolled back toward my apartment, listening to my shoes tap on the concrete in the cool night air. "You don't use bait for whales." I laughed again and thought about how those few words triggered a whole scene in our heads, a whole memory.

Every once in a while there are discrete moments in time when an unrelated train of thought will trigger a rushing conclusion to some problem you weren't even consciously thinking about. This was one of those slap yourself on the forehead epiphanies. I ran to a street light and pulled out the transcript. I read it again, carefully this time. There it was. "It was in the alley," I'd said. "Right there near North off Quaker."

Why would I say that? It's Morph and Quacker on every sign I'd seen in ten years. They were zapped over as soon as the city repainted them. No one called streets by the right names except the police and the mayor. I'd left myself a clue only I would understand.

Chapter 7

When I got home I began pacing, trying to figure out what I'd been trying to tell myself by using the correct street names in the forget session. By three in the morning I decided that a month before I'd given myself too much credit for intellectual capacity. I gave up and went to bed.

My unconscious mind did not solve the dilemma for me during the night. I woke up ridiculously early and showered and wiped hair removal cream on my face for the first time in a few days. It felt good to be clean, but a clean body doesn't think any better than a dirty one.

I must have known Forget What would send me a bill, and I must have known I wouldn't pay it. I also must have realized the forgotten memory would bug me until I figured out what memories I'd had them delete for me. Yet, I'd been stumped to find out. If it weren't for Chen and Paulo happening to know Carla who worked for Forget What, I would never have acquired the transcript. I must have expected to somehow get hold of the transcript and eventually notice the street names.

I tried to picture the alley, tried to pull the memory back even though I knew I wouldn't be able to. I closed my eyes and imagined a walk down Quacker. Not only could I not evoke anything about the death scene, I couldn't remember an alley being there at all.

I decided to go to the alleged alley and look for myself. I walked fast to Morph and Quacker, then went south on Quacker. I remembered the street well, but even when I came upon an alley, I had no recognition of it at all. Standing there, staring at the gap in the buildings that formed the alley, I felt unbalanced, wavering with a bit of vertigo. My inner ear didn't like the discrepancy between what was there and my memories of what was there. The sight made me nauseous.

Forget What had been efficient and complete. It wasn't so much that I remembered the two corners being connected, but more that I just couldn't place anything between them.

Looking down the alley, I could see some dumpsters, one was overflowing with yellow bags, the other had a long trail of ancient grease and other liquids, which had leaked from it over the years, flowing to the pot-holes in the alley asphalt. Little black and white bees floated around the dumpsters.

There was some broken glass strewn in small piles, mostly clear bottles, but also some of the dark brown ones favored by derpal makers because light degrades derpal's potency. The alley smelled faintly of urine. Instead of a street sign, there was only a pole where one used to be.

It took effort to walk into the alley. Everything felt wrong, eerie. It went back about fifty meters to a brick wall. There were a few doors along the way which had no handles and, "Keep Exit Clear," signs mostly hidden behind barrels, a pile of sagging tires, two dead refrigerators, the remains of a battle-scarred wooden creche, two rotten sofa carcasses and piles of smaller trash. The door at the far end of the alley had a torn, faded awning and a single light bulb, now broken. Beside the door it said, "Carma Alley Blues." I thought the alley must be named Carma at first, but then I saw that the sign had been zapped like all the street signs. Readable under the white paint, was 'Carla.'

The alley's real name was Carla, just like Paulo's friend who had given me the transcript. I stared at the sign while I tried to comprehend how this odd piece of information fit with everything.

Before the forget, I would have known the alley's name. I hung out a lot in this area with Chen on his thatching expeditions. I'd also used the correct names for the streets in my transcript. If Carla was the correct name for this alley, maybe this was my clue for myself. Or maybe I was tying myself in knots of self-deception.

I thought back on my dinner with Carla. She'd said she thought she knew me, but couldn't remember from where, and I felt the same way about her. That sort of thing happens all the time, of course, but the feeling had seemed especially strong. I began to wonder if I'd already known Carla before Paulo hooked me up with her to get my transcript.

I had Carla's phone address, so I went into a coffee shop, picked up a used cup, so it would look like I had purchased something and used one of their PALs to back up her phone address to her street address. It's not as hard as it sounds if you have the right database codes. It turned out she lived in the Unapartments just like Chen and Paulo. Not a big surprise since Paulo met her somewhere and where they lived seemed as likely as most places. She lived near the top floor. It wasn't as noisy up there, if you could afford it.

I went to her apartment building, a trip I'd made many times before while visiting Chen, but everything along the way was suddenly more interesting. I looked at every detail and found it distinct and unique rather than just another store or window display or protruding hydrant pipe. There was a lot of stuff between the alley and the Unapartments that I'd never noticed before, but nothing as big as an alley.

Even my way of finding her apartment felt unusual. I just went up the vator and walked to her door. I didn't need to take detours as I usually did at the Unapartments when going to Chen's.

I knocked. Carla opened the door a moment later. Without thinking, I breezed in past her as though I went there every day. She had a tiny apartment, even compared to mine. The kitchen and the bed were right there together. There were only two doors, one to the hall I'd come through, and one presumably leading to a bathroom. The couch lay opened into a bed, taking up almost the whole room, and the blankets were in disarray. She'd painted the apartment in shades of blue like old German plates. The small table that held her PAL was white plastic with a blue stripe around the edge. A matching plastic chair was tucked under it.

"I heard about Chen," she mumbled. "I'm sorry."

I suddenly realized it was Monday afternoon. "Why are you here? Shouldn't you be at work, or did you forget to set your alarm clock?"

She looked at me, dark brown hair, mussed up, and light gray eyes. Her face a little wrinkled from sleeping. "I don't have a job. I got fired from the grocery," she said as though it were true. "Do you want something?"

She wasn't trying to hurry me up. She went over to the sink and drew a glass of water. "I'm afraid it's all I have at the moment."

"No, thanks. You don't work for Forget What?"

"No. I've never worked for them, why?"

Carla seemed a different person from the one who had met me at the Tucuman. At dinner she had been lively and clever, now she was subdued and reticent. "How did you know Chen died?" I asked, changing the subject temporarily. "Have you seen Paulo?"

Carla sat down on the only stuffed chair. I sat on the edge of the bed and waited for her to say something.

"I heard at the front door, from his neighbor, that the police are saying Chen killed himself after he killed Paulo. I am sorry. I guess they found a lot of derpal in the apartment. The police think they were drinking it through their noses and overdosed on it enough to make them crazy. The neighbor heard a lot of yelling and breaking things. He called the police."

She said some more I didn't catch; my mind had wandered. I hadn't known Paulo was dead too. The police hadn't let me in on that. It explained why the detective had thought it funny when he suggested that Paulo had killed Chen. I didn't especially like Paulo. He worried a lot and nagged Chen about going out, but his death still took me aback.

Carla sat with her knees together and the glass of water held tightly in both hands resting on her knees. I watched her gently swirl the water while I thought about Paulo and Chen yelling and throwing things at each other. I knew they nosed derpal sometimes. It could well have gotten out of hand. Much as I wanted the police to be hiding something or making stuff up, their answer really seemed reasonable, even probable. But if they already knew who killed Chen, why had they interrogated me about it later?

"You have a marketing job at Forget What, remember?"

"No I don't."

"You got me some transcripts from there. Transcripts from my memory forgetting session." She looked at me with her head tilted to one side, like a dog that hears an unusual, but unworrysome sound. "We had dinner," I said.

"Oh, yes. I remember dinner. We should do that again sometime," she said, and she smiled. She was real pretty when she smiled. I smiled back. Someone had given her a forget session too, but hers was recent and probably gratis. I hoped her change in personality was temporary disorientation from the forget.

Instead of focusing on the problem at hand, I noticed that she was wearing a nightgown that didn't hide much. She had a friendly body and her just-awakened sleepiness made her appear especially warm and soft. I wanted to run my fingertips over the cloth that covered her breasts and feel that warmth and softness.

I stood and went to the door. She stood up and followed when I opened it, as though she were walking me out, but it was just a step. Like an idiot, I reached out and touched her hair. Her eyes opened wide for a second, then she looked down. I took a deep breath for no apparent reason, then left.

Walking home, I stopped by the VRcade and played a walk through a gang infested neighborhood, saved the pretty girl and shot the female gang leader in the head, but I was playing by rote. I wasn't in the mood. Carla had made me think, and I couldn't get her off my mind. Why had I pointed myself toward her in my forget session? Who was she? Why was she important? She didn't seem to remember, and that was either because she wanted to forget me, or because someone else wanted her to forget me. Paulo hadn't wanted her to be the one to give me my transcript. He'd balked when Chen suggested it, so Paulo probably knew why she was important to me, but he was dead. Chen probably knew, but he was dead too.

I went home shaking my head and stomping along in frustration, coat open, not feeling the cold and trying to forget the whole thing by focusing on the fall mist on my face.

This time Doorway and the detective with the yellow goatee, whose name I still didn't know, were waiting for me at my apartment.

Chapter 8

The detective pushed me against the wall. "So you thought Chen was dead a month ago, huh? The forget you never paid for says otherwise. Let's go to the station and talk about it." He nodded to Doorway, who handcuffed me again.

"Couldn't we just talk about it here? We could relax and have a beer and discuss the whole thing without having to make the trip." I didn't have any beer, but I didn't really expect them to accept my offer.

The detective didn't bother to respond, he just nodded to Doorway and off we went, back to the ceramic cat house. My neighbors didn't even give me a send-off this time.

In the car, on the way to the police station, I decided that the transcript I was given must have been made up, or the police wouldn't be taking me in again. If they'd read the same version of the transcript I had, it would not have elicited any more questions from the police than I'd already answered. I hadn't put it together until then. It seemed that someone else had used North and Quaker instead of Morph and Quacker. I'd thought I had been very clever to have found a way to help my post-forget self track down the woman I loved, even after forgetting all about her. How annoying that the alley being named Carla was just a coincidence. That especially bothered me because now it appeared I was just making a sap of myself. I hadn't left a clue for myself after all. Someone else had messed up, and I'd been out-thinking myself. Not that I was surprised by that.

We went past the sniffers and down the hall. Doorway showed me to the same back room again while the detective ducked into a side room.

I sat down in my usual chair. "Haven't we been here before?" I said.

Doorway removed my left handcuff and attached it to the table. "Detective Kumar will be back in a minute," he said. He left me alone in the silence with nothing to do but think. I decided I didn't like the name Kumar. The guy himself didn't do much for me either.

A few minutes later, a guard entered with the detective close behind. Kumar walked in rubbing his yellow goatee as though in deep thought. "Benny, why did you think you could get away with lying about your forget?"

I looked at him, but didn't answer. It was one of those questions you couldn't answer without incriminating yourself, like, "Have you stopped kicking your dog, yet?"

Kumar continued, "The company must have told you they were going to report you. Are you remembering anything you should tell me? Are there any memories coming back to you?" He sat down in the other chair. He was doing his chummy act again.

I showed Kumar the transcript I'd been given. "It's all I had to go on. You can't blame me for not remembering what I forgot. No one does. And anyway, who's to say which transcript is the real session and which one was faked?"

Like an idiot, I smiled. I saw the anger build in his eyes, but he didn't hit me, or the table. He just smoldered for a while, thinking.

I was mixed up in something. He knew it, and I knew it, but neither of us knew what it was. I found that amusing. He didn't.

"Are you playing a game with me, Benny?"

"I like games," I said. "But the police don't generally play fair."

He leaned in close. He'd eaten curry. "Well, maybe I'll change the rules. Police are allowed to do that, you know. You've shown me your transcript, now I'll show you mine."

"Go get it," he said to the guard while keeping his eyes on me.

The guard came back a minute later with a video headset and a memstick. Kumar had a video transcript of the session. He knew which transcript was the real one. This game was no fun.

I knew he would be watching my body language. Respiration and other indicators would be watched electronically in the next room. I tried to settle into the chair and watch objectively, but, to be honest, I was scared.

I put on the headset and watched myself talk through the memory I wanted forgotten. It wasn't related to Chen or Paulo at all, but it was related to the alley and there was a dead person with his head bashed in. In fact, the transcript Carla had given me matched this one very closely but for one important detail. The dead person was not Chen, but someone apparently unknown to me. I told the doctors I wanted to forget I saw the body, just as my version of the transcript reported, but here, watching myself, I could tell there was some other memory I was hoping would vanish along with the memory of the body: the real thing I wanted to forget. I watched myself telling the doctor that I wanted to forget all about that alley, and I kept saying that over and over. The description of the body and the bone sticking out and all the other details were the same.

When the film ended, I reached up to hit the replay button, but the guard yanked the viewer off my head.

Kumar was in my face again. I decided it was a north Indian curry he'd eaten, maybe Pakistan. "Do you admit this is you?"

How could I not? The video could have been doctored, but it didn't seem likely. The person on the screen sure acted like me. "Yes," I said. "That certainly seems to be me."

He climbed out of his chair and glanced at the wall to my right. "Was there anything surprising, anything different that you think might give us a clue about who the dead person was?" He looked at me closely now, expecting a reaction.

"I can't think of anything. I obviously don't remember things as happening differently." We stared at each other for a while.

I had hoped to see Carla in the video of my forget session, but she wasn't there. I didn't recognize anyone in the room.

There were dubious things about this police interrogation, though. I had always been told that the police were not allowed to show the forgetter any written transcripts of their sessions without a court order, that way the integrity of the forget wouldn't be compromised. In this case, Kumar had shown me actual video and hadn't even bothered to mask the employees' faces. I also thought the forget companies weren't allowed to abet a crime, and allowing me to forget the dead body should have gotten their license revoked. What's more, I should have been under arrest for having the forget done in the first place, or at least for not paying for it. There was something else collateral to the whole situation which I didn't know about, a missing angle. "Let me watch it again." I said. "Maybe I'll notice something new the second time."

"I think once is enough Mr. Khan. Perhaps you noticed the difference between what you really had forgotten and what your transcript showed."

I worried that he would ask me how I acquired the transcript in the first place. I didn't think I would be able to lie my way out of that. How would he react if I told him I wanted to talk to a lawyer? He didn't ask about the source of the transcript though. Maybe he thought Forget What sent it to me to prove I'd had a forget done. The other possibility was that he already knew how I got the transcript from looking through Chen and Paulo's apartment. That scenario I didn't like at all. Maybe Carla wasn't someone I'd loved before, but I still didn't want to see her get into trouble.

I thought about the differences between my transcript and his video. "The only difference I could detect was the obvious one. I didn't recognize the dead guy in your version."

"Why do you think that is?" Kumar acted like he was sharing his job with me, letting me in on his analytic process.

"I have no idea. You're the policeman. You're the one with the training." I meant that to sound encouraging, but it came across cynical and snide. The guard grunted.

Kumar ignored me. "Why would someone go to the trouble of replacing an unknown, someone you didn't know, with Chen in your transcript? Who would go to that trouble?" He posed the question as though it were as much to himself as to me. He gazed at the wall.

I had spent some time thinking about why myself. "I really don't know. Perhaps it was Chen?" Certainly Chen couldn't disagree with me, and he seemed as likely a suspect as any. I figured blaming a dead guy would be a good strategy.

Kumar looked at me for a moment longer. He seemed to make up his mind to tell me something, but then he hesitated and finally decided not to. He was hiding something. I had the feeling he knew details about me I didn't know myself, details I'd lost with my forget. But he wasn't going to tell me. At least not yet.

"You can go, Mr. Khan," he said. "Keep your head low and stay in the area." The guard took back the handcuffs and he and Kumar left me sitting there alone in the room as though it were my place and they had just been visiting.

I went home, a twenty minute walk. I was hungry, so I leaned back against the sink, ate an apple with peanut butter and reran the video transcript on the back of my eyelids, trying to remember my body language and every word I spoke. Kumar had kept my paper transcript, so I couldn't consult that anymore, but by now, I'd read it often enough to remember it pretty well.

With a shock, I realized I had named Morph and Quacker by their correct names even on the video. I smiled at that. I still wasn't sure if the names were a clue to myself or not, but I felt better about having believed there was some meaning behind it.

Mostly though, the video was the same as the paper. I kept saying I wanted to forget everything about the alley. I could see myself saying that several times.

It dawned on me that if the video the police showed me was real, the only reason they would show it to me would be because it was already public knowledge. They already knew all about me finding a dead guy in that alley. That was why I wasn't still at the police station. They had been testing me, seeing how much I remembered of events they knew more about than I did.

Perhaps the dead guy could help me catch up a little. I decided to search the public databases for murders and figure out whose body I'd actually seen.

Chapter 9

If the murder I'd seen was already known to the police, I figured it must have been in the news. The major news companies had inside people who leaked everything of interest to the public—a public who willingly paid for first gossip rights to the newest information.

The library, a huge brick building with gargoyles on the corners down on Incongruous, is about a half hour walk. I decided to do my searching there. My own PAL could have handled the retrieval, albeit somewhat slowly and with an enormous quantity of ads, but that would have left my machine's fingerprint on the database search engine and you never knew who had a sniffer running. It's not that I was paranoid, just that I was cautious and practical.

The library didn't loan books anymore because changes to fair-use laws made lending impractical. However, they kept up a solid collection of reference books, and still bought magazines, and newspapers that you could read while sitting in their stiff-backed wooden chairs. They also had PALs, ugly art, and rest rooms that were open to the public. The library was only open during regular working hours, so if you had a job and paid the taxes to support it, you couldn't use it, but I didn't have that problem.

I followed a vile smelling woman with enormous matted hair and dirt caked clothing through the revolving door. She headed for the rest rooms, and I went to the main desk and took a wait card off the stack. They would buzz me when a PAL became available. If the number of waiting patrons was high enough, they gave out the cards to avoid a long, curving, quarrelsome line.

I wandered around waiting for my card to buzz, studying ceiling panels and other artwork. A ceramic wall mural depicting dramatic details of the Pittsburgh cave-in completely covered the north wall of the atrium. The coal under the mountains ignited by miners and left smoldering for a hundred years had sucked in oxygen and burst into yellow flame after the burnt out coal deposits and old mines collapsed under large parts of suburban Pittsburgh. The mural showed housetops sticking up through what used to be the ground level, sprouting long flaming tendrils in the semidarkness. People with anguished, tear streaked faces pulled themselves out of the burning earth like so many dead drawing themselves up from hell. The wall was called Suburbia.

I was studying a black dog lying on his side, tongue hanging out, eyes open and dull when I was buzzed. The ceramic wall was creeping me out anyway. The woman behind the desk pointed to an available PAL sitting under a hanging sculpture which appeared to be a bent boat propeller, parts of which had been eaten away by cavitation or perhaps chipmunks. When I took my seat, I looked up. One of the blades pointed down toward the top of my head.

I worked fast, browsing back through old news stories around September tenth, looking for deaths. I found it easily and whacked my forehead with the heel of my hand for not looking earlier. There I was in the background of a news video at a crime scene. A woman wearing a magenta blazer, puffed blonde hair, and enormous breasts talked to the camera about the murder of Judge Kimbanski who had been investigating narcotics distribution in the city. Apparently I'd found the body. I could see myself in the background talking to a woman, my hands in my pockets, nudging the edge of a pot-hole with my right foot. Closer inspection revealed that the woman I was talking to was the detective Kumar had sent with Doorway to arrest me the first time.

Detective Kumar had implied, but never said, that they didn't know whose body it was that I'd actually seen in my forget session. He'd been testing me, trying to see how much I'd forgotten, and I now knew I'd forgotten a lot.

A sidebar linked to the video explained that the alley was named after Anton Carla, a former Alderman for the district. He was best known for buying a piece of inaccessible land, an island really, which had been created as the lake receded. He'd built a small house on it, and then demanded that the city build a causeway because by law they had to provide unimpeded access to all residential areas. The law was meant to correct some snow removal problems, but Anton Carla had seen a way to make his land worth a lot of money. It was a new island off the coast of Chicago and everyone wanted to live there. He wanted to put up a ring of condominium buildings and have a park in the middle.

It cost the city more than three hundred million to build a low land-bridge and to pay for the court costs accrued while fighting building it. Then the lake level rose back up a little and the island, instead of growing, shrank to nothing. Now the causeway was an expensive ersatz cruise ship dock and fishing pier.

This information was provided to library patrons by Death News, a news company that reported only on events in which someone died, preferably in some gruesome, violent way, though sometimes they would include articles where pets or zoo animals died as well. As the ads rolled by, I sat back and looked up at the prop again.

The police hadn't arrested me when they received the transcript because I'd reported the body to the police in the first place. I'd already told them everything about finding it. The murder was already public knowledge. When I showed up at Chen's, they recognized me from Kimbanski's murder scene and that was the reason they were interested in why I was there. They were thinking I'd found Kimbanski because I was involved in the killing, that maybe I was the murderer. Apparently I'd satisfied them that I wasn't. Or maybe they were still watching me to find out who I talked to and who I went to see.

The police blackout period was over, so, when the Death News ads finished, I looked up the news reports of Chen's and Paulo's deaths. The neighbor, who had identified the bodies, was on the videos talking about it to a reporter from Good Dirt Press. He'd put some pants on for the interview. He didn't know much, he hadn't actually looked at the scene of the crime, but he talked fast and waved his arms around a lot, so the reporter couldn't get away. I was surprised the neighbor even knew what Chen looked like. After scanning through fifteen minutes of coverage, I decide there wasn't much more in the news that Carla hadn't already told me.

After watching the Good Dirt Press ads flash around the screen for a while, I found a later report that had more information from the investigation. The police listed Paulo's death as a murder and Chen's death as a suicide, Chen being Paulo's killer. Chen was listed as not employed. No surprise there, but Paulo was listed as working for Forget What.

That stunned me. Paulo worked at Forget What. I remembered Chen saying that Carla worked at Forget What, and that she could get the transcripts for me. Paulo called me later with Carla's phone address. Now I figured Paulo must have worked a deal with her to give me the modified transcripts in exchange for a free forget of her choice, which would also include her forgetting she ever gave me the transcripts in the first place and forgetting that Paulo worked for Forget What. She had seemed anxious when we had dinner, and that was probably why. I had no idea what she got out of it, what her primary forget was, but she certainly wouldn't remember either.

If Paulo had created the fake transcript, then it was Paulo who put Chen in the dead man's spot. I could only guess that Paulo was mad at Chen for suggesting Carla give me the transcripts in the first place and he had used the modification of the transcript as a passive-aggressive way to get back at Chen. It seemed a bit too ghastly for Paulo's bouncy attitude, but then I'd been surprised to find out he worked for Forget What in the first place.

Carla was apparently telling the truth as she knew it when she said at her apartment that she never worked for Forget What. I smiled at that. I hadn't liked the idea that Carla would change her story about something so obvious. It had seemed stupid and unfriendly.

So I was back to where I started. I'd forgotten something, and I still didn't know what it was. The only person who was directly involved in some way and still alive was Carla. And, for some reason, I wanted to see her again anyway.

Chapter 10

I went back to the Unapartments and took the vator to seventeen. I met Carla at the door as she was going out. She was wearing a blue, knee length coat over black slacks and black shoes. Silver globe earrings glistened when she turned her head. "Hello," I said, "Do you have a minute?"

"I was just going out to get something to eat," she said looking more alert and determined than she had the last time I'd seen her. I hoped she was coming back to herself after the forget. She looked me in the eye with what I hoped was a sort of invitation.

"Can I tag along?" I said, feeling stupid and uncouth and suddenly warm.

"Sure, but I'm going somewhere cheap." She clutched her handbag as though it contained everything she owned in the world and gave me a forced smile. She had a job either at Forget What or at a grocery not long ago, so she wasn't used to having no income at all. She'd have to move out of her Unapartment and into civic housing like mine soon, unless she found another job. Finding another job seemed unlikely if she had been a clerk at the grocery, more likely if she really had training in marketing and had worked at Forget What, but I was doubting that more and more, and she couldn't remember it anyway.

We walked without talking down to a noodle stand and stood slurping from steaming cups and watching the bank's street screen display mechanical avatar boxing results. I used to bet on them years before, but when the results stopped feeling real to me, I quit.

"Carla?"

She turned to me instantly, like she was just waiting for me to say something. "Yes, Benjamin?"

Benjamin? Nobody called me that. Khan maybe, Benny, usually, but Benjamin, never. I liked it though. She said it distinctly, pronouncing every syllable clearly and separately. It sounded like an important name. Not like Benny at all. I rolled the name soundlessly around on my tongue, liking it more and more. Finally I pushed it aside.

"How long did you know Paulo? How did you meet him?"

Her shoulders sagged a little, and she sighed. She looked across the street toward an older, dark-skinned man in a dark gray suit who was playing the harmonica and stomping out some blues for a small crowd near the VRcade.

"I don't remember meeting Paulo exactly," she said after a moment of listening during a pause in the ground traffic. "He was friendly and we just got to talking in the vator or waiting for it sometimes. He came into the grocery once in a while. I didn't really know him. He was just an acquaintance. I knew he lived in the building, but I didn't know where."

She paused then looked back toward the bank. "Do you think they fix the outcome in avatar boxing? It certainly looks real to me. Isn't it regulated or something?" She wanted to change the subject, but I needed to know a little more.

I slurped the last of my noodles and tried to look relaxed. "When was the last time you talked to him?"

"Oh, I don't know. A month maybe." She looked me in the eye. "Why do you care? Were you and he—close?" She said close like she meant having-an-affair close. She was watching me, expecting a reaction. The pepper in the noodles made my face flush. Why was I so attracted to this woman? I had to admit she was pretty, but there was more to it than that. I'd been around pretty women before and they didn't have this effect on me. Some of them even wanted to affect me, though I admit I didn't know why.

"No, we weren't *close*. Paulo and I didn't interact much, but there are just a few things I don't understand."

I folded the noodle cup and put it in the bin next to the vendor's stand. Bits and pieces of the music filtered through the noise while I waited for her to finish her dinner. The harmonica player was singing, "Key to the Highway," and playing fills and turnarounds as he went along.

Carla folded up her cup, threw it in the bin, then looked at me expectantly. I asked her if she wanted to go for a walk.

"I'd like that," she said, holding her hands out in a which-way-should-we-go gesture.

I pointed up E'Clair toward Morph Street and we started walking that way. Our hands brushed, and I nervously pointed at construction equipment across the street to hide my confusion about taking her hand. "The city is digging low-income housing there; twelve stories deep. They haven't been able to find anyone to develop the above ground part yet." I thought I sounded like a tour guide.

"You make it sound like they're going to bury poor people," she said. "Actually, from what I've read the developers have orders for three more of those below ground apartment buildings for upper class people. They're going to be terribly expensive. Sunshine piped in through mirrored light tubes, or the fake stuff when it's a cloudy day. They shine it in behind display windows showing any scene you want in hologram so it changes as you move around in your room. They're planning to place little camera posts in a few select places in the world then pipe in the actual scenery. You get a view out your window of a sandy beach or a winter mountain top. Sounds pretty nice to me." She described the pit as though she would love to live there, but I knew the apartments they were creating at this location wouldn't have piped in light or scenic views. They would be little concrete coffins far below ground level where gov could hide the indigent, so people with jobs wouldn't have to look at them anymore.

We crossed the street and looked down in the hole, which was already lined in plastic concrete to keep out the water. Morph was a long normal street in Chicago except here, where a tooth had been pulled leaving a hole in Chicago's jaw that I thought would get infected quickly enough.

"For the people who can afford them, the amenities will be nice, but I doubt this pit will have piped in sunlight."

Carla leaned on the fence and stared down into the dark. "No, probably not." She sounded wistful.

We turned right on Morph and walked into the evening wind which was blowing from the lake. The air smelled of dead alewives and rust. We passed a canned meat market and Carla said, "I like their lamb when I can afford it. The real stuff is a bit strong, but the fifty-fifty is good."

"Yeah, lamb is a favorite of mine, too. My brother has meat all the time."

"Maybe the next time we go out, we should go to your brother's house," she said.

I looked at her. She was suppressing a smile, but not doing a very good job of it. I hadn't been teased in years.

"It would be an improvement over the noodle stand, and I'm sure Arno wouldn't mind," I said, imagining Arno's reaction to my bringing my own date instead of trying to work with someone he thought was a match. I laughed out loud. Arno would not like the idea that I might do something better than him, even if it was picking my own girlfriends. I guided her right, onto Quacker.

"My brother would like you too much, and besides, it's not a romantic place."

She stopped.

Women have a way of displaying several emotions at the same time when they want to. Men can't or don't do that. We are creatures of a single emotion at a time. It's one of the reasons men tend to make a firm decision that is wrong rather than hesitate and waffle and appear unsure. Whatever we're thinking, we're positive about it.

Carla stared at me with her head slightly tilted and a wisp of an enigmatic smile on her lips. She looked coy and happy and intensely sensuous at the same time. I wasn't sure exactly what I'd said that produced that mixture, but I liked the look. I wanted to wrap my arms around her and hold her for a while. She slowly turned forward again and we started walking. I could tell she was thinking, but I didn't know if that was a good thing or not.

When we arrived at the alley, I stopped, took a deep breath and looked at her. I wanted to see if she had any reaction to the place. She looked up at me expectantly, so I leaned over and kissed her. It seemed like the thing to do. Her lips were warm and friendly, but I felt like a clumsy lout. When I pulled back, I wasn't sure if she would feel like I'd pulled back because I didn't like it or what, but she smiled a relaxed smile and leaned against me. In my mind, I fought a battle between feeling like we'd known each other for years, like she was a part of me, and feeling that we'd just met, that I was smitten with a kind of puppy love reaction to closeness and emotional eye contact. It's what love was supposed to be, I guessed. I'd heard people say that. But the strong feelings made me uncomfortable. I just wasn't used to that emotional level. It invigorated me and tired me out at the same time.

"Come back in the alley," I said, "I want to show you something." I didn't want to, but I had to know what her reaction would be.

She lifted an eyebrow, but followed me back anyway. The sun was low and hidden behind the buildings, but we could still see. I showed her The Carla, now Carma, Alley Blues Club sign. "I don't even remember this alley being here," she said, "and I walk by here all the time to go to the grocery. It's just around the corner. Doesn't look like the club's been closed very long either."

Things were beginning to make sense. If Carla couldn't remember the alley, then she must have had a forget session that included Carla Alley just as I had. I wondered if Carla had been there when I found the body.

"The alley's named after Anton Carla, some politician, but I like the name."

Carla smiled a tight, cursory smile to acknowledge the compliment, then turned and walked back out to Quacker Street. I followed her out. There was a restaurant neither of us could ever afford legally on one side of the alley entrance and a surveillance and voyeur supplies store on the other. "Do you remember the restaurant and that store?" I said pointing to one then the other.

"Sure. Like I said, I walked by here all the time. At that store they have displays in the window that show who's looking in the store. You can see yourself in the display, which is nothing special, but you can also see what you look like from behind. I guess they have cameras on the other side of the street. It's kind of weird to see yourself that way. Why don't we go somewhere else? This place spooks me. This alley isn't supposed to be here. It's like they created it yesterday just to blink me."

I had to admit it made me feel that way too. Every brick, every bag, every piece of broken glass looked too defined and distinct, as though it had been painted too perfectly. The rotten smell of garbage and decay and the lack of any breeze made the whole scene feel overdone.

But I had one more question. She was looking at the window of the surveillance place. I watched her in the reflection. "Did you know Judge Kimbanski?" I didn't expect any reaction at all, just a "no, who's that?"

She spun around, eyes wild, breathing hard. She grabbed my arms. "Oh, no. I mean, yes. I knew him." She turned around and ran down the street a few stores. When I caught up with her, she was crying. I hugged her, but I wanted to ask her who Kimbanski was to her, and why she had said, 'Oh no,' like that. Instead I waited. Which wasn't like me at all.

I had no doubt then that Carla must have been there when I found the violently beaten body. I must have sent her away before I keyed the police to report it. And I decided that I'd been right in the first place; I had left myself a clue. I must have wanted to find Carla after things simmered down. I looked down at the top of her head, which lay against my shoulder, and I understood why I wouldn't want to forget a woman like her. I could feel my heart in my chest.

I figured I also must have wanted to forget she was at the scene of the murder of Judge Kimbanski in case the police followed up with more questions later. I wouldn't have wanted to ever implicate her in any way. If I couldn't remember, I wouldn't have anything to hide. I'm not a very good liar.

She settled down a bit, and I edged us next to a building, so we weren't in the way of pedestrian traffic. "What do you remember?" I asked, still holding her.

She looked up at me with stricken gray eyes, and I almost kissed her again. "I remember his name, and I remember being really upset about him. I cried for days about it, but I don't know why. That name makes me shiver though. I remember being on this street with him. I think he was a client." She turned away from me suddenly.

A client. Carla was a pro. She hadn't wanted to admit that to me, but it explained her affording her apartment on a grocery clerk's wages. I held onto her. I wanted her to know I wasn't rejecting her just because she had clients, but I'd expect her to stop now that we—well..., I felt like an idiot again. "Carla, was that about a month ago?"

"Yes," she whispered.

"Did he take you anywhere?"

"Yes, to that restaurant next to the alley."

"He was murdered in that alley."

I regretted saying that immediately. She shook all over. "Oh, no. I knew that didn't I? I was there wasn't I?" She turned around and faced me again, tears running down her cheeks. She grabbed my shirt. "Did I kill him? Benjamin, did I kill him?"

I tried to come up with all the reasons why she couldn't have killed him, or at least to come up with a better a suspect. I wanted a scenario I could believe, so I could convince her of its possibilities. "No," I said, "but you saw somebody do it. I found you and the body, but I must have told you to leave before the police arrived. I guess I didn't tell them about you. Paulo must have seen me find the body, and he must have figured out that you were there too. Paulo worked at Forget What. He must have made you forget what you saw. I can only guess that he blackmailed me into having my memories removed as well, or maybe I got a forget to forget I saw you there so I couldn't incriminate you later. I don't know. Either way, I left myself a clue."

I'd left myself a clue, so I'd find her again. I hadn't cared about the body or the police investigation or even that Paulo knew who killed the judge. Or even if he'd killed Kimbanski himself. I had just wanted to make sure I found the woman who I'd last seen, or maybe just met, under circumstances I'd be forgetting.

OK, I knew I could be wrong. It was possible that she had killed the judge, but, still, I wanted to believe it was someone else. Paulo seemed a good choice. Thinking of him as the murderer left Carla innocent in my mind. And besides, Paulo was dead and Carla was in my arms crying, her eyes shining and reflecting the street lights and she smelled so lavender-sweet and blameless and her body felt so comfortable and agreeable against mine.

We walked slowly back south, my arm over her shoulder, her arm around my waist. We talked about the lake freezing over the year before and, when a buzzcar flashed past us at 10 meters doing 100, we talked about how loud buzzcars were; we had a common enemy.

We also talked about her family. Her father had drunk some bad milk and died a couple years before. Her mother lived in the Pine Tree, a mixed apartment and business office building that looked very much like a thirty-story white pine, branches and cones and everything. The Tree was the last architectural marvel of the AIN, Architecture Imitating Nature, movement.

Carla laughed at my jokes, but not too hard. She asked me if there were any apartments open in my building. I told her that it was a bit of a dump, but that there were empty units. I'd ask.

When we arrived at my apartment, Detective Kumar was there waiting again, but he was alone. He didn't seem surprised to see Carla. We'd probably been observed the whole time we were together, but there are times when nothing is worth getting upset about. I was feeling mellow.

He studied Carla carefully for a moment, "What did you find out?" he said. Carla closed her eyes and leaned against me.

"Paulo killed the judge, didn't he?" I said.

"That's the easy answer." He raised an eye brow and rubbed his goatee still looking at Carla. "She doesn't remember anything, does she?" he stated.

I felt Carla stiffen then she tilted her head up. "Remember what?" she said.

I squeezed her shoulder a little in what I hoped would be a comforting gesture. "No. She doesn't remember the alley at all. She said she walked past it all the time, but didn't ever notice it."

"It's creepy," Carla said.

The detective sighed. "Keep your head low," he said, as though he expected someone to be shooting at it, but I thought the line was just something police said as a sort of see-you-later thing. He stared at Carla for a moment, then left, but his stare lingered in my mind. He was thinking something I didn't like. He was thinking Carla had more to do with the murder, but that she had forgotten about it. He was thinking she was a suspect, and I guess maybe I was thinking he was right.

I palmed the lock and ushered Carla into my apartment. Looking around as she scanned the apartment, I realized how dull, even lifeless, my apartment was. No color at all except for the orange PAL on the table. Only government issue PALs were orange. I felt a bit queasy with shame for living there. I was poor. I was the poor the city was digging holes to hide. I'd never really felt poor before, I just didn't have any spending money. The gov gave me enough money to eat and buy some clothes once in a while. That had always been enough. Carla looked out of place standing there looking over my apartment, a polished sapphire tossed in a dirty paper sack.

Carla took off her coat, kissed me as though she would always be kissing me, then laid down on the bed hugging the pillow under her face. I suppose that might have been an invitation, but she was tired, and I'd put her through a lot of emotional trauma at the alley. In any case, she fell asleep quickly.

She slept for hours and while she slept, I paced, pausing once in a while to look at her. If, when I'd been doing my forget, I thought she had killed the judge, I wouldn't have left the clue for me to follow to find her. I wouldn't have wanted to find her. I knew I might still be giving myself too much credit for intellectual capacity, but who was I to argue? I laid down beside her on the narrow bed. She opened her eyes enough to see it was me. She snuggled closer and went back to sleep.

I fell asleep trying to imagine what it would be like to live with someone and what kind of job I could get that would be legal.

Chapter 11

I woke up struggling to come up with any believable motive for Paulo to have killed a judge.

I could see Paulo killing someone, don't get me wrong, but he'd need a powerful reason. Something that would get him sufficiently upset and angry to make him do it. Paulo might kill in an emotional rage, but I didn't think he would kill for money or power or any of the other reasons that might make a person commit murder even after careful consideration of the options and the consequences.

I rolled over and stared at the ceiling, trying to piece together old memories and implications.

It would have to have been Chen. Paulo would have killed for Chen. Not because of jealousy, they'd been together far too long and were too cozy for that. But he would protect Chen if he had to, or if he believed he had to.

And I could imagine Chen needing to be protected once in a while. He irritated a lot of people and seemed to like to make enemies of those who he thought had no sense of humor. He couldn't comprehend why the guys he thatched didn't want to talk about the experience a few days later. Chen got beat up several times because he talked to his victims and laughed at their angry indignation.

What's more, I couldn't figure out just what Chen did to make money. He always seemed to have enough for gadgets, wild costumes, restaurants and a nice apartment, but he never had to be at work. The news report had said he wasn't employed.

Also, I'd accepted his propensity for wearing odd makeup and modifying himself as something he just liked to do, but what if he had been disguising himself to avoid the police? And what about his rules for getting to his apartment? All these oddities had been apparent for as long as I'd known him, I just didn't think about them much; the subject never came up. I guess I'd always known he was into something illegal but didn't care.

The news had said the judge was investigating narcotics distribution in the city, but I just didn't see Chen distributing or selling illegal drugs. He used them, mostly derpal, but he didn't seem mean enough to deal. Yet the more I thought about it, the more I felt it was possible. After all, he must have known how much his ass thatching hurt. I learned how painful that could be when he thatched my finger. The searing heat lasted for hours.

Then I realized Carla wasn't lying beside me anymore. I got up and found a note written on the back of a hardcopy of a Forget What bill. "You are sleeping peacefully, so I'm leaving. Call me." There was no signature. I looked back at my bed. Somehow I could picture her there naked even though she hadn't taken off her clothes. I breathed out, and my mind went blank for a moment. I was in deep, and I didn't even know her. I felt like an adolescent boy with a crush, all knees and elbows, hesitant and worried if she liked me as much as I liked her.

But, there was still a tiny rock in my shoe. Who killed the judge? Was it Carla? I couldn't be sure it wasn't, and that concerned me.

Another thing that bugged me was that the neighbor identified Chen's body. Chen looked different just about every day. He grew a beard and shaved it off, sometimes he would shave his head or wear a wig. He paid for injections to make his lips big. He always wore different makeup when he was out. One time, he had his nose made smaller, then a few months later, he had it made larger than it was in the first place. One day he would look like a successful gov official, then the next day he'd look like a bum. How would his neighbor even know what Chen looked like?

I decided to go down to the city morgue and take a look for myself. I didn't think anyone would have claimed the body.

●●●

The city morgue was next to a city garbage incinerator. Up Your News once reported that the city was burning unidentified bodies with the garbage. The city responded by saying that that would be illegal, that the city had to use licensed cremation facilities, but the number of cremations of unknowns had dropped forty percent before the release of the article.

The trash was separated into the basic material that could be burned and the material that had to be carted off and buried in a dump outside Rockford. The stuff destined for burial was covered with people searching for anything of value. A young girl dressed in gray was holding up the card cage from an old computer and trying to carry it down the precarious mountain. She fell and disappeared, but soon climbed back out of the hole triumphantly still holding the cage, a prize worth only the value of the metal.

I walked past the trash junkies and pickers and into the converted meat processing plant, which was now storing bodies. At the front desk sat an older man wearing glasses and an attitude. Apparently, he didn't believe in having his eyes repaired. He stared fixedly at his PAL until I rapped my knuckles on the table. He glared at me, brows down, probably thinking I was a trash junkie asking to use the bathroom.

"Hi," I said, trying to act as though coming in to look at a body was no big deal, "I'm here to see the body of Che Chen. He would have been brought in a couple of days ago."

The old guy sighed the sigh of old bones and walked around to the metal door to let me in. "Sure, why not. Everybody else has." I wanted to ask who else had looked, but I didn't want him getting interested in me. I was just an acquaintance coming down to see the body. Nothing more. "You got to sign in," he said, pointing to a tablet on a stainless steel table. This table looked the same as the table at the police station, right down to the little metal loops for hooking handcuffs to.

I signed in slowly while looking at the previous signatures. None were familiar, but I knew as I signed the name Wolf Irishman as illegibly as I thought I could get away with, that, just like me, anyone who came to visit Chen would not want to leave any useful clues. Then I walked past the cameras and decided that in the future I would need to plan more before I acted.

I expected drawers, but the bodies were laid out on rolling gurneys in a huge cooler. The old man looked at a screen near the door, nodded, and said, "Yep, 104."

We walked past rows of white bags tented in the shape of men, women and children, seemingly floating three feet above the floor, then he stopped and zipped one open. The makeup had been wiped off, leaving smears of red and yellow. The wig had been removed. The hole at his temple had been cleaned. It wasn't Chen.

"Beandogs!" I said before I thought enough to realize I shouldn't do anything to bring attention to myself. It wasn't Chen, it was Sukey, a friend of Chen's who did look a bit like Chen now that I looked for the resemblance. He looked enough like Chen to fool an acquaintance or a neighbor, but not to fool a friend. I turned and looked at the old guy. "He owed me money."

"You won't get it back now, will you? Not unless you go after him." He grinned. I thought he looked a bit maniacal.

"Why, you think he took it with him?"

He glared at me for a moment. "Let's go. It's too cold in here to stand around and crack wise."

I didn't know Sukey that well, but I felt like another friend had died. He'd had some hard times lately, and I was saddened by his death, but I was also a little mad at him for being there where Chen was supposed to be.

I walked out, frustrated that things were getting worse rather than better. Now, I not only didn't know who killed the judge, but I didn't know why Sukey's body was on Chen's gurney at the morgue, or where Chen was, or why I hadn't looked at Paulo's body too, just to make sure he, unlike Chen, was actually dead.

Chapter 12

I bought some jerked beandogs and vitamin water on the way to Carla's, but she wasn't at her apartment. I sat down in the hall, enduring the stares from the tenants standing by the vators, and ate while trying to figure out what to do next. I finished my dog and started on hers before I decided Jon Tam was my best bet for reducing the number of open questions. He and Chen had always been close friends. He lived south of Incongruous, and I decided to walk off some of the beandogs' sleep inducing effects.

Sunny, clean air blew across dusty brown pavement, and the air didn't seem to mind. People passed by with purposeful strides, but me, I drifted along. I felt the need to relax and clear my thoughts, listen to the sounds and smell the scents of the city. I unfocused my eyes, and walked along, head down, and among the crowd, so I wouldn't get hit by a car.

Chicago was a town of motion. The wind was strong and almost perpetual, the people moved in swarms along the wide sidewalks, the political environment was always stormy, and the lakeside buildings were following the level of the lake and sliding into the lake basin. Immersed in all that movement, my life felt still; the same for many years. Before, I hadn't considered that a bad thing. I got along, had some fun now and then, taught myself things. Now I thought of Carla and knew she wouldn't want just that. She was used to more. She'd want more, and I'd want more too if she were with me.

The people who walked along beside me had jobs they were hurrying to, or perhaps families they were hurrying back to. I had nothing like that, which had never bothered me before. Seeing these people rush around used to make me feel superior because I didn't have to be anywhere at any particular time, and I didn't have to spend eight hours a day working for a company or six working for the gov. I'd always felt rich in time and vocation. Being poor isn't so bad as long as you don't know what you're missing, as long as you can convince yourself that you don't want or need what everyone else has. It becomes a focus, though, it becomes an obsession, when suddenly, everyone you look at seems to have what you just realized you want. You start to feel unlucky, and you start to feel down.

Jon Tam lived in the rooms behind the reservation desk of an apartment building that used to be an upscale hotel. When travel became so difficult and expensive that people didn't come to Chicago anymore, many of the hotels were converted to living spaces. A small room with a bathroom was the standard apartment for the working poor.

No one in their right mind lived on the first floor in this area of town, but Jon Tam never seemed worried about that. No one bothered him.

I waited outside for a buzzcab to lift off from the driveway in front of the building, then walked in behind a fat woman and her skinny kid.

As soon as my eyes adjusted to the low light in the dark green lobby, I saw that Jon Tam's apartment was a crime scene. The whole area around the front desk had been marked off with tape, and a uniform leaned up against a square pillar to the left near the entrance to the apartment. I figured there was probably a flat camera on me at that moment, so I didn't try to act like I came in with the woman and her son, or like I was coming to visit someone else. When they reviewed the tape, I'd be digitally ID'ed and Goatee Kumar would know I'd been there anyway. Instead, I walked right up to the cop and said, "What happened here?"

He stood away from the pillar, his eyes narrowing as his arms went from crossed to hanging ready by his side. "Who are you?"

"Benjamin Khan," I said distinctly and with confidence as though he should know who I was, but I could see myself in the mirror that hung behind the old reservation desk and realized I wasn't fooling anybody. That was also when I saw Chen's reflection. He was walking out of the elevator and toward the door behind me. He had on a gray overcoat, gray pants and black businessman's shoes. He was bald, but it was undeniably Chen. He winked at me in the mirror, then turned and angled out the door.

"So, what's going on," I asked the uniform again, trying my best not to seem agitated. Actually, I was trying not to look annoyed. Chen knew I was being monitored, yet he walked right by smiling and winking as though this were some kind of acting school and this whole thing was a test of my ability to appear calm under stress.

I suspect he thought my predicament was amusing.

The cop harrumphed. "I think Detective Kumar will have some questions for you. Why don't you sit down here and wait?" It wasn't a question. He put his hands on his hips, which put his left hand just above his holster. OK, I should have just acted like I knew someone else in the building and walked on when I first entered the building and saw the tape, but I didn't have any other leads at that moment.

Detective Kumar came out of Jon Tam's apartment about then and saw me in a stare-down with the cop. "Well, Benny," he said, "What brings you to Mr. Tam's apartment? Just coming to see a friend?"

He said "coming to see a friend" like that's the answer a bad liar would give, so I said, "Yes, that's exactly right. What brings you here?"

Kumar came around the front desk. He motioned the cop toward the door to Jon Tam's. "Go lock the place up. Make sure about the windows too." The cop looked me over one last time as though he thought he might have to identify me in a lineup someday and didn't want to make any mistakes. He scowled, took one step back to get out of range of me making a reach for his gun, then turned abruptly and swaggered back to the apartment.

Kumar turned to address me.

There are two kinds of bully. There are the ones that are mean and obvious. They get right in next to you and tell you they're going to break your legs, or your nose, or your balls. They might wave a gun around. They might yell and stomp. They get on their toes and in your face like a male bird fighting for a mate or an alpha dog asserting her dominance. And then there are the ones who act like a friend trying to do you a favor. They might act like they're making you a deal, "I'm trying to help you, but you need to help me a little too." They might put an arm around your shoulder, talk quietly, use your name a lot, but all the while there remains a subtle undertone of violence. They move around the real issue like a gently circling shark or like an eagle soaring above its prey. An eagle will suddenly fold up its wings at just the right moment and drop like a cannonball for the kill. Kumar was the second kind of bully.

"You're always turning up just when you shouldn't, aren't you

Benny?" he said in a conversational, sympathetic way, as though we were chums.

"I guess I have a knack. Is Jon Tam dead too?"

"No. He's at the station. Maybe I should bring you in too, Benny. I bet you remember something about the judge's death you haven't told me yet. Isn't that right?"

I watched him closely. He thought I knew something. In fact, he appeared sure of it. I wished at that moment I knew what it was he thought I knew, because I felt completely ignorant. "Look," I said, "I just came to see him because he was good friends with Chen and Paulo, and I thought he might need a little consolation. I thought maybe he'd want to go out for a beer or something."

Kumar leaned against a post. "It'll be awhile before Mr. Tam can go out for a beer. We arrested him for running a derpal kitchen right here in the hotel."

Derpal was one of those drugs that people liked to use for years and years. Those I knew who used it weren't in any hurry to quit. It was cheap and easy to make. For most people it made them drunk about four minutes after one swig. But for those hardened users, you could drink it through your nose and get a special woozy that was as intense as it was fleeting. People who used it that way would become very mad when it was gone. I'd thought that was what happened to Chen and Paulo, but knowing that at least Chen was still alive made me wonder.

I nodded solemnly to Kumar. Just like any other work based on commission, detective work was unfair and biased. I felt like pushing Kumar's buttons because he was working so hard to push mine. I guess I just felt mean at that particular moment; and more than a little frustrated. "How much you get for bagging a derpal kitchen and making the arrest?" I said. "Can't be much. Do all the big jobs, the ones with the big money busts, go to the chief's kids? Maybe you should think about a different line of work if this is the type of bone the department is tossing you." I turned and walked toward the doors. I tried to swagger like the uniform had.

"Hey," Kumar said to my back. "I know it wasn't Chen who died. If you'd told me that, I might have let Carla out, thinking you were on the good guys' side."

I spun around, "Carla?"

"Carla's in custody too," he said. He actually smiled. I wasn't overly surprised to find out he enjoyed my predicament just as Chen did, but he wanted to make sure I knew he enjoyed it. That, I found especially maddening, which, I suppose, was his intent. "She was seen at the restaurant next to the alley with the judge right before he died. I'm holding her on suspicion right now."

I wanted to smack him. I wanted to scream at him. But my mouth opened and closed and nothing came out. The usual wise-crack was nowhere to be found. Fear had ripped even the interest in a smart response right out of me. I must have looked like a hooked fish gulping air.

The cop came back out of the apartment at that moment. While I thrashed on the line, Kumar turned toward him and said, "Turn on the cameras, Carmine. I want to know who else comes visiting tonight." He turned back to me and smiled. If smirking were a performance art, Kumar would have been able to sell tickets. "Let me know if you find out anything else of interest, won't you?"

"I know right where to find you, detective." I couldn't look at him anymore. The swagger had been taken out of me, so I plodded out the door.

Carla was locked up, and, as I stomped toward the street, I felt more alone than I'd ever felt in my life. Not much affected me before I met Carla, but now I had something to lose. My loneliness was like a lens magnifying my anger. I shoved my fists in my pockets hard enough to hurt my hands and my jacket. Ineffectual, idiotic lout. Saying that to myself over and over didn't help either. Usually, I could use reverse psychology. If I kept telling myself I was stupid, I would eventually admit that maybe that wasn't really true, and that I was being too critical, but even my self-deprecation wasn't working. I was accepting my insults as a completely accurate assessment.

The third person I walked into gave me a shove, and I cursed him. I stomped on.

I felt sure Carla couldn't have killed the judge, and I felt sure that if she knew who had killed the judge she would tell the police, but my reasoning wouldn't hold up for anyone who wasn't in love with her. I had to get her out of jail, and I knew the only way she was going to be released anytime soon was if I figured out who murdered the judge. To do that, I needed to talk to Chen.

I tramped North on Bigbash, trying to decide if I could watch Jon Tam's apartment building long enough to meet up with Chen without the police noticing. Maybe he lived there now, maybe not. I didn't know if he would return to the building at all, but it was the only lead I had.

A guy in a gray coat brushed passed me. When I glanced over to scowl at him, he winked at me and said, "Meet me Under The River at seven," then he sped up and turned left on Gripe Street.

Chapter 13

Chen must have thought we were being watched when he passed me on the street, and I suppose we were. Much of the city was under surveillance at any moment. If Kumar wanted to see where I went and who I had talked to, he could do it, but he'd spend hours looking through memsticks from each store's outside cameras. I doubted I was worth that effort.

Under The River, where Chen had asked to meet, was an abandoned, below-street-level train station the size of a soccer stadium, which was actually alongside the river, rather than under it. The east side was open to the weather and looked down onto the mud of the Chicago River. The homeless and the hoboes and the bums used Under The River as a place to stay warm and somewhat safe in a chaotic mix of boxes, barrels, rummage tables, and day-old-food markets. It was a cavernous place, bounded by a low wall dividing it from the river on its east side and a maze of underground offices and apartments called the Warren on its west.

The Warren housed criminals who could no longer show their faces topside. Everyone called them Gnomes because they would die, or at least be arrested, if sunlight touched them.

The homeless who lived Under The River could have made it difficult for the Gnomes, but it was a symbiotic relationship. The Gnomes of the Warren, who had money if not mobility, paid a group of techs to keep electricity and plumbing and some data flowing. Apparently to keep the metaphor intact, people called the techs who did this work Elves. The homeless acted as a buffer between the Gnomes and the police.

There would be no surveillance cameras Under The River. The police left Under The River to itself. It had law. It had justice. Just not police. The sentence for just about any disturbance was to toss the perpetrator out over the east wall and into the river without trial.

Resting on top of Under The River, were office buildings and apartment towers, their residents mostly unaware that under their feet there was a hidden little Chicago.

I knew Chen would want to meet by the west wall. That's where he often went to buy secondhand gadgets and absurdly inexpensive photonics. Chen had said seven. It was four, and I knew those three hours would last forever if I didn't do something with my hands and my mind other than twitch and fret. I decided to go back and search the public records and even the individual traffic for more references to the judge and his death.

So I went to the library and searched and read and even took notes, which was not a Benny thing to do. I decided it was a Benjamin thing to do though, and compiled a list of questions which I sought to answer. The ones I couldn't find an answer to at the library, I was hoping Chen would help me with. Like, who killed the judge?

One thing I did find out was that the judge wasn't investigating criminal narcotics dealers after all. He was exploring corruption within the narcotics division of the police force, and the investigation was aimed at police who used their surveillance equipment and techniques and a group of prostitutes for blackmail.

The source of this new bit of information was an anonymous police officer on the payroll of Up Your News. Up Your News was chaotic and impudent and irreverent and sometimes silly, but they were always a whirl to read. They had no sense of propriety, and I could never figure out how they avoided being shut down for one reason or another. Not the most dignified news agency, but the most entertaining, and sometimes, the only one with the truth. Sometimes not, but in this case other news agencies claimed they'd also dug out the same information earlier and just didn't report it because the police department asked them not to. Yeah.

They closed the library at six, so I headed for the river. It was a short walk, but the weather wasn't cooperating. The wind made the trip seem like a hike up the Circus Tower. On the positive side, there were few people out in the wind, and I could see anyone who might be following, but no one went my way. I did a few extra circle backs and side trips and came into Under The River by the north stairs.

Under The River was humid, and brightly lit from high intensity lamps and a few low intensity fires. I picked a paper napkin up off the concrete, wadded the cleanest corners into ear plugs and burrowed my way through the crowd along the west wall. Previously, I had been there only during the day, when many of the people were away, out on the streets above scavenging or begging. At night, it was a tight squeeze and the place felt and smelled like the inside of a sweaty old sock. They could have used a little of the wind from topside.

I cruised the tables looking at memstick players where the screen fit right over your eyeball, solar powered personal air conditioners, soap, boots, stuffed birds, even touchpoint jewelry that could make you happy if you went near someone else who wore the matching jewelry. I stopped at a wrist unit table and noticed the time was about ten past seven.

I glanced around and saw Chen a few tables away looking at belts. He'd changed from a gray businessman's look to a sort of pirate garb, wearing a large gold loop in his left ear and a bandana stretched over his head and tied in the back. He had no parrot, yet he gave the impression that he usually had one, that it had just flown off looking for something to eat. I moved generally in his direction, picking things up and putting them down as though browsing.

"I think you need a bigger one," Chen said when I picked up a thong. I'd picked it up without realizing it, but Chen seemed amused.

I had a million questions. I even had the top five written down on a piece of paper somewhere, but all I could come up with was, "What's going on, Chen?"

Chen winked. I was really starting to hate that. With a slight tilt of his head, he motioned for me to follow him. We wove around a bit and ended up at a huge stapled-together box. One piece of the cardboard had a doorknob sticking out. He stuck his hand in a ragged hole near the door, and I heard a click from the palm lock. Chen opened the door and motioned me in.

The inside of the cardboard box was paneled in dark wood. It contained a kitchen, a couch, two easy chairs, and a bath tub. The air was conditioned and comfortable. It was relatively quiet.

Chen took off his coat. "Want a derpal?"

"No," I said, dropping into a chair. I actually relaxed. For the first time in days, I knew the cops didn't know where I was and weren't viewing me. I still had all my troubles, but Chen's relaxed attitude and apparent lack of concern made me feel like things might not be so bad.

Chen quick-frosted a derpal shot and sat down, putting his feet up on an ottoman that slid out smoothly from under the couch. He grinned at me. "Been to see Jon Tam?"

"Yeah, you already know that. I saw you in the mirror. They took him to jail for making derpal."

"Actually, Kumar took him to jail because he makes derpal and because he knows me. I'm surprised Kumar didn't arrest you too. Why haven't they arrested you, Benny?"

I felt suddenly chill. Chen was accusing me of something, though I didn't know what, exactly. And I thought, what if Chen is a murderer? What if Paulo made me forget that? What if Chen brought me here to kill me too, because he thinks I remember too much?

Chen stared at me and sipped his drink. I didn't know what to say. I had planned to be the one to ask the questions. I had planned to be in control.

"I don't know," I said. I looked at the bottom of his shoes, pink gum and part of the wrapper from a straw. I built up a little nerve staring at his soles. "Who killed the judge, Chen?" I looked into his eyes.

He looked back at me. I think he was trying to decide whether to lie to me or not. Finally, he smiled humorlessly and winked. "You killed the judge, Benny. Can't you remember whacking him over the head with a piece of angle iron? No of course not. You forget anything that ties you to your own past. You want to live for the future only, tear off the rear view mirror and act like your history is just an inheritance."

He paused while I reeled. I killed the judge? Could I do that?

"Of course you had the judge's murder forgotten didn't you, Benny? You don't even remember how much you like to forget." Chen continued while he stood up and quick-frosted another derpal. "Do you remember where you went to high school, Benny? What kind of car you used to drive? Do you even remember your mother's name?"

He'd become angry now. Like this was all my fault. But he was right, I couldn't remember my mother's name. Was I an orphan? No. I could picture her clearly standing at a shop's service counter complaining that her new refrigerator had ordered eggs four days in a row when we didn't need eggs, that the refrigerator was faulty, and the refrigerator company should pay for the eggs because she sure wasn't going to. She wore a pale gray shirt and blue pants with a black stripe that wound slowly down her leg like a spring. The spring was more compressed at the top and bottom. Her shoes were white and reflected the sunlight that shone through the plate glass on the shop's store front.

The appliance shop was in Glen Ellyn and faced the CAT tracks. She'd bought a cowboy hat for me that same day. She was upset about the refrigerator, but had been unusually happy the rest of the day. "Clean air," she said. "Enjoy it. It wasn't always like this," and she smiled and we walked hand in hand across the tracks. There was a breeze that blew up the tracks from the west, and she turned toward the afternoon sun then closed her eyes. I remember doing the same thing and feeling the warmth and seeing the red glow of the sun on the inside of my eyelids, imagining I was a plant absorbing the sunlight and growing. The wind caused a cool evaporation on my face, and, as the wind built and dropped, I could sense the sun more and less on my skin. It hadn't rained for a while, so I could smell the dusty tang of the bed gravel that lay between the rails. I opened my eyes and looked at her again. She was looking at me. It was the first time I'd studied her face, and it may have been the first time she looked at me as a young man, I don't know.

Sitting in Chen's box I could remember my mother, just not her name.

Chen came close and leaned down at me. "I keep telling you that forgetting is supposed to be a one-time thing. That each time you use it, you lose more and more other memories, associations, important things, but every time you have something bad happen, you run off and forget all about it. I like you Benny, but forgetting is a drug with you and this time, it cost Paulo his life.

"Paulo?" I was shaking. What had I done? "Sukey killed Paulo, didn't he?"

Chen dumped his derpal down his throat and poured another.

"The world revolves around you, Benny. History changes for you. Things never happened that you don't want to have ever happened. How can you live with yourself? You're a stranger. Don't you ever wake up and wonder who you were the day before? Don't you ever notice the holes, the spaces left blank? Those spaces are emotional things, tragic things, maybe illegal or evil things, but they're part of you. It's the foundation of your personality, and it's full of holes. I don't know what Carla ever saw in you." He turned and went to the sink again.

"Carla?" I grasped onto the only thing that made sense. Carla made sense. I tried to refocus on getting Carla out of jail. I briefly thought about going and giving myself up, but that would only implicate Carla more. Did I actually kill the judge? Dumbfounded and suddenly cold, I sat there feeling very alone.

"Yeah, Carla. You don't even remember who she was to you, you pathetic sap. Things get tough and you forget."

"Who was Carla to me . . . before?"

"Benny, leave her out of your life. I shouldn't have reconnected you two. I thought things had blown over. It's bad enough you made her forget this business and who knows what else from her life as a result, but she's not at fault for anything. Just drop it, or forget it if you have to. Your brain's Lorraine Swiss already. What's another forget one way or the other? Just go in and have everything removed. Your whole life. Start over." Chen frosted another.

"Carla's in jail," I whispered. "I've got to get her out."

"They've got nothing on her. She'll be out in a few days whether you help her or not. Maybe even quicker without your help. You're more likely to mess things up, Benny. You might make them wonder why you want to get her out so badly, make them think maybe you're worried about what she might tell them."

"But I've got to do something." I felt my eyes welling with tears and my face grew hot. I put my head in my hands. I guess I sobbed.

A moment later, Chen slapped me hard on the back of the head. "Get out of here, Benny. I don't want to look at you right now."

I looked up at him. I could see the derpal dripping from his nose.

Chapter 14

I stumbled out the door into the confusion and noise of Under The River. People swirled around me as I plowed my way to the north gate. I ran up the stairs, and once outside, darted across the river to Hacker Drive before I slowed down. Head bent against the wind, I turned north along the river, trying to figure out why I would have killed the judge, what I had done to cause Paulo's death, and why I would have done anything to endanger Carla.

I tried to remember being with Carla at any time previous to the day we had dinner together. I tried to put her at various corners, at restaurants I went to, on the rocks at the lake, in my apartment. She just wasn't there. Trying to find her in my memories made me frantic as though I were searching for my life's savings, which I had somehow misplaced.

It started raining sideways and in my face. It rained and blew hard enough to hurt, but I didn't mind. I was working on bringing Benjamin out from under Benny. Whatever my past, the current situation demanded that I get Carla out of jail. I didn't share Chen's opinion that Kumar would let her go just as quickly even if I did nothing. She was in because of me, and I would get her out.

I started thinking about what Chen had said. I could believe I had killed, but I thought I would need a reason. It just didn't feel right, me killing the judge because he was paying Carla as a client. That seemed the only obvious reason, but since it didn't bother me that much when I heard about it this time, why would it have bothered me more back then? Chen said I caused Paulo's death in some way, but he hadn't said how, and I couldn't imagine it. Could Chen be displacing his guilt onto me? Was he there when Sukey and Paulo had their fight?

I thought about my mother again. I remembered the Glen Ellyn scene, but that was all I could dredge up. The house we had on the west side when I was a kid was painted white with green shutters and had an evergreen shrub on either side of the red door, but for some reason I couldn't remember the inside, only the outside. The image of an angel fish we had named Jerome popped unexpectedly into my head. But I couldn't remember my mother's name. I splashed on, following the sweep of the river toward the lake.

I caught the CAT at Mythagain Street, rode it to Morph, and then walked to the Unapartments. I stood outside the building in the rain, staring up at the dots of silver light falling toward me from the sky, staring up at the wall that disappeared into the darkness. A buzzcar roared by on its way north, probably someone with a family and a dog. Someone with meat on the table and a refrigerator that ordered whatever they needed.

I kept resolving to go talk to Kumar; to ask him what he wanted to let Carla out of jail; to make a deal with the shark. I'd tell him I killed the judge because of Carla, but that she wasn't involved. It was just jealousy. Plain old jealousy, I'd say. But when I'd get to that part, I wouldn't believe it. I knew I couldn't say it with enough truth in my voice. Kumar would know I was lying.

I started shivering and shook myself like a dog.

The more I focused on Chen's words, "You killed the judge, Benny. Don't you remember?" the more I didn't believe them. Chen must have been lying about that for some reason. Killing the judge at that time would have put Carla in danger, and Chen had said Carla meant something to me even before the murder. I knew I wouldn't have purposely put Carla that close to a murder.

Chen wasn't lying about my tendency to forget things, though. I was tempted even at that point to just go forget it all; start over like Chen said. Forgetting was a seductively simple solution, but I would lose Carla again, and I couldn't do that.

There, standing in the rain, blinking up at the Unapartment building, I realized I would not have forgotten the last time either, for all the same reasons. That was the basic fallacy of all my assumptions. I wouldn't have forgotten the murder, even with the street name trick, because I would have had to forget too much about Carla. I knew there was some important piece to the puzzle I was missing. I trudged home still trying to remember what Carla was to me before the murder.

I opened the door to my apartment, turned on the light and stood dripping on the floor. I looked at my apartment with new eyes. Not much of me was there. The furniture was an aggregation of whatever I could find lying out on the street on garbage collection day. I had an orange gov-issue PAL, hooked to a base station, sitting on a small desk. My bed, one corner resting on a stack of bricks, sat under the only window, which was too high on the wall to see anything out of except the clouds and an occasional pigeon sitting on the sill. I had no pictures. No personal items. It was as though I'd survived a fire, but lost all my life's possessions. I had some books, but they didn't look too interesting. I'd found them somewhere and hoped to sell them. Two hardcopies of Forget What bills lay wrinkled on the floor. I had a plastic chair and a metal folding chair.

It didn't feel like home. I didn't know what home felt like, but I somehow knew this wasn't it. The problem with forgetting the past and starting over is that you don't get to take yourself with you. It was why forgetting was used so much by the government. They could correct bad behavior with a quick wipe. Delete the person. Let them start over. For the most part, they didn't need prisons any more, the criminals were new, innocent people immediately after treatment.

Only I'd wiped myself. I didn't know who I was. I wanted it all back. The pain of any memory would have been better than this sudden feeling of emptiness. Starting over isn't as clean as it sounds. It's clumsy and confusing. I felt like a nonperson, not important enough to arrest. Chen didn't even kill me for causing Paulo's death. He'd just sent me off like I was a schoolboy, with a lecture and slap on the back of the head.

I was a walking shadow. Physically, I matched the Benny who should have been, but only in profile. I was just a silhouette. The real me, the accumulation of my experience and thoughts did not exist. I had forgotten him and his mother's name.

I climbed up and stood on my bed to look out my window. From there I could see the metal side of the next building glistening with the rainwater's reflection from a street light. There were two dried out Carrot Doodles on the sill and to the right of them, "Arno has your stuff," was written in the dust.

Chapter 15

My brother didn't seem at all surprised to see me. "I was wondering how long it would take you this time," he said, leading me back to his detached two-story garage.

As we passed the kitchen window, I saw Denise looking out the window at me. She looked unhappy, perhaps concerned. She often looked that way. Arno didn't treat her well. She always tiptoed around like she was worried she would break something. I liked her, but I didn't think there was much I could do to help her.

We entered the garage through the side door. Arno kept his Moto on the first floor and his Milwaukee buzzcar on the second. "Seems like it takes you longer to remember your stuff each time you do a forget," he said. He just stood there gazing at me, waiting for me to say something.

I said, "So?"

He grunted, flipped a switch hidden behind the door, and a section of the ceiling lowered. On it were three open plastic crates a half-meter or so on a side, and a couple of identical handprint-sealed metal containers each the size of a briefcase. I stared at Arno until he got the hint.

"I'll be in the house," Arno said and then he left, closing the door behind him. He acted insulted, but I had more important things to worry about. I was alone with myself, and we'd never met.

I approached my stuff cautiously, as though it were sacred. I looked through the crates first, resisting the urge to look in the locked boxes. I wanted to ease up on my history. The parts of my past I'd felt the need to hide, I didn't want to expose yet.

The open crates were full of the things we collect in life that we have no need to save, yet can't quite recycle.

One crate was packed with books all old and worn, Aristotle on rhetoric, The Complete Wilde, Emerson and De La Mare—"Memory, that strange deceiver! Who can trust her?" The crate also contained books on pattern languages, architecture, timber framing and cabinet construction, harmonica playing, Shaker societies and bookbinding. I'd read, no, I'd studied all of them. I'd also forgotten most of what I might have learned except for an errant quote now and then and maybe a glimpse of understanding about construction or music at particularly lucid times.

Another crate contained pictures of people who I knew were important to me at one time, yet I couldn't place them. A toy buzzcar that would hover a few centimeters above a surface and fly in circles. The power chip still worked. There were labeled disks, some music, some film, some immersion. I saw there was an immersion headset, but I didn't try it out.

The last open crate had tools; wood planes, chisels, auto-lock-picks, a glass cutter, an articulated bolt cutter, knives and two padded wooden boxes containing lenses.

Here was everything I should have had at my apartment, but didn't. My life's accumulation, my only connection to the past, had been stuffed into a few boxes hidden above a secret panel in the ceiling of my brother's garage.

But, in the end, none of this seemed like mine. I felt like I had broken into someone else's garage and was looking at their possessions. I felt like an intruder, embarrassed and a bit criminal.

Finally, I pulled a handprint-locked box off the pile. There were two, but they both looked the same, so, in a fit of superstition, I took the one farther from me. I put my hand on the reader, and opened it. Inside were six bundles of swipe cards held together with rubber bands and seven bundles of cash each marked "fifty thousand" on a paper label. A quick glance through the cards showed each had nine thousand on it. At twenty cards per bundle, that totaled up to more than a million four. It was a shocking amount of money. Enough money to live like the mayor for the rest of my life.

I stared at the contents of the box in stunned amazement. Wild thoughts ricocheted around in my head. I could spend money, real money. I could buy an apartment for Carla and me. I could afford to have a kid and fix whatever was wrong with him right off. I pictured a house.

But then I started to wonder. Why would I have so much money? How had I acquired it? What's more, I'd had the money to pay for the forget in the first place, but I didn't use it. Why? I admit, I'm cheap, but cheap is a relative thing. To a rich person, a couple thousand is not a big deal, and I was a rich person.

The other box seemed ominous now. I squinted at it fearfully.

I knew it wasn't more money. Somehow I just knew that. I'd packed them, then forgot them; some residual memory must have remained. I pocketed a few swipe cards and set the first box aside.

I palmed the lock on the second box, but hesitated to open it. After a deep breath, I flipped the lid and pulled my hand back as though a snake might strike out at me. The box contained two guns without holsters, each with three clips banded to them, two unlabeled metal vials, which I knew immediately were some type of poison. The blue one would be a gas and the red one a liquid. Both were deadly. I knew this. It bothered me that I knew this, yet I recognized that these tokens of death were how I made the money in the other box.

Inside this box was another. This one with an eyescan lock. This third, smaller box contained a few gadgets including a thatcher that said "slice" on the side, which I pocketed, and a block of nitroceramic used to start a fire when you don't want anyone to know it was started on purpose, two egg-sized grenades painted to look like silver ornaments or possibly ben-wa balls, and a dime-sized stun plate, called a slapfaint, that you could smack on any open skin to incapacitate your victim. One block of nitroceramic was rigged to sensors on the box. The box would self-destruct in a burst of flame if someone tried to by-pass the eye scan.

There was also an envelope taped to the inside of the lid. I sat down on the floor and pulled out the pencil and four hand printed sheets of paper. The sparse first page had many dates across the top, each lined out except the last; September 7, just before what I thought was my last forget.

The letter started out with: "If you've found this then you're on the way to recovery from your last forget. Make sure you add any new information now, as you may not have a chance before you have to forget again."

I pushed the pages away as though they had started to burn. I could feel what was coming next, and I didn't want to know for sure. A tight fear gripped my stomach. I took two deep breaths, consciously calmed myself and cautiously picked the pages back up.

The second page was divided into horizontal rows, each containing a name, a number in the thousands that increased going down the page and a check mark. The last name was Judge Omar

Kimbanski. The number next to it was two hundred thousand. The last column was blank.

Chen was right. I did murder the judge. I'd been paid well for it. It's what I did. I murdered people for money.

The list was on old paper. The first kill was Dujo Kay, nine years before. There were fourteen more names, some carefully written, some written with a flourish. The judge's name was written with an unsteady hand. It looked as though I wasn't happy about it.

I had trouble reading the other names. My hands trembled. I started sobbing as I scanned through the list of people I'd killed already. I couldn't remember any of them. I couldn't remember their faces, I couldn't remember how I'd killed them. I had listed their names, so I would know just how good I was.

I scooted back against a wall and pulled my knees up against my chest. I put the paper down, wrapped my arms around my knees, and stared at my distorted reflection in the curved bumper of Arno's maroon Moto. How I could have murdered all those people? I stopped crying, but the air left my lungs, and I barely had the will to suck more back in.

Hysteria lay just below the surface of my consciousness, ready to reach up and pull me under. So that's who I really am, I thought. I murder people for money.

I wiped my eyes and tried to envision Carla's face, her navy blue dress with the cream collar she'd worn to dinner, her bouncing foot, the hole in her shoe. I picked up the letter again and pushed on.

The third page included a brief inventory and explained the use of the vials, the guns and how they were used, everything I would need to do my next assassination. The letter used that word, assassination, but I knew I was a murderer. There was no doubt of that.

The last page explained the history of my murdering techniques with a clinical evaluation of method. The letter sounded dry and factual, as though I didn't really remember the information when I wrote the letter, just that I'd read it in the previous letter or someone had told it to me. The descriptions made me wonder why I'd murdered Kimbanski in such an unprofessional way. Why hadn't I poisoned him, or shot him, or used the slapfaint on him then slit his throat?

The letter continued with advice on how to get more money out of my brother for an assignment. He found the clients and was the middleman, but I did the killing, and I admonished myself to make sure I received sufficient remuneration for it. The letter used the word agent to describe my brother's relationship to me, but he was more like a pimp.

I thought back to that day on the CAT tracks in the sunshine with my mother. How did two brothers like us emerge from such a sweet childhood? I suspected that my first forget was related to this inconsistency somehow, but I'd never know.

The last bit of information was that I sometimes worked with a woman named Carla who was often able to maneuver the victim into a trap because she was so pretty and was a good actress as well as an accomplished assassin in her own right. Her assists were marked with an asterisk, it said. There were five marked that way, including the judge.

Arno knocked on the door. I tried to control my voice. "I'll just be a few more minutes," I yelled.

I held the pencil from the eye-scan box and carefully put a check mark beside the judge's name. Looking back at the list, I saw that most of the other check marks were clean strokes, as though I were checking off a grocery list. The one I'd just made by the judge's name was shaky and small. The check mark before that one wasn't much steadier. Maybe I'd started down the path of guilt before the last one, before the judge.

While I packed up the boxes, I took the rest of the cash and swipe cards. I distributed my wealth around in my pockets, putting most of it in pockets in the inner layers and keeping a petty cash pocket in my coat. I wasn't sure if I could really come back. The desire to know more about my history was fading fast. I felt leaden, and it was hard to breathe. I locked the last box, noting that the tamper-proofing nitroceramic gelpacks were in place, and put it on the panel. The memorabilia of my life looked meager sitting there in a stack. The boodle in my pockets felt conspicuous, like a lie about to be found out.

I had considered myself opportunistic, but not evil. Maybe there's a thin line between the two, but I knew which side murder for money was on, and I thought I was no longer on that side of the line.

There were obviously others, however, who I'd worked for, who paid me for murder, who might suspect that my box contained more secrets than it did. I was a hired assassin who might have second thoughts after any forget session, and there would be people who wouldn't like me walking around if I was no longer in their pay. The government was willing to let killers go after they'd forgotten whatever made them killers. Apparently I'd forgotten whatever had made me a killer, but I would be a potential liability to anyone I'd worked with before, so my own life was in danger.

The killing and forgetting sequence must have happened many times before, perhaps as many times as there were murders on the list. Each time, my brother would have had to evaluate me to see if I'd changed too much to accept another job. How had I acted the previous times? What would give me away this time? I had to bank on my employers viewing me as a valuable resource, too important to throw away without knowing they'd used the last drop. Being quiet and noncommittal would keep them wondering, but opening my mouth would remove all doubt.

Arno was there hovering and smiling when I opened the door.

"We still partners?" he said.

I thought it best to sound like I was willing to kill again. "Yeah," I said, "we're still partners," but I couldn't smile, even as an act. Did he know I suddenly didn't like him at all? Did he know I felt nauseous?

We walked back past the kitchen window. Denise was still there. She wasn't doing anything. Just watching, sad faced.

"I can give you a ride home," he said without looking at me. We had already walked to the front of the house away from the garage. I knew he didn't really want to give me a ride home. He stood with his hands in his pants pockets and his eyes scanning the hedges, giving me the feeling he was distancing himself from me already.

"No, thanks. I'll walk." The train would have taken me most of the way if I'd wanted a ride, but it was only about an hour walk, and I decided that I needed the time to come to grips with being a murderer and to accept the idea that Carla was a murderer too.

I tried not to feel guilty about those murders. They were done by someone else. It wasn't me. I started life around September tenth. Before that, there was someone who looked like me and who left me a lot of money in his will. Yeah.

The police were right about one thing. Forgetting can change your whole persona. I used to be a murdering bastard and now, all I could think about was Carla and getting her out of jail.

Since Carla was an assassin too, when she'd said Kimbanski was a client, she probably meant he'd hired her to kill someone. Did she even remember what the word client might have implied? If she still remembered who she was before, she hid it well. Was she still a killer? I didn't know, but I knew I had to find out.

I figured Carla must have a stash somewhere too. I hoped I could get to her before she was able to find hers. I hoped to save her from that devastating moment of discovery. I also hoped she wouldn't be the one assigned to kill me when my brother determined I wasn't his pet murderer anymore.

I fondled the money in my pocket and thought about bribing Kumar, but I didn't want to end up in jail myself. Who would I be of use to then?

The doorman was sitting in his spot by the door when I walked up to my building entrance. I went over and settled down on the cool concrete beside him. He eyed me suspiciously. "This is my spot," he said in a gruff, put-on voice. "Get outta here."

I reached in my pocket and pulled out a five. I handed it to him. "I'm not looking to take your spot, or your patrons. I just want to sit for a few," I said.

The doorman stared at the five. It wasn't a huge donation, but it mattered to him, I could tell. He grabbed it and stuffed it down his shirt. It was then I realized the doorman was a woman. A man doesn't stuff things down his shirt that way.

I leaned my back against the wall. "You ever had a forget?" I asked.

"First you sit in my spot, then you talk." She paused for a while. "No, I never did. Thought about it. If I had the money, I might, but I don't think so."

"Why not? You could forget whatever it was that put you here. Maybe get help from the agencies. Get back on your feet."

She grabbed my coat by the shoulder and stared into my eyes. I could see her focus switch back and forth from my left eye to my right eye and back. She was looking for something, or maybe trying to get my attention. "Then who'd I be? I'd be somebody else wouldn't I?"

She let go and straightened her hats back into a neat stack. She smelled of sweat and urine and shit, but not of alcohol or derpal. She gazed up at the underside of the entrance roof. She said, "You've had a forget or two haven't you?"

"Yeah. Is it that obvious?"

"You look scared, that's all. Maybe a bit lost. You used to kick me as you walked past. You seemed to think it was a joke or something. Kick the lady on the ground. Then you just quit doing that. Now you're all chummy and giving me money, like I should forget all that, like I should forgive you. But those kicks hurt you know." She kicked me hard in the calf. It hurt. She was crying and trying not to show it.

"I did worse things than kick people," I said. "I've had enough forgets that I can't even remember my mother's name or who I am. I'm sorry I kicked you. It wasn't me."

She kicked me again, even harder. "Yes it was. Now get out of here. Your five is all used up."

I stood up. I had a bit of an urge to kick her back, but I didn't. I said, "Thanks for your time," and headed up the stairs to my apartment.

She had a point though. It was me, and I couldn't get away from that. I had to face my past whether I could remember it or not. Other people remembered me as I was before, and, although I wanted to keep the deeds of my past selves separate, I just couldn't do that.

I would have to atone for my past sins, not just forget them.

Chapter 16

I was tired from walking to my brother's house and back, and emotionally drained from what I'd found there. At least Kumar wasn't waiting for me at my door this time. He'd left a message, though. He wanted to see me the next morning at eleven. That was just as well. I wanted to see him too. He knew things I didn't know, and I had a feeling they were important. What's more, Carla was still in jail and Kumar had the keys.

Kumar was fishing for information and not just to help him track down Kimbanski's murderer. I'd thought he was looking for Chen and was using me to find him. I appeared to be the bait. That made me nervous. But there had to be more. He didn't even ask me where Chen was.

Kumar had arrested Jon Tam for running a derpal kitchen, meaning Kumar actually worked for the drug enforcement division. Kimbanski was investigating the drug enforcement division. So it was certainly possible that Kumar was under investigation. It was also possible that Kumar was helping Kimbanski investigate someone else, maybe Chen. Either way, I had the feeling Kumar and Chen were playing cat and mouse, with each one thinking he was the cat and the other was the mouse.

But I still couldn't place Chen in the equation. His only link to my mess seemed to be Paulo's death, and that he suggested Carla would be a good choice to hand me my transcript. He also knew I'd killed the judge, and he hadn't told the police about that. He didn't even provide an anonymous tip. Why not? Because I was his friend? No, there was some ulterior motive behind Chen's largesse. I decided to talk to Chen again if I could find him in time.

But first I had to keep the bureaucracy happy. I brought my latest rent receipt to the dole house and stood in line for two hours waiting to have it registered so the money would be reassigned to my pitiful account. Later that month the same amount would be automatically withdrawn to pay the next month's rent. They could have done it all automatically, but they wanted to make sure I paid for my apartment in some way. Having people stand in line fulfilled that bureaucratic need.

When I returned home, I resolved to get some sleep, wake up early the next morning and try Under The River. Chen didn't get up early, so if he was still hiding there, maybe I could catch him before my appointment with Kumar.

The morning was raw and windy, but clear. I held my coat together in the front, using my hands tucked in the pockets and folded across my belly. I ducked through an Egyptian restaurant and used the back door out to a garage to avoid the bitter wind. Taking short cuts through buildings kept me warm, but it also allowed me to see how the person who followed me was doing. I knew the buildings. He didn't. That was obvious. I had to wait for him twice.

He had tried his best to look like an indolent slacker, but I knew what indolent slackers looked like. For one thing, they didn't wear anything that retained creases, nor did they walk with their head held high with arrogance.

Finally, head down, scratching a nonexistent itch on my face for cover from the cameras, I went into a bank, crossed the lobby and slipped out an emergency exit. While the alarm sounded, I ducked down a flight of stairs that led to the lower level CAT, immediately circled and came back up another set only fifty meters away. Looking back at the bank exit I'd come through, I could see a guard holding a gun on my follower. The follower happened to look my way. I waved, took three steps back down the stairs, hiding myself behind the railing, paused, then returned to street level. He was gone, the guard peering down the stairs after him. I stepped into a travel store where I attracted an appraising glance and no more. The guard had let my shadow continue to follow me, which meant the shadow was police. Strangely, that made me feel better. At least I knew who it was.

I waited ten minutes, then walked over the bridge and entered Under The River by the north entrance.

The dupe was fun, but it had wasted time. I headed for the west wall. The stainless wrist units at the third table showed it was already eight thirty and the cat house was about a half hour away. I had two hours.

I meandered a bit, making sure no one was watching me too closely, then I wandered toward Chen's box. But the box was gone. Completely gone, bathtub and all. There wasn't an empty space where it was either. Under The River abhors a vacuum. Chen's box, large as it was, might never have been there.

Someone nudged me, but their hands didn't wander. I looked in another direction for a second then, casually looked at the nudger. He had dark skin, slick black hair, a bulbous nose, and was wearing the coveralls of a city street cleaner. "He moved," he said.

I looked away. "Clue?" I said.

"Where The Sun Don't Shine," he said, then he strode off.

Where The Sun Don't Shine was not in the dark back places, but rather, out near the river. Here was an area that, even though it was exposed to the weather, was shaded by the tips of a few buildings and never saw sunshine. A bad combination. It was where the outcasts of the outcasts lived, the poorest of the poor. The woozied out, the insane, the people who didn't even bother to go topside and ask for a handout. The lowest of thieves lived there too; the ones who would steal from others Under The River if they could.

Pulling my coat around me, I took a roundabout path to Where The Sun Don't Shine.

I found what I thought was Chen's box, noting a cheese stick emblem in a high corner. I circled the area, trying to decide if I should simply go up the entrance and shake the door, or if I should just leave. Two women followed me the last half way around, and when I paused, they stopped to whisper to each other. One of them left, but the other continued to watch. The one that stayed was older, perhaps fifty, with black hair and a sallow complexion. She wore a dark long coat and bright white platform shoes which seemed absurdly out of place. She didn't try to hide the fact that she was watching me, and I didn't try to hide the fact that I knew she was watching me. We were waiting for something. I hoped it was for Chen to approve my talking to him, but it also occurred to me that we might be waiting while the other woman went to retrieve five or six men to grab me, shove me in a box and take my money and clothes. I leaned against an unlit fire barrel and waited.

Most of the construction Under The River was relatively new, built after the fast and furious fire that swept through the fields of cardboard and people about seven years before. When they moved back in, the homeless refused to accept the sprinklers installed by the Elves and continued to use fire barrels for heat and for disposal.

The Gnomes were forced to turn the fire detectors off.

Three things happened while I stood there. A tall, thin man was brought out from the inner part of Under The River by four others and summarily thrown over the railing into the muddy part of the river. One of the throwers turned to the onlookers and said, "Liked kids too much," and strode back into the gloom. Then an enormously fat woman made me move because that was her fire barrel and, even though the fire wasn't lit, I could only stand there if I paid her. I moved a few feet away, but she continued to glare at me. Finally, the man who'd given me the clue emerged from the growing bustle and nodded to the woman with the white shoes. She moved toward me and opened her coat for a moment to let me see she what she was wearing underneath, a pink merry widow, garters and stockings, and, of course, the outlandish white shoes. I nodded and took her arm, hoping this was a ruse to make anyone watching think I was after sex, not Chen. I suddenly worried that I'd given her the impression that I was really after sex for money and that perhaps that was what she was expecting.

She took me to a wooden crate, which was barely out of the weather under the protection of the concrete foundation floor of the buildings above. The younger woman, who had long red hair and enhanced lips, stood by a door. She opened it to let me in as though she were running the brothel. Inside, it was a hallway with open doors leading to many tiny rooms with just enough space for a bed and a little area in which to get undressed. I guessed it was too early to have clients.

Chen was in the next box, which was connected to the first by stapled together flaps forming a short passage. He sat at a desk in a low, mostly dark room. A lamp lit his desk and a bit of floor around it, but left the rest of the room in shadows. Chen was reading the top page on a stack of paper. A larger stack, turned upside down, sat to his left as though he'd been reading for quite a while.

He looked up when I entered, held up his index finger indicating he would be a minute, then went back to reading. I looked around for chair and found a sturdy box against the far wall. I sat down and studied the back of my hand.

Finally, Chen wrote rapidly on one of the sheets of paper and looked up. "What is it you want, Benny?" He sounded hostile and wary.

"I know I killed the judge, Chen. I guess I've killed a lot of people, but I don't remember."

"What do you want from me? Sympathy? Forgiveness?" Chen turned the lamp shade up so the light was directed toward the ceiling. The walls were covered in gray foam. A tall man would have brushed his hair against the ceiling. The only things in the room were Chen's desk and chair, a narrow bed, and the box I sat on. There was another door which presumably led to the room I'd been in when his box was on the other side of Under The River.

He turned over the page he had been reading. "You kill people for a living, Benny. There isn't any forgiveness for that." He drummed his pen on the desk. He didn't have time for me.

"I don't expect forgiveness from you. I wanted to let you know I won't kill for money again, and I'm looking to start over, not by forgetting, but by atoning. I'm not the same person who killed those people, the judge. I know I'm still guilty, but I'm not that person." I said it like I believed it, but I was trying to convince myself as much as I was trying to convince Chen. I leaned back against the foam and sighed. The wall insulation felt warm against my back.

Chen stood and paced across the room twice, then turned to me again. "Benny, who were your clients? Who paid you?"

How could I answer that? Arno was a murderer just like I was although indirectly. He never did the killing, but it was close enough, yet he was my brother and turning him in was still betrayal. Of course I didn't really know who I would be turning him in to. Chen wasn't police, at least the thought hadn't occurred to me until that moment. Why would he want to know who paid me?

"I can't tell you that right now. There are some things I have to work out before I tell you that. Anyway, why do you want to know?"

Chen leaned back against his desk and crossed his arms. "You don't trust me? I guess that's not surprising, but there's nothing I can do to make you trust me more, and there's nothing I can do to make you tell me if you don't want to, so you might as well go." He walked around his desk and dropped back into his chair. He swung the lamp back down to light his papers.

"Chen, I've got an appointment to see Detective Kumar at the Cat House at eleven. I think if I tell anyone, it should probably be the police."

I had his attention back. "Kumar's not the person you want to tell. If you have to, just call in an anonymous tip to the central line, but don't tell Kumar. He's not who he makes out to be."

Chen wasn't helping me, but he still wanted me to follow his directions. "If I tell him, he'll probably let Carla out. That's important to me. Why should I tell you? Can you get Carla out of jail?"

"Still thinking of yourself, Benny? What's in it for you? That's all you care about. You've not changed as much as you've let yourself believe. Carla will get out anyway. They'll wipe her and release her, whether you tell them something interesting or not. Kumar will make you think the only reason you got even that much was because you told them about your clients, but it'll work out the same anyway."

Chen paused and adjusted his light. "And he'll probably try to get you to tell him more about me."

That surprised me. "I don't even know anything about you."

"Get out Benny. Don't come looking anymore, I'll have you thrown in the river as a topside spy if you do. I have to move again because I let you in here, and that in itself is making me mad. I'm tired of moving, and I'm tired of you. Why don't you just forget the whole thing and turn straight if you're so pure now? Go out and get a job." He went back to staring at the papers on his desk, ignoring me.

I sat there for a moment trying to think of something smart to say. Instead, I said, "Tell me how I was responsible for Paulo's death? You owe me that much."

"I don't owe you anything." He didn't even lift his head.

I went to the door and stood fixed there for a moment thinking he might tell me anyway. Chen never liked a silence. He finally looked up. "Sukey borrowed my old thatcher, the Zorro one, and was waiting in our usual spot for a likely victim. Carla brought the judge into the alley with you not far behind. He witnessed you and Carla in action with the judge. He asked Paulo for a forget favor and Paulo obliged, but Sukey found out he'd had a forget and wanted to know what it was. They were arguing with each other, so I left. I didn't want to listen to that." Chen put his head in his hands. "If I'd stayed, they'd both be alive, but I couldn't know that." He considered me again. "And you didn't know he was there when you killed the judge, but you ended up killing Sukey and Paulo along with your mark. I know you didn't do it on purpose, Benny. You sent Sukey off with a threat when you realized he'd seen you. You could have killed him too, but you didn't. You were already getting squeamish about murder the last time you had your forget. And now you think one more forget has provided you with a conscience."

A conscience. Yeah, I guessed that was what I had, and it was getting as heavy as a dead body. "Chen, are you with the police?"

That popped a derisive laugh out of him.

"How do you know about the murder?" I asked.

"You told me, Benny."

"That's no answer."

"It's all you're going to get. Now, I need to have this done in twenty minutes, but please don't tell Kumar what you know. You will regret it."

I went back through the cardboard passage to the brothel. The woman with the enhanced lips swayed over to me, took my hand and smiled at me. Her teeth were sharpened. She looked like a smiling opossum. "Would you like to stay awhile? A friend of Chen's would get a break."

"Sorry," I said, "I have an appointment with a shark."

Chapter 17

The front desk at the police station was originally a deep mahogany color, but years of cuffs and guns and hands had removed the stain and left the wood worn and dirty. The woman behind the desk was much the same. She shifted her gaze to me without moving any other part of her body.

"What's your business?"

"I'm here to see Detective Kumar, but if he's not around I can come back later."

"Uh-unh, wait over there." She pointed with her eyes at a long bench full of men in orange uniforms, each handcuffed to a stout bar that ran across the wall behind the bench.

"You know something I don't?" I said.

"Just have a seat."

I went to the opposite side of the room and sat on the floor beside a girl with bowl-cut straight black hair and a skin sculpture of a bloody hole on her forehead. I smiled and said hello, but she didn't respond. She looked unhappy.

While I sat on the floor, cooling my jets, I watched people; a woman frantic about her missing son, a crazy demanding to be handcuffed for having urinated on the lamp post outside the police station, and any number of police coming and going. The girl beside me never had her name called and didn't move from her spot.

About an hour later, Kumar arrived by the same door I had. He motioned for me to follow him as he walked by. I stood and nodded to the girl as though we'd been talking the whole time. She sneered, crossed her arms and looked the other way.

Kumar led me to a small room with a steel desk and two chairs, one behind the desk, the other facing it. The left wall was stacked solid with unlabeled cardboard boxes. There was a window with a set of metal blinds, but the slats were bent like someone had leaned on them, and they let in sunlight. It was not an interrogation room, but apparently an unused office. He sat down in the chair behind the metal desk, and I sat in the other chair, which was an armchair with metal posts sticking up where the arms would have been attached. Someone had scratched "You're fucked," into the paint on the front of the desk.

Kumar had a note pad and a pen. He tapped the pen against the desk twice, then said, "What did you learn from Chen?"

I tried not to look startled, but I'm sure I failed. The police must have had people Under The River watching things and just happened to see Chen. I wondered if Chen would be trapped Under The River forever. They would be watching for him at the exits now.

I decided to startle Kumar back. "He told me I killed the judge and then had the memory forgotten." I waited for a moment, watching him. He didn't seem surprised. He just looked at his pen. "Then he told me I'd caused Paulo's death somehow and that Carla was not involved in all this and that you'd release her in a few days whether I tried to help her or not." I dropped the last part in, hoping to get an indication if Kumar had anything on Carla.

Kumar sat back in his chair causing it to creak like a front porch step and tapped his pen against his lips, blowing air out past it each time. He looked thoughtful, then said, "Actually, we're releasing her today. She's had a few memories wiped by judicial order and with her consent. Apparently she had an uncle who was quite mean to her as a child." He said it as though he knew it was a blink. He was holding back information or making it up, I wasn't sure. I ached for Carla. I didn't know what part of her they'd wiped exactly, but I had the feeling Kumar had orchestrated the forget to cover himself. Which was odd because I hadn't thought of him being a bad cop until Chen implied it earlier.

Kumar was involved in the investigation of Paulo's murder and the arrest of Jon Tam, and he was paying a lot of attention to me. He had to be part of the explanation of my mystery.

I shifted forward in my chair. "So, are you going to arrest me? You probably have the evidence for a conviction. I don't remember doing it, but that shouldn't stop you."

"I want to believe you're on the level, Benny. I want to think you don't remember any of it. If that's the case, your punishment is already complete, but I need to know why you killed him. What was your motive?"

I thought about that for a moment. My atonement came to me then. I had to turn in my brother and if Kumar was in on the whole thing, on the wrong side, I had to out him too. "Money, I guess."

"Money? You're poor as dirt. You should have been flush when you got paid if that was your motive." Kumar was fishing again.

"I put the money in my brother's garage. I hid it there, so I wouldn't be caught with it."

Kumar tapped his pen against his lips some more. Again, he didn't seem surprised and that made my hair itch. His icy gaze chilled me. "Well, Benny, I don't know if you're square or not. We'll have to wait and see. I have an interrogation this afternoon, and I need to be in on a raid tonight, but tomorrow morning we'll go over to your brother's house and see that stash. If all goes as you say, we can show a judge the evidence and your forget transcript. With my recommendation, I imagine we can keep you out of jail."

"Can you keep me from getting wiped?"

"Sure, Benny. You've undoubtedly forgotten the important stuff, and, by turning yourself in, you've shown you're no longer a danger." He didn't sound exactly convinced and neither was I. It was a nice thing to think might happen though.

There was a tap on the door. A uniform came in and whispered into Kumar's ear. Kumar listened while staring at me, then said, "We're done for now Benny, but I want you here at eight tomorrow morning." Kumar stood and hurried out the door.

I sat for a moment, thinking I'd set myself up for some real trouble. I wished I knew what the trouble was, and from which direction it would come.

Chapter 18

I decided to go to the library to find out who I'd killed and maybe why. I could remember only five of the names from the list, but I figured five would be enough.

The first person I'd killed was Dujo Kay, but I could find no information on him whatsoever.

Gerard Bonarubi was next. The news reported that he was suspected to be chief financial officer of a clique called the River Pirates. This particular clique catered to rich deviants who wanted people to torture and sometimes kill, or for more long-term sexual slavery. The River Pirates would take the order and kidnap someone who fit the exact need. Bonarubi had had two small children and a wife who gave lots of money to charity, but apparently didn't spend any time at it. I didn't feel real broken up about that one. I felt for his kids, but, if the news reports were correct, he was doing things worse than killing for money. He knew what he was getting into.

Another remembered name was Galasta Chavez, who also appeared to be a member of the Pirates. She was suspected of renewing the Pirates' money through various commercial ventures and running an on-line protection racket. If you paid the clique money, they would protect your on-line presence from attack, presumably from themselves.

The third was another woman. Killing women felt especially vile to me for some reason, even though the idea that Carla had killed didn't repel me that much. The victim's name was Yuni Mukawski, and she ran a fabric store. She was unmarried and the press didn't seem to know much about her. It wasn't obvious to me why I would have been paid to kill her, until I noticed that she had owned the secluded house Arno now lived in. Could he have paid me to kill her just so he could buy the house? That seemed unlikely, yet I couldn't find any other connection.

A singer named Agasey was next. He was known to have gambling debts, and he liked to have violent sex with women, then settle out of court when he was sued for causing permanent damage to their breasts and the bottoms of their feet.

The person I'd killed just before Kimbanski turned out to be only fifteen. He was a forward on the soccer team at the private high school where Arno's son was second string in the same position. They made a big deal of a promising sports career gunned down in the street by clique violence. It wasn't clique violence. It was Benny violence.

The news reports included a video of Arno's son, who I knew as Little Arno, on the verge of tears talking about his best friend and their rivalry for the position and how much he would miss the other boy.

I had expected to find out that Arno was methodically killing off his rivals for some clique job, or perhaps getting revenge for some past injustice. But going through the old cases, I began to suspect he had me kill anyone who he felt was causing him a problem of any kind or degree. It became so easy, he'd even used me to get his son on the first string soccer team.

Everyone has things in their past they wish they'd not done. Everything from trying to sing Volare *a capella* at a party, to getting woozy and using their car as a blunt instrument. Me, I'd killed for the most insipid of reasons, money, and I felt wretched and despicable.

Arno scared me. He'd paid me to kill a fifteen-year-old boy, yet he didn't forget anything. He didn't need to. He felt no remorse.

"Buddy, you going to sit there staring at the screen, or give it up so someone else can use it?" The man stood over me, talking loud, so everyone in line could hear. He was a tough guy, standing there, fists balled, leaning forward on his toes, red-faced and belligerent, aware of his audience and playing a part. I had an urge then. Something worrisome, an arbitrary sort of irritation, like you get when a fly keeps landing on your hair. I figured that's not what normal people feel. I figured that most people just get angry or hostile. But I could kill him. I could rid the world of this obnoxious nit and feel good doing it. All I had to do was grab him long enough to shove the slash thatcher deep in his ear and tic it. If I yelled, "What's wrong!" before I grabbed him, no one would suspect a thing.

Instead, I shut down my session and walked along the waiting line. They all glared at me and looked me up and down as though trying to figure out just what a loser looked like, so they could identify one should the need arise. I smiled, just to disconcert them.

Their opinions didn't matter to me.

I walked out onto Hackson and into the slanting sun, which glinted through a break in the clouds. The wind was shoving its way west and stirring up the sandy dirt from the construction site next door. The dark mass of moving clouds made the building appear to be tipping over me and the verdigris gargoyle perched on the corner of the library seemed about to take flight. I didn't wait.

I plodded north with my head down, looking up only at the traffic lights. I knew seeing Carla would be a mistake, but I had to go.

Everyone who's feeling down has that impulse to feel more down, to wallow in self-pity and martyrdom. I told myself I needed to hit bottom, so I could imagine things only getting better.

Somewhere in the back of my pathetic psyche, though, there clung this hope with its head down and its feet worn raw from walking on broken glass. Somewhere down there I hoped that she would remember me and, if not, would at least still be the same person, the same Carla I'd fallen in love with. The same Carla who seemed to like Benjamin just fine.

Gov wipes people specifically to make them into someone else, someone who will be a better member of society. I didn't know which personality shaping events and people had been removed from Carla's memories. I didn't know what other unrelated memories had been lost simply because of their proximity in the brain. But I still had that barefoot, hangdog hope.

I had had an immediate affinity for Carla after my last forget because I'd known her for so long and, I thought, loved her for so long, that just erasing memories of her didn't erase her from my mind. She must have been more to me than just the memories. She must have been there in everything I did and thought. I had erased her physical presence from my memories, but her essence was still there. I was able to reconnect the dots when I saw her again, the same way you find your way to some place where you haven't been in years, by looking around and, without remembering any specific landmarks, just going the direction that feels right. Carla was unforgettable.

The wind picked up and low dark clouds shuttered in to obscure the tops of the taller buildings and block the sunlight. I could feel the rain coming, I could smell it.

I arrived at the Unapartments around five. While I was walking up the stairs, my stomach began to hurt. I told myself it was because I hadn't eaten all day.

Once at her door, I stood for a while staring at the paint, noticing the drip just below the number, then seeing the cross-swipe where the painter had tried to remove it with the brush after the blob had dried. What if she had no memory of me? What if she remembered more and knew I was a killer? Scenes played out in my head, a series of quick movies each ending with her calling the police to report a suspicious man outside her door.

A lean woman holding two bags of groceries in her arms and wearing a purse belted to her waist stumbled out of the vator, down the hall and around the corner, not sparing me even a glance. Perhaps I wasn't so suspicious looking. I knocked.

I heard Carla's voice, "Hold on a minute."

It seemed like more than a minute before she opened the door. She wore a loose sky-blue oxford shirt and a stainless necklace, sand colored pants with open-toed black shoes. Her hair hung down and curled under at the ends. No longer was it up and away from her face, but rather enclosing her face like a dark picture frame. "Benny, I was hoping you would come by." she said, opening the door.

That she still remembered me, was an instant thrill, a shot of exuberance that went through my whole body. That she called me Benny took that feeling away almost instantly and replaced it with a sense of dread. I didn't know why, exactly, but her use of my nickname scared me.

Other than cosmetic changes, at first glance she looked like she'd looked before the police arrested her. But closer inspection revealed a lighter, easier stance, the tenseness was gone from her shoulders. Even her face hung easier on her cheekbones.

"Hello, Carla," I said, "I haven't been by in a while, so I thought I'd drop in and say hello."

She'd been working at her PAL. I sat down in the soft chair and asked, "Do you still need a new apartment? There are two open in my building which would be a whole lot cheaper than this one. I could probably get you in."

She looked at me with a smile. She didn't smile at me as she had at Dinner that day at the Beef Tucuman. This was different. Her smile wasn't sweet or happy or enticing. It was a placeholder. "No, I'm fine here. It's small, but I like it."

I'd been worried that Kumar would have her completely wiped clean. Now I was worried that he had instead accidently given her the key to her past and that she had opened the lock.

She sat down at her PAL and asked where I lived. I said, "I live at the Hacker Skyhigh on Obyeo near LaSally."

I suddenly realized her typing was unrelated to what I had to say. I stood up to leave.

"Please stay. I have some citrus if you want some."

"No," I said. I had a bad feeling. I thought maybe she was telling someone I was there, asking what she should do. I had to get out. "I've got to be somewhere, I just had a moment. See you again."

I ducked out and started down the stairs. I was running from something, and I didn't even know what it was. Carla had scared me. I didn't know what she was thinking, and it could be anything from, "Gee Benny's a nice guy," to "Benny's the guy they said I was supposed to kill next."

I ran down the stairs, out through the E'Clair Street exit and headlong into a slashing, wind-driven rain. I didn't slow down for two more blocks.

Then I wanted to go back. She was probably just finishing whatever she was doing when I'd knocked. Maybe she was ordering dinner. She might have gotten a job and was still working. She could have been doing any of many things. I'd been spooked by an unknown shadow.

But I didn't go back. It would look silly, and I would feel stupid. Instead, I kept sloshing along, waiting for my breathing to slow to a gentle wheeze. I couldn't decide if I was happy that Carla still knew me, or if I was terrified that she knew more of her past than just me. Was I being paranoid? Maybe I was, but seeing Carla made it clear that there were things I had to do before I got to know her again. I couldn't afford to be entangled or distracted when Kumar and I went to Arno's garage.

Chapter 19

By the next morning the rainstorm had gone by and an oily smelling wind blew down LaSally. It was much too early to be awake, let alone outside, and the bright sunlight shining directly in my eyes and reflecting off the wet pavement made me squint.

Let Kumar wait a bit, I thought, while I ambled over to the cat house. It wouldn't hurt him.

I knew I should try visualizing exactly what would happen at Arno's house. I could have planned the day's events while I walked. I could have thought through the possibilities in my head. I could have thought about consequences.

But I didn't make myself think ahead. I had this feeling that Providence would guide me. I'm not a big believer in anything greater than luck, but at that moment, I didn't know if I was in the right or not. Allowing things to happen as they might made me feel less responsible for the eventual result, which Providence would select from all the possible futures. It's like flipping a coin to decide important questions that have no obvious answer. Let the universe choose for you.

So, instead of devising a strategy, my thoughts lingered on Carla. I'd fallen for her without understanding why, only to discover she was from my past; that I'd been in love with her before. Could I hope for the same from her? Was her love for me, if indeed she'd ever had a love for me, as deep-seated as my love for her? Were the memories and burned-in synaptic paths that caused her attraction to me far enough away from the scrambled places in her mind to be saved? What exactly had the police forced her to forget, and what doors into her past had their interference opened? I didn't know, I couldn't know until I tested it out. That would have to wait.

Outside the police station, their electronics and their dogs sniffed me up and down to make sure I wasn't carrying any bombs or weapons into the police station. The guy behind the raised desk looked knowingly down at me, but I wasn't sure exactly what he knew that he thought I knew. I looked knowingly back and hoped that was the right thing to do. He said Kumar was waiting for me.

Kumar came cruising out of a side corridor a few minutes later, long coat swaying behind him as he walked. He said, "Follow me," in passing, and I followed behind him out the front door. He stopped at a black four-door car. Wire screen and bulletproof plastic divided the front of the car from the back.

Kumar slid into what appeared to be a cockpit rather than a driver's seat. There was a steering wheel, but that's where the similarity to a regular car ended. Touch screens and displays wrapped around him as though he were playing a VRcade game. They lit up when he started the car. He ignored them. For the first time in my life, I climbed into the front seat of a police car. I felt disoriented, like I shouldn't be there. Kumar gave me a surprised look. He'd apparently expected me to sit in the back, but he didn't say anything.

I focused on a tiny flashing red light perched atop a display, which showed a street map centered on the police station. I was already regretting the decision to trust Providence or the notion that some universal constant should decide my fate. Suddenly, I wanted to plan the whole thing. What if Kumar wanted to take the money with him without a receipt? What if Kumar wanted to arrest Arno, and Arno pulled a weapon on him, or even me? How mad would Kumar be when he found out that the money was in my pockets, and no longer in the garage? What if Arno's kids were right there, watching? Possibilities blossomed in my mind and crowded out all useful thought.

"What else can you tell me about Chen?" asked Kumar, glancing sideways at me as he drove through another red light.

"I don't really know him all that well, and why are you so interested in him? Has he done something illegal?"

Kumar grunted. "I guess he has, and more than once I might add. Do you know where he is?"

"No, he moves around a lot. I don't know where he moved after I saw him last."

"Don't fool with me, Benny. I know you know more than that. Give me something, so I know you're on the level." Chen had said Kumar would try to get more information about him from me.

I leaned on the door, scrunching into the corner between the door and the seat. I wasn't trying to get away from him, but I didn't want to be close to him either. Looking out the side window, I could see the traffic behind us in the side mirror and this was the third time I'd spotted a blue Fairchild a few cars back. Kumar had apparently arranged for backup. I supposed this was good, but I knew he would have assigned hand-picked allies to the job. They would be of no help to me if things got difficult.

Kumar kept glancing at me. I finally said, "Look, Kumar, if you can't find him, maybe you should consider a different line of work." He almost drove into the stopped car in front of him, but the autostop slammed us to a halt with a hand's width to spare. His reaction gave me some extra measure of confidence.

I was proud of myself for that slice. I was trying to be tough, trying to get in the mood I'd have to be in to handle Kumar and Arno at the same time, along with the backup that followed us.

"Benny, don't start getting slap with me. I can still put you in jail and have you wiped clean without too much trouble. I just want to see if you're with the program. I'm on your side remember? I get credit for arrests leading to convictions. That's how I get paid, and I could use the commission on an arrest as big as the killer of Judge Kimbanski. So why should I keep you out of jail, keep you from getting wiped?"

I was wondering the same thing. "You mean like you had Carla wiped?"

He again looked startled, then he said, "Yeah, Benny. Just like Carla." We were driving in the shade of a building, but he still squinted.

There have been a few times in my life when I've been truly scared. The worst was when a city bus was bearing down on me, the driver leaning on horn, and I stood transfixed in the street staring at it, unable to decide which way to go. I looked at the logo between the headlights and calmly imagined the imprint of that logo which the forensic evidence specialist would dutifully report finding on my forehead during the autopsy. Then a big dark-skinned guy dressed all in black grabbed me by the collar and pulled me back to the sound of screeching brakes. All he'd said was, "Damn fool." I couldn't say a thing. All I could do was stare at the asphalt and imagine my body lying there in a splatter of blood, a lump of smashed meat.

And I worried that if the moment came, and I had to act, I'd freeze again, just as I had in front of the bus. I'd always been in control before. I was never in a hurry, so I always had the best hand. Except for that time with the bus.

Now, I was letting the future get out of my control. That logo was still coming down the street toward me, and there was no one to pull me out of its way at the last second.

Kumar had something else in mind and it had to be more profitable than arresting me. He was quiet while we drove to Arno's part of town. There were houses and trees and parkways and little kids playing in front yards. Everything looked clean and fresh from the rain the night before. There was a wet, slippery shine on the concrete and the tires snickered as we drove down Arno's street.

I looked in the rear view and didn't see the Fairchild, but they would know where we were going.

We pulled up to Arno's, and Kumar turned in under the overhanging maples. He drove up to the house and stopped the car before I realized I hadn't told him where to turn. Kumar had been to Arno's house before. I could tell because he didn't look around; he didn't scan the place like a cop. That bothered me a little. I started to have a bad feeling. "Come on, Benny. Let's get your brother out of bed."

How did Kumar know that Arno always slept late?

Chapter 20

I rang Arno's door bell. We waited. Kumar watched me, I watched the door. Denise answered. "Hello detective," she said. Then she suddenly realized I was there too and added, "Oh, Benny." She looked wide-eyed for a moment then backed up letting us into the house. She was shaking.

Arno came out of the kitchen drying his hands on a towel. "Detective, Benny." He nodded. "What can I do for you?"

"Benny says he keeps a stash of money here. We'd like to see it." Kumar seemed too relaxed for what might be a confrontation.

I hadn't heard the Fairchild pull into the driveway yet. They probably weren't backup. They were probably there to keep other people from pulling into the driveway while Kumar was there. It wouldn't do to have visitors.

There was a polished brass stallion, which reared on a table by the door. I watched Arno, but in a reflection on the horse's hind quarter I caught Kumar shaking his head. They were talking without me.

I'd thought I was going to be in the middle between them, but it turned out I was on one side, and they were both on the other. I tried to back slowly up toward the wall, but Kumar put his hand behind my back.

Arno said, "We can go out to the garage if you want to. Benny, is that all right with you? Do you want me to wait for a warrant?" Arno didn't wink at Kumar, but he might as well have. He was still evaluating me. Was I still a killer for hire, or was I a liability? The dreadful part was, Kumar was evaluating me too.

"No," I said, "let's go." I offered to follow Kumar, but he pushed me forward. Denise's eyes were full and wet. There were no tears, but I knew she was in pain. This time, her pain was for me.

We walked through the house and out the back door. Arno led the way, and Kumar continued to follow me as we walked single file to the garage. I glanced back down the driveway and saw only the police car there. No Fairchild. Maybe the car hadn't been following us. Fewer witnesses fewer problems.

Once we were inside the garage, Arno pressed the button and

the deck came down, just as I'd left it. All my stuff right there.

"We can take it as it is," I said. "All the stuff is moveable. We can take it to the police station and open it up under video."

Arno produce a grunt from his stomach. "That's not necessary, Benny. I'll be your witness."

Kumar motioned me to open the boxes. "Go ahead, Benny."

I pulled the crates off the pile and opened them. I showed Arno and Kumar pictures of our dog. They smiled as though to a lunatic. I almost cried. We'd put Gusset down because he'd bitten my mother's boyfriend on the ass while they were in bed. "You can't have a dog that bites," my mother had said. "There's no reason for a good dog to bite no matter what somebody does. He's better off dead." Actually, I couldn't remember much about Gusset, but even at the time, I had doubted he would be better off dead.

"Open the handprint boxes, Benny," said Kumar. He didn't bother to obscure the threatening tone.

Without me, they would need an expert and a lot of time to open those boxes and that assumed I hadn't set traps with explosives, which, of course, I had. The traps were incendiary and easily triggered. They would have suspected I would set up something.

Sometime between getting out of the car and looking in the crates, I'd decided that Kumar and Arno were going to have to die. Just like the dog. Just like Gusset. Fire wasn't the best way to go, but they had to be put down. Maybe they wouldn't be happier dead, but I knew if I was no longer there to kill for them that they would hire someone else instead. Maybe they would even hire Carla, if they could get to the old Carla, and, if they couldn't get to the old Carla, they would have to kill her eventually just as they planned to kill me.

They only needed me until the boxes were open, until they had access to the money, enough to pay for many more murders, and access to any incriminating evidence I'd stashed with the boxes. Then they could do what they wanted back in that garage.

"Sure," I said, "I'll open the handprint boxes, but don't you need to put this on video or something to use as evidence at my trial?"

"Just open them Benny, if you agree they're yours, then we don't need any more proof do we?" He was still holding on to the pretext even though we all knew they planned to kill me as soon as the boxes were open.

I knelt down next to the first box. I could feel their eyes on my back. I could feel them waiting, not taking a breath.

I could imagine Denise in the house wringing her hands like little wash rags. She would wonder, but she wouldn't interfere.

I put my hand on the lid and popped the clasp, taking care not to dislodge the trigger of the fire bomb. I palmed my slash thatcher out of my pocket as I stood up. "Watch out for this little knob right here," I said pointing to the trigger. I wanted them off guard. I wanted them thinking I might still be unaware of their decision to kill me.

I looked for a reflective surface to see what was behind me. The side of the Moto was shiny. I couldn't see their faces clearly, but I could see their hand motions and their posture in silhouette.

"That one has all the money in it," I said. "The other one has the weapons and things like that." Kumar bent down to peer into the box. Arno was watching him.

I let the thatcher peak between my fingers, pointed it at the box and ticked it. The beam hit the incendiary and the gelpack exploded into flames. Kumar leapt up, swatting his face and lunged toward Arno and me, his face melting, covered with the sticky, burning gel.

Arno reached for his gun, which he had hidden in a pocket in his sleeve. I tried to punch Arno, but he slapped my fist away like I'd thrown a piece of paper at him rather than a punch. Kumar danced around the garage, screaming, trying to swat out the fire. He'd leapt around enough to ignite a box of filters, a bird house, and some wood fencing.

"Benny, you bastard. What have you done?" screamed Arno.

He raised his gun to shoot me. Kumar, now completely in flames, not even screaming anymore, ran into Arno, knocking his gun aside. Arno pushed him, then shot him in the chest. Kumar staggered, then dropped silent against the wall next to a stack of boxes which instantly lit.

I hit Arno on the side of the head, driving my flat palm against his temple with my whole body. He stumbled. Some of the gel had come off Kumar and stuck to Arno's hands and chest. He dropped his gun and started flapping his hands trying to put the fire out.

I grabbed a set of hedge shears and whacked him over the head with the flat of the blades and he fell to his knees with a sickening crack, then pitched forward onto the floor.

I glimpsed someone with wiry black hair turning away from the window.

The fire spread. A gas can heated up enough to pop its lid and the fumes gushed fire, igniting some shop rags. I checked Arno. He wasn't going anywhere without help. I thought to drag him out, but realized that I couldn't do that. This would be my last murder, but it had to happen. Arno knew too many people in the right places to ever be convicted or even brought to trial.

I acted as a vigilante. I acted as a cold blooded killer. I still had it in me, and I found that vile, yet I hoped my disgust with my own actions indicated some good too.

Through the smoke, I found the other box, handed it open, pulled out the incendiary and tossed it into a back corner. The fire would reach there in a minute. I flung the contents of the box out into the garage floor. The police would find the weapons, the two bodies and the empty burned-out boxes.

I stood in the intensifying heat and considered staying, basking in the irony that the vigilante kills himself as retribution for past deeds. But I couldn't do it. I was too weak. I opened the door and walked out into the cool morning air.

As I walked slowly down the driveway, I heard the second gel-pack ignite with a whoosh. I didn't turn around. I could feel the heat billow at my back.

Denise looked out the kitchen window at me when I walked past. She could see the fire, but she wasn't on the phone. Her finger tips were at her lips, almost as though she were praying. I could see her tears. I've remembered her in that pose ever since, the picture etched in my mind. I kept walking. I figured she would either tell the police I was there, or she wouldn't. Or maybe the person whose hair I saw as they turned from the fire and ran might be calling the police at that moment to report me. Either way, I would be at ease with the result. I wouldn't be happy, but I'd be at ease.

Out on the street, the Fairchild drove up beside me. The window rolled down. I was prepared to get shot in the head and actually accepted the idea, but Chen stuck his head out. "Get in, Benny," he said.

Chapter 21

I climbed into the back seat of the Fairchild next to Chen. A woman with blonde hair pulled severely back into a ponytail was driving. I couldn't see her face. The guy with the wiry hair was in the passenger seat.

Chen tapped him on the shoulder. "Send a team to the house, it'll be on the police net soon enough. We want to be the first there." He turned to me.

"I told you not to trust Kumar. I had a feeling Arno was in on this too, but I could never link him in. He always kept his hands clean."

"Arno was my agent," I said. "He set up the kills. Even the kid who kept Arno's son off the soccer team. Even the woman who used to own his house. She wouldn't sell. He didn't even have the murders forgotten. Somehow he didn't need to." I was nervously trying to convince myself I'd done the right thing. I was shaking, staring at my trembling hands. My muscles sagged on my bones.

Chen didn't say anything for a while. The wire-haired guy got through to someone and talked in low, urgent tones. Finally, Chen asked, "Did you leave anything behind that might incriminate you?"

I thought about the kill list. The history I'd written down that included Arno, and Carla and me. Yeah, that would have been incriminating. "No," I said. "There won't be anything left at all." Gel-packs burned hot and long and left no residue. The fire department would think Arno had accidently set off some of the extra buzzcar fuel bars he stored in his garage.

I sat staring at the back of the wire-haired guy's head while we drove back to town. "Who was Judge Kimbanski? Why did Arno have me kill him?" I didn't really want to know, but I felt like I should learn. It would deepen my guilt and I had the need to do that. I wanted to wallow in guilt. The more blame I gathered to myself, the more deep my ache. Wallowing made me feel like a martyr.

"Judge Kimbanski was investigating the blackmailing scheme that Kumar, and maybe your brother, ran. The judge got too close, and Arno apparently hired you to kill him. Maybe Arno, acting as your agent, was paid by Kumar, maybe he was a part of it. I doubt we'll ever know.

"I knew you'd killed before, but I thought you'd forgotten it all. That's why I didn't turn you in, but somehow you remembered." Chen was silent while we waited for a light to change.

"How are you in this, Chen? Why did you pick me up? Why do you care?"

Chen thought about that. You could see him trying to decide how much to tell me, or what story to feed me. Then he shook his head. "I work for Up Your News. I was following the Kimbanski case. The judge was a friend." Chen dropped his head. He cleaned a nonexistent spot on his shoe, then looked up at me and said quietly. "You killed a good man, Benny."

Chen watched my reaction. He needed to know if I was a danger to society or not.

"Yes. I killed him."

I said it like a confession; as though it were for the record; as though I were making sure I wouldn't ever change my story. "I'd like to think it wasn't really me. That it was a past me, but I know that really isn't going to help your feelings about the murder or about me. Arno and Kumar were the last, Chen. Even so, I'll understand if you turn me in. You've no way of knowing who I am now."

Chen was thoughtful. He flicked his thumbnail against his teeth. "Do you want me to hide you for a while?" He didn't sound enthusiastic.

"No, I'll take whatever comes my way. I'm not sure whether Denise will tell them I was there or not. There are probably some police who know I was there, but I doubt they will want to tell how or why they knew. I'll just let things happen."

The driver pulled the car up to my building. I reached for the handle, but Chen grabbed my arm. "Arno and Kumar used you to kill. You were a willing partner, but you don't remember that. If you were arrested for Kimbanski's murder, they would release you because you already accepted the punishment. Killing Arno and Kumar, that was planned. That, they would wipe your memories for, even if it was self-defense. Maybe you could put all this behind you by confessing, or by getting another forget. But I don't want you to forget. I want you to remember, Benny. I want every last detail to stay fresh and hot in your mind. You killed your brother, Benny. You feel guilt now, and that is what's going to keep you straight. If you do go in for another forget, I'll spill everything I have to the police, and I have more than you know. They will wipe you clean as a new born babe."

We locked eyes. "Be good, Benny," he said. He released my arm.

I nodded, climbed out of the car and closed the door behind me. They drove off.

I trudged up to the front of my apartment building. The doorwoman was there, asleep, or faking it. Inside, the lights were out, so I knew the elevators would be too. Climbing the stairs, I thought about Chen being so sympathetic yet stern, but at the same time making it clear with his eyes that he didn't want to see me again. He already considered me a stranger.

When I opened the door to my room, I saw that the place had been stripped. The only things remaining intact were the table and the bedstead. The mattress had been ripped up and a blanket lay in a pile below the window. All my clothing, all my food, my PAL and even my one chair had been taken. I guessed they took everything that might have hidden evidence or secrets. Kumar probably sent them to clean my place as soon as he knew I was at the police station.

We spend our lifetimes collecting physical representations of memories, but the stuff is so ephemeral. The thievery here didn't bother me that much. My real past was gone in a few minutes of fire at my brother's house, and I didn't even know I'd had a past until a few days ago.

Everything here could be replaced, but people were going in and out of my apartment like it was a thrift store and not leaving any money for what they took.

I stood up on my bed and watched the swirling clouds through the window. The note in the dust was still there on the sill as were the carrot doodles. I pushed the doodles onto the floor and wiped off the note about my stuff being at Arno's. I'd been there and didn't like it.

The old life was completely gone now except for my memories of Kumar's face burning and Arno lying on the floor as I left the garage. Carla was alive, but changed in ways I didn't understand. My stomach hurt. I wanted to forget. I climbed down from the bed, sat on the floor, and cried. A tough guy killer sitting in the middle of an empty apartment, weeping and rocking and holding his stomach. I wanted to forget.

Lying back onto the floor and looking at the ceiling, I thought back on what Chen had said in the car. "I'll spill everything I have to the police, and I have more than you know," he'd said. What else did he know that he would tell to the police? And how had he known I was going to Arno's house with Kumar? I hadn't told him about my appointment. But what made me stand up and start pacing was the realization that Chen had allowed me to kill two people. Whether guilty or not, he should have stopped me. His wire-haired proxy should have stopped me.

Chen had told me not to take my information to Kumar in the first place. Why? Was Kimbanski really investigating Arno and Kumar, or was he investigating Chen? He'd said that Kumar would try to pump me for more information about him. But what could I have told Kumar that he didn't already know?

Thinking back on it, when I first went to Chen to talk about the bills from Forget What, he'd suggested using Carla to get my transcript. He'd known I knew Carla, and he apparently knew we worked together too and thought it a great joke to get us back together when neither of us remembered that we were killers.

What's more, he'd said Carla could get my *last* transcript for me. It was a minor distraction at the time. I thought it a slip of the tongue, but obviously he'd known I'd had other forgets. He also said later that he knew I'd killed before. Could Chen be a danger to Carla? If I determined he was, would I kill him?

Paranoia is insidious. It starts with a little thing, something you hardly notice, but you still question it. Then, when you start looking for more evidence to prove that they are out to get you, you start to see it everywhere. Repeatedly pacing the five steps from the door to the bed wasn't helpful either. It just fueled my obsession.

My chair had been removed, so I flipped over what was left of the mattress, pulled the bed away from the wall, and wrapped the blanket around the mattress like a bandage to contain most of the stuffing. It looked like a fresh-made army cot. I laid down on top and forced myself to smile and think about Carla's face.

I laid there for quite a while, feeling better, until I fell asleep. A *fwoop* sound startled me awake and I immediately rolled away from the sound and off the bed. I landed on my elbow and stifled a groan. Light expanded into the room as the door swung open, and I could see under the bed as two sets of boots and dark pant legs strode into my apartment. The palm lock lay smoking on the floor. I could hear my breath easing in and out. I sounded like a tire pump.

"He's not here," a man said.

A woman replied. "Look in the bathroom, quickly." She sounded like she was in charge. Her voice was familiar.

"If he's in there, he's going to shoot me."

"I'll be right behind you, just go. I don't think he's here at all."

One of the sets of boots took small shuffling steps toward the bathroom. If he turned to his right and looked between the bed and the wall, he would see me. I rolled further under the bed, using the noise from his shuffling to mask my movement.

He stopped for a moment, probably listening, though why he couldn't hear my heart pound, I didn't know. My lungs ached from consciously focused breathing. I hoped his vision was poor coming from the lit hallway into the dark room.

The bathroom light went on. The shower curtain screeched suddenly across the bar breaking the silence. "He's not here."

The man strode back to the door. "Looks like his bed hasn't been slept in either. They're going to be mad. We've tipped him off, and he'll be more careful now. I told you we should have kicked the door in. He won't believe this break-in was just burglars. He's going to know."

The woman moved into the kitchen area. Cupboard doors thumped closed as she searched. "It looks like he's moved out," she said, "but let's get out of here anyway in case he comes back. You never know what a guy like him is carrying."

They kicked the palm lock out of the way and pulled the door closed behind them. A pool of light from the hallway still shone through the hole where the lock used to be. I waited, elbow throbbing, still trying to breathe slowly.

These two assassins didn't know that Kumar had had the place stripped, which meant only that they weren't associated with Kumar. They could still be police, though the police had shown previously that they have easier and quieter ways to enter my apartment.

I counted to a hundred before I lifted my head and peered over the edge of the bed. No one was there, but I waited ten minutes, listening and rubbing my elbow, before I stood up shakily and padded over to the door.

Someone knew I was a killer, and they wanted me dead. Chen was the only one I could think of who knew and was still alive.

Chapter 22

My PAL had been taken with everything else, but I figured it to be about two-thirty or three in the morning when the assassins left my apartment. Since someone wanted to kill me and they knew where I lived, I said good-bye to my desk and what was left of my bed. I walked out the door knowing I couldn't return for a while. Everything I owned was in my pockets, cash and swipe cards and the slash thatcher I'd used to start the fire that burned Kumar and Arno.

The laundry room in the basement was a dank hole, but under the sink I found a pair of huge greasy pants that would fit over my own. Stuffed behind a broken washing machine I discovered an oversize coat with a burned left sleeve. Judging by the dust and layers of cobwebs it must have been there for years. A piece of torn green undershirt, which I tied over my head, completed the look. I put a little of the money in the outside pants and put the rest in two mismatched socks in the pockets of my own inside pants.

If they were watching the entrances, there wasn't much I could do about it, but I didn't think they would recognize me with the alterations. I certainly didn't smell the same.

I walked out the front door. No one moved on the street. The one street lamp lit a few cars parked on the far side of Obyeo. A light drizzle made everything shiny. I sat down beside the doorwoman

She kicked me. "What do you think you're doing? And in them clothes."

So much for my disguise, at least at close range. "I'm hiding," I said. I pulled out a five and gave it to her. "You mind if I sit here for an hour or so?"

She looked at the bill. "Yeah, OK. But don't make it a habit. I'm not a landlord."

"I thought this was your real estate."

"And don't be thinking of any long term leases." I wasn't sure, but I thought she might have snuck a smile in at that point.

"Did you see a man and a woman dressed in black, maybe carrying weapons, go into the building about twenty minutes ago?"

She grunted. "How could I miss them? They came by like they were invading the place, jack boots and all. Were they after you? Is that who you're hiding from?"

"They blew off the lock in my room, but I hid under the bed."

"You hid under the bed?" She laughed showing white teeth. "That's a good one. And they didn't look? That's even better. They weren't pros, that's for sure. They approached the door like they'd read a book about how to approach a door, but they kept talking to each other in a whisper so loud I'm surprised they didn't wake you up from down here."

"What did they say?"

"The woman was pointing and saying, 'Go over there,' or 'Don't make so much noise.' You'd think they were in training. She called him Soybrain a couple times. He called her Rela."

"Was the power back on by then?"

"Yes, the lights woke me up a little while before that."

"What did they look like?"

"She had medium hair, blonde and wavy and in a ponytail, silver nails—bad color for her light complexion. She was much shorter than he was. He had dark stiff hair about as long as hers, some stubble—pretty much nondescript other than that."

I stared at her. "That's a remarkably good description." I pulled another ten out of my pocket and gave it to her. She'd just described perfectly the driver and the wire-haired guy in the front of Chen's car. I couldn't be positive that this Rela was the same one I'd had dinner with at Arno's, but the matching name and hair would be an extraordinary coincidence. Paranoia is instinctual for a reason. Sometimes it saves your life.

"I used to be a couturier—you know, a fashion designer. The way people looked was my business." She stuffed the money into her shirt. "You could use a fashion consultation yourself."

A buzzcar flew past overhead, but other than that there was still no movement on the street. "What happened? Why did you quit?"

She looked at me curiously. "You're just passing time here. I got to stay. Don't get me thinking about old times. I don't need the heartache."

"Yeah," I said. "I know what you mean."

"I don't think you do. You aren't down low enough. Live awhile in those clothes. See how it feels. It changes your life. Just the way people look at you changes your life."

I thought about that for a while. I couldn't figure out why people like her lived on the street. Even if you had no money, you could get an apartment as long as you took the rent receipts down to the gov every month, and, although the dole wasn't really enough money to buy all the food you needed, with some odd jobs and some scratching, you could get along. Yet there were a lot of people who chose not to accept public assistance. They would rather sit outside, unprotected and hungry and let their life get sucked into the concrete. It seemed like a self-enforced misery, a kind of righteous martyrdom. What was the point?

I sat for another twenty minutes. My ass was falling asleep and getting cold. "My name is Benny—Benjamin. If you need anything, let me know. I'll help if I can. I won't be back for a while, but after I've straightened a few things out, I'll move back in."

Big sighs can mean a lot of things. This one I think was her way of saying she didn't think I would be back. "I'm Myra, but everyone calls me Hattie." She reached up and patted the top hat on her stack, which this night was a purple beret. She gazed intently at me for a moment then kicked me in the calf. "I think I still owed you that one. Maybe we're even now."

That last kick irritated me at first, I was getting tired of being kicked, but then I decided that it was her way of keeping me at a distance. She didn't want friends. She certainly didn't want any that would be dead in a day or two. She'd lost enough already.

If someone was still watching the apartments, they had more patience than I had. I stood up to go, and rubbed my butt to get the circulation going again. I didn't know which way to turn. Under The River was the only place I could think of, so I waddled over to LaSally, getting my circulation going, then headed south.

On the way, I thought about Chen. The more I thought about him, the more I thought he was a self-absorbed, nasty, ass-thatching bastard. I just hadn't really taken notice of that fact before because he was a friend. You can put up with a lot of crap from a friend. You just ignore the bad behaviors. Especially when he is the only friend you have.

I didn't have any close friends, and I started wondering why not.

I guessed I'd forgotten them all, or pissed them off before they turned from acquaintances to friends. Or maybe I just kicked people too often. I suspected that before I had my last couple forgets I had acted a lot like Chen acted. Maybe I was a self-absorbed, nasty, ass-thatching bastard too. Perhaps removing all those experiences and memories had allowed a conscience to bubble up to the surface.

Since he didn't succeed in killing me, Chen would think I would be out to kill him now. He must have determined that if I tracked down Kumar and my own brother, found them guilty, and killed them, that I might start thinking more about it, and I might track him down too. His people had already made the first move. They wanted to kill me first.

At least it wasn't Carla who came for me. I would have died twice.

I wasn't quite sure what I was going to do when I found Chen. I probably wouldn't kill him, but I was having a tough time coming up with a good reason not to. Guilt was one, but guilt would pass. The only guilt that remained over killing my brother and Kumar was really over my not feeling especially guilty about it anymore.

Fear would be my best weapon against Chen and his pair of hired guns. I was a killer from their point of view. They were scared of me, and I had nothing to lose.

Chapter 23

There were people walking Chicago's streets at four in the morning, but they stayed away from each other. If they had to pass by someone, they would look straight ahead and walk fast. I imagined them chiding themselves for fearing every stranger they saw and believing he was a killer. Yet sometimes they would be right.

OK, I knew I was obsessing about being a killer. I'd acted in self-defense with Arno and Kumar, well, sort of. The others I could not explain away so easily, but I couldn't remember them either. It really was a different Benny who had killed those people. I felt like I should try to be Benjamin now, Benjamin was not a killer, yet I knew I could slip easily into old patterns if I didn't continue reminding myself. A derpaholic needs to continuously remind himself that he is a derpaholic. It's part of the therapy. It's part of how you avoid taking another snort, and you always feel like taking another snort. Sometimes it's easier than not taking one.

I obsessed for a while about Carla being a killer too. My visit with her at her apartment had alarmed me. I wasn't sure who she was anymore. Was she the woman I took to dinner? Was she the woman who was so tearful when she thought she could have had something to do with the Judge's murder? Or had she found her history, and had that history reminded her that she was an assassin, and had she slipped back into that natural detent in her psyche? And would they send her after me? And what would I do then?

The LaSally bridge was empty and windy. I crossed the river and walked Hacker Drive to Crackson, then continued back over the river and entered Under The River through the southeast stairs. That entrance comes out near Where The Sun Don't Shine.

People wandering around Under The River that late at night, or that early in the morning, depending on how you looked at it, were viewed with suspicion just as they were topside. I strode purposefully as though I had a destination, so I would avoid being questioned. I didn't want to attract attention. I wouldn't be able to give good enough answers, and I could easily end up in the river. That time of year, and at that time of night, I would not survive the cold.

Tiredness grew in my head like a fog rolling in from the lake. The last few days had not left much time for sleep, and what sleep I'd had was disturbed by bad dreams and worries, not to mention intruders at all hours. I tried to focus, but mostly I focused on staying awake.

I walked quickly past the spot where Chen's place and the brothel had been located the last time I'd come to meet him. I wasn't surprised to see that the area had been taken over by a beandog stand and a blanket and overcoat resale shop.

The Elves, a fanciful name for the people who kept Under The River working with electrical, photonic, and structural repairs, were working on the main data feed server and had a conduit open with its contents spilled out like so much multicolored vermicelli. The Elves always refused to say who paid them, but in the far depths of Under The River, away from the entrances and from the river itself, lived some people who could afford to keep the plumbing, data, phone and the power all working. They needed the Under The River people as a shield against police incursion. In return, the people who lived there ignored the relatively rich Gnomes who never went above ground, who always lived in hiding.

The warren of offices and apartments stretched under the buildings all the way to Instead Avenue. I'd been back there once, though I couldn't remember anymore exactly why. The dim halls wound around without any pattern or any right angles as though created by blind moles randomly searching for bugs. The doors were unlabeled. There were also dead ends, which would make it easy to catch someone if they didn't know the layout well. If I were Chen, and I didn't want it to be generally known that I was alive, I'd be moving my office and apartment there, if they had any vacancies.

I continued north and a little west, past the other place where I'd seen Chen, where he'd slapped me on the back of the head and told me to get out.

At the time, Chen had blamed me for Paulo's death. I suspected now that Chen had been trying to blame me because he knew it was his own fault. He'd been more mad at himself than at me that day.

The previous location of his abode had disappeared into the ubiquitous jumble of boxes, drums, tents, tables and left-behind junk. The layout of the little city had changed so much, in fact, that I couldn't find my bearings, and I couldn't stand around in indecision for fear of being stopped and questioned. I marched on past and up the north stairs, weary and chilled, though I'd sweated while Under The River.

After I emerged, two men approached from across the dimly lit street. They headed straight for me. I veered to the left, and they changed their angle to intercept. I stopped, figuring to act complacent, then surprise them.

With a start, I realized that this was a tactic I'd used before. For a moment I felt a wave of fear, but it disappeared as quickly as it came, replaced by a cocky assuredness. I knew I could handle these two even though I had no idea what I would do.

At four-thirty in the morning, no one would be watching. The rest of the street was empty and silent. There was just enough light to see their teeth. Their type was written all over their shaky smiles and open gestures, which they made to allay the suspicions of anyone who might be watching out a window. Probably used to rolling drunks and maybe a few old folks for pocket change, they would be surprised to find any resistance. At a distance they would try to act friendly and loud, then, when they were close, they would try to bully me quietly. They were young and eager and a little nervous.

I relaxed and hunched over a little.

"Hey, you look cold, old man," said one when they were close.

The other whispered, "Give me everything you have. Don't hesitate, or I'll just kill you. We don't have any patience." The first slapped my back in an apparently friendly way.

I slammed the heel of my right hand into the second one's nose. The impact flung his head back. I kicked the first one in the balls, which bent him over. I grabbed their shirt collars, smacked their heads together then threw them on the ground. I didn't have any patience either. I wasn't a street fighter, but they were both groaning on the ground. I could have killed them and I didn't, which pleased me because it showed I had some restraint at least when I had no special emotional involvement, when it wasn't about me or about Carla.

I briefly thought about what lesson the two muggers might take from the incident. In the future, they would probably carry guns and get themselves shot.

Walking away, I tried to think of a safe house. I would have to sleep, and I would be naked by the time I woke up if I tried to sleep around there. I hadn't eaten in more than a day. The violent burst of energy had taken almost everything I had.

Carbide would help a friend in need, and he could use the extra money I would give him for the use of his floor. He was a muscular, hard working man I'd worked with sometimes, doing odd jobs, mostly hard physical labor moving boxes and crates around in the office buildings or making deliveries Under The River where the regular services don't go. He did more than his own share of the work. His apartment was only a ten minute walk. I circled back once to make sure no one followed me.

Exhaustion echoed on every step as I climbed the stairs to Carbide's third story walk-up. I stumbled up to his door just as he was going out. Carbide started his day early.

"Hello, Carbide," I said, trying to sound healthy and in control.

He stared at me for ten seconds before he replied. "Benny?"

I'd forgotten my affected appearance. "Yeah, it's me. Can I crash on your floor for a few hours?"

"I was just going to a job. I have to rent a truck and move an office into storage Under The River and clean—"

"I'll give you ten if you let me in." The stress of the whole week was leaking out of me all over the floor.

Carbide was a big man. He towered over me, making me feel small and even more tired. I must have started to fall asleep, because he grabbed me and hauled me back into his apartment. He shook me. "Benny, I have to go. Are you going to be OK? You stink something fierce."

"It's a disguise," I said and laughed, perhaps maniacally.

Carbide gave me an uncertain look. He left me lying on the floor and retrieved a glass of water. I drank it and told him to go. I pulled out a ten and handed it to him. He looked at it with what I believe was disbelief, then I fell asleep.

•••

When I awoke, I stood shakily and went into the bathroom.

When I came back out, I noticed Carbide sitting at his table looking at me.

"Sorry to drop in on you like that. I needed some sleep."

"Yes, you did. A log has nothing on you."

"What time is it?"

"It's after three. You need something to eat?" Carbide still had that uncertain look even after a day's work."I gave you a ten didn't I?"

"Yeah, but you already owed me twenty." He wasn't asking for more money, just making a point.

So my gesture wasn't so big after all. Carbide was a bit of a sucker, and I'd taken advantage of him a time or two. I guess I did that time too. There I was with a million in my pockets, and I'd given him a ten. I pulled out the last twenty I had in my outer pants and handed it to him. "There," I said, "that makes us even plus ten, but I'd like to stay here for a few days if I could. Eat some of your food, take a shower, wash my clothes."

Carbide looked at the money, grunted, then shoved it into his pocket. "OK, Benny. I especially like the shower and washing your clothes part, but who's after you and did the birds clean up all the cookie crumbs behind you?"

I smiled. Carbide knew me well enough. "I'm not perfectly sure who they are, but I know I didn't lead anyone here. If you don't tell anyone I'm here, anyone at all, then there will be no one who knows. I'd like to stay indoors for a few days and wait things out." Actually, giving Chen a few days to worry might be to my advantage, I decided. Let him stew for a while. Let him think that maybe I'd left town or that someone else had already killed me.

Carbide nodded. "So you want a vegiburger and a beer?"

My stomach made my reply for me with an unusually loud growl. "That answer your question?"

After I'd washed my clothes and myself, Carbide let me sleep on the couch instead of the floor. I slept a lot. The previous events had taken more out of me than I supposed. I used his PAL, watched movies and read the regular news.

Death News had some repulsive pictures of the bodies in the garage, which didn't do my opinion of myself any good. They said the police had determined that the blaze was an accident, which must have occurred when Arno was trying to refuel his own buzzcar. It was illegal for anyone but a licensed refueler to even touch the fuel bars, but they had determined that Arno had gotten hold of some and refueled his own car regularly. Apparently Denise had admitted to this.

Up Your News carried the same basic story, but with pictures of the burned-out garage after the bodies had been removed.

The guns weren't mentioned in any of the news accounts. I wanted to search for more details, but I didn't want to draw attention to my safe house by doing specific lookups on Carbide's PAL. I'd have to go to the library for that. Which brought up my dilemma. What to do next. I didn't know how to approach the problem, well two problems really.

First, I wanted to visit Carla. I paced, thinking about what I would say, and how I would act, and what I would ask to elicit a response which would reveal her nature. I couldn't stand not knowing, yet there was the second problem which got in the way of the first.

The second problem was, of course, Chen. I wanted to talk to Chen, preferably without killing him, and especially without him killing me. And, although there was evidence against him, I didn't even have enough proof to convince myself absolutely, let alone a judge. I'd decided I didn't like him anymore, if I ever really had, but I wasn't absolutely sure he was guilty of anything more despicable than ass thatching.

I was pretty sure that the two who attacked my apartment were the blonde driver, who I now knew was Rela, and the wire-haired guy who worked for Chen, but I couldn't be positive that they weren't sent by someone else. They could have been working freelance.

I also knew the police wanted Chen, or at least Kumar had wanted him. If I determined that he had paid for any of the murders I'd committed, I would be able to point the police toward him and let them wipe his memories as punishment. No need to kill anyone.

So, I needed to find out what the police knew and what they wanted Chen for, other than for hiding Under The River and as a witness in the deaths of Paulo and Sukey. I needed to talk to someone in the police department who I could trust, which, at first analysis, left no one at all. Yet I knew that by myself, I wasn't going to figure out who was trying to kill me. I would need some honest police help.

I felt I could trust Doorway. Oddly enough, I'd liked his manner, and he seemed guileless. If he'd taken part in any illegal activities for Kumar, I'd know quickly enough.

I decided to go find Doorway and have a talk.

Chapter 24

I sat across from the police station in an automat, drinking machine-dispensed coffee and waiting. I'd put my bum disguise back on. It was cleaner now, but I still looked the part well enough. Two hours after I'd arrived, I saw Doorway go into the station. He looked fresh. It would be the start of his watch, so I'd have to come back about six hours later and wait again. On the bright side, he'd walked to work, so I could follow him back home on foot.

The library was open while Doorway was working to keep the streets safe, so I hiked down there to use a public PAL. I bought a jerked beandog at the stand on Bigbash then chewed on the beandog and my plan as I walked south.

When I entered the library, the people inside stared at me. It was unsettling, as though they had seen a wanted poster of me on the wall, or had seen me rushing under the sink when they flicked on their lights at night. There weren't enough people to bother with the pocket buzzers, so I stood in line, but everyone continued to stare at me even harder. It actually took me a moment to understand that my clothes represented a stereotype that required me to use the public bathrooms, then leave. Knowing this, I smiled back enthusiastically, and, I hoped, somewhat insanely, at anyone who looked my way, trying my best to unnerve them in return.

After a half-hour standing in line and playing psychological games with library employees and the other patrons, I finally got to a PAL. The first search I did was on Kumar. I wanted to see what he'd been doing for the last year or so.

He had a fair arrest record in drug enforcement. I couldn't find any stains on his character, or really much of anything else. Up Your News, to which I paid special attention since Chen had admitted to editing it, mentioned Kumar briefly as the arresting officer, or as someone who would share in the arrest for accounting purposes, in various crimes. Doorway showed up in two of the photos with Kumar. He was in the background doing the real work in both of them, and in one they mentioned his name, Hero Fish. I had to laugh when I read that. He was an unlikely hero, but an even unlikelier fish.

Since I had discovered his name, I looked him up too. He was in many crime scene photos, but he never shared in the arrest because he wasn't a detective. This made sense because only detectives were paid by the number and quality of arrests and convictions. The regular guys, like Doorway, just got paid by the hour. Nothing remarkable there either.

Next I looked up Arno. I couldn't find him at all. He wasn't even listed as the owner of a company. Even the purchase of his home was done entirely in Denise's name. No Arno.

There really wasn't any good reason to methodically keep your name off the public records, but Arno had done it. Admittedly, I'd done it too, but more by accident because there wouldn't be much for me to show up on. The dole listings were not public.

Che Chen was there, though. He'd coached some women's soccer a few years back, and he was listed as a backer for a play based on the life of some dancer who married a pathetic slob. It was too sappy even for the play-going crowd. There were a few other things of no great consequence. He was not mentioned in any article or database related to Up Your News. There was no public connection. He was also never mentioned by Up Your News, which had to be on purpose. Chen had been in the Navy. I found a picture of him and his mates on the deck of a sub, saluting the flag. He was third from the right.

Finally, I looked up the detailed news coverage of the murder of Kumar and Arno. I'd hesitated, and I'd put it off. Although I'd looked up the basics at Carbide's apartment, here at the library I could search for the details. I'd seen what Death News had, and they wouldn't have added any more detail, maybe more pictures and some gruesome writing, but no additional details. Up Your News had left it alone, except for its initial and basic reporting. I figured Chen put the slow-down on any further digging by his reporters.

It was Next Day News that seemed to have the most detailed information. They specialized in only telling the news when it was old enough to be correct and then, not only telling what happened, but also what it meant to the average person and why anyone should care.

Next Day News said they thought the scene deserved more investigation and they gave their reasons, which included the speed of the fire, the completeness of the devastation, and the fact that a neighbor, who had been questioned by the Next Day News but not the police, said that a blue Fairchild had picked up someone outside Arno's house just a few minutes before the fire. They said the police hadn't been interested in their interview results, even though a police officer had been killed in the fire. They even speculated that the police either had a further investigation going on, or they were covering up an internal squabble between police factions. They didn't mention the guns.

Police factions were a myth invented by some of the less scrupulous news organizations to explain odd police behaviors. Never mind that these actions were more easily explained by stupidity. The public likes to think the police are smarter than average people, and so they like turning idiocy into conspiracy. In fact, police are not smarter than the people at large. They are basically the same, and the fact that people in general are stupid enough to believe in things like police factions, should serve to remind us that, as members of the general public, police are fallible too. The police hate the factions myth, but angry denials only serve to fuel the speculation.

I watched some ads flash around the screen. They showed trips to the Seabase that included train tickets from Chicago, walls that duplicated exactly what was outside a building which was standing somewhere considerably more interesting than your own, and full body orgasms from opto-magnetic stimulation, whatever that was.

Finally, I did a quick search for Carla. Carla Shoen was listed as having been picked up and released as a witness to the murder of Judge Kimbanski. They didn't report that she'd been wiped before they released her. She had her right to privacy for her forget, in fact the judicial system didn't want her to discover her forget by reading about it in a news article. They didn't mention me, because I wasn't detained, just brought in for conversation and general bullying.

Carla had also starred in a commercial for a latex glove dispenser where you just put your hand in a hole in the wall and, when you pull your hand back out, it has a perfectly fitting glove on it. "As used by hospitals worldwide, for your hygienic convenience." Useful for an assassin too. The ad only showed her hand.

On a whim, I looked up Sukey. All I'd known about him was

that he hung around with Chen and Paulo sometimes and that he was an Elf. I found his community college graduation picture and some news items from his volleyball captaincy there. In July, his girlfriend was featured in an article about women who are kidnapped for sexual slavery and torture. She'd been dumped from a car in front of the hospital after which she was listed as critical for almost a week. They had a quote from Sukey about how he couldn't comprehend a slaver's mind. After that, he also disappeared from the on-line record. After some thought, I went back to the news reports of Chen and Paulo's deaths. There wasn't much additional information since they weren't well known, but I was unable to find a follow-up saying that Chen's body had been misidentified, and I knew by now it would have been cremated. Sukey's name didn't occur anywhere after the slavery article. Kumar had known the body found was not Chen's, but he never released that information to the public. Also, Chen must not have had any relatives or friends who decided to yell loudly that the body was not Chen's

I did one final search. I looked for the origins of Up Your News. Since Chen's name wasn't associated with the company, I wondered whose name would be. I found the answer in the person of Denise Okipa—my sister-in-law's name before she married Arno.

Chapter 25

Doorway wandered out of the police station at about three in the afternoon. He turned right and headed north. I quaffed the last of my chocolate tea and set off after him. I didn't have any trouble keeping up. He seemed to be in deep thought and kept stepping aside to let people pass.

I caught up to him just as he walked into a local pub. I entered right behind him. When he sat down at a table, I sat down beside him. I had planned to pull him into an alley, but he was quite a bit bigger than me, and my recent associations with alleys were not so good.

He was surprised to find that someone had sat down in the other chair, and he looked at me wide-eyed for a moment. "Bug off," he said. "I don't have any money for you."

I pulled out a ten and said, "How about I buy you a beer Hero? We can talk a little about Detective Kumar and about Che Chen."

Hero stared at the ten, then at my face, then at the ten again. He squinted in concentration. "You're that Benny guy. What do you want?"

"Yes I am, and I'd like to buy you a beer."

"Why would you want to buy a policeman a beer?"

"I've offered one to you before and you declined. You seemed to think we should talk at the police station rather than in my apartment. I figured I'd offer again."

"I don't want any beer on your tab. I've got my own money."

"Of course you have. You get your hourly pay." I pressed the talk button on the table and asked for an Indian beer. Hero did the same, but asked for a different brand.

"What do you want?" he said again.

"I want to know why the fact that Che Chen isn't dead never made the news."

He stared at me. "Che Chen is dead. Personally, I think somebody killed his live-in, which made Chen kill himself, and I wouldn't be surprised if it was you."

"Unless he died in the last few days, Chen's very much alive. Kumar knew that. The body they took out of Chen's apartment was that of Sukey Mack. They look a bit alike, but I've talked to Chen a few times since his supposed death. Didn't Kumar let you in on that? I went to the morgue and looked at the body. So did Kumar. He knew."

"Why would he lie about a thing like that?"

A helper bot delivered our beers. I paid for both of them. Hero didn't complain. He looked a bit miffed. "Beandogs!" he said. "We'd been after Chen for almost a year. The trail had just gotten warm. We figured out where he lived. Then we get the call saying there had been a big fight and then silence. The neighbor thought something bad had happened, and he was right. We thought the trail had gone dead cold then. We thought we'd lost Chen to suicide."

Hero considered his fingernails. "Chen's still alive, huh? Maybe I should have bought you a beer. I thought you were his friend. Why are you telling me this?"

I took a long drink and thought about that. "Because I thought you already knew, and I guess I would have told you anyway. I need your help to figure out who's trying to kill me."

"Yeah, everybody's got someone trying to kill them nowadays. What makes you different?"

"They cut the palm lock off my door at two or three in the morning and came in with automatics. I hid under the bed until they went away, but they talked about killing me while they searched my place."

"You hid under the bed?" He peered at me over the edge of his glass.

"Yes, I hid under the bed."

"And they didn't look?" He set his glass down and leaned forward. I could tell he was preparing himself for a good laugh and just wanted to make sure it was really as funny as he'd thought it was.

"No."

He laughed like an expert laughing at an amateur, the same sort of laugh you get when you watch a male dog with one hind leg try to lift that leg to pee. It was a silly giggling sort of laugh. He took a sip of beer, then laughed some more. "Do these people scare you?"

I sighed. Their incompetence was diminishing his view of the seriousness of my situation, and if I wasn't careful it would make me careless too. "Yes, Hero, they do scare me. Their guns scare me. Someone paid them to kill me. If they don't succeed, the backer will find someone more capable. It doesn't take an expert to kill someone. If someone wants me dead, sooner or later they will succeed. It's just a matter of time."

Hero sat back, ran his hand through his hair and sighed, but he was still smiling. He was trying to decide about me. "You hid under the bed while two thugs searched your apartment, and they didn't find you?"

I laughed this time. I had to admit. The image was a good one.

"Where is Chen now?"

"I don't know. Why have the police been after him for so long?"

"Tax evasion."

"Look, I gave you something, can't you give up a little in return?"

"You didn't give me much except the headache I thought I'd lost permanently a week ago, but OK. Kumar was looking for Che Chen. He said Chen was blackmailing public officials using newspaper surveillance techniques and equipment, then threatening to publish secrets or videos or something on his news channel, Up Your News."

"Did you personally ever see any proof, hear from any of the sources?"

"No."

"What did Chen's apartment look like after the murder, after it became a crime scene?"

"Why should I tell you? It's police business. Anyway, I'm still not so sure you didn't kill them both."

"I didn't kill either of them, Hero."

"Did you kill Kimbanski?"

Guilt has tremendous gravitational pull for other guilt. The greater the guilt we feel, the more guilt we attract and place on top of it. It feeds on things that only might be your fault as though there was no question. I'd believed I killed the judge, but I actually had no proof except Chen's word, which I no longer thought was worth all that much. I'd said only a few minutes before that anyone could kill, they didn't have to be an expert. But I'd been paid to kill him. I was an expert. Did it seem likely that I would just bash in

Kimbanski's head in an alley? No. It didn't seem likely at all.

"You know, I don't think I did." I smiled and took another drink. "I thought I did until just now, but the more I think about it, the more I don't believe I did." Hero was looking at me as though I'd suddenly declared I was the Pope.

"So, you don't believe you killed him, but you haven't entirely convinced yourself."

"No. What did Chen's apartment look like the day of the murder-suicide?"

"You asked me that already."

"You never answered."

"Yes, I did. I said I wasn't going to tell you."

"Actually, you asked me why you should tell me. Well, I don't think it was a murder-suicide either. I think it was a double murder."

"It's not that easy. Chen, or this Sukey Mack guy, shot himself in the head. The prints were just right, the right position, the right pressure, everything. It's not like you can just put a gun in someone's hand and fool the police. We're better than that."

The straight line left me gasping to comment on how "better than that" the police were, but I swallowed my retort. "What did the scene look like?"

Hero heaved an exasperated sigh and drank the last of his beer. "Stuff was strewn around all over and things were broken against walls. There were a lot of empty derpal bottles. Both their noses were wet with the stuff. Paulo's was bleeding. They'd been snorting all right. Paulo Mui was lying half on the couch with two shots through the chest. Sukey Mack was lying on the floor near the piano, the gun was near his hand, but he wasn't holding it anymore."

"Who owned the gun?"

"Unregistered."

If it had been Chen's space gun, Hero would have mentioned it. "Were there only three shots fired from the gun?"

"Look, you've got more than a fair exchange for your flimsy lead. So Chen's alive. What am I supposed to do with that? You haven't told me where he is. You've told me you don't *think* you killed Kimbanski, not much of use there. And you've bought me a beer, which is sounding more like a bribe than a friendly gesture. You bring me something else, something with some bite, and maybe we can do business, otherwise, I'm not interested."

Hero sounded like he wanted to be a detective, but hadn't made the cut for some reason. He certainly acted the part.

"Did you know Kumar was dirty, that he was running a blackmail operation? That's really why he had Carla Shoen wiped, because she might reveal too much."

Hero stood up. "Nobody wiped Carla Shoen. She was questioned and released. And Kumar doesn't concern you, Benny. Drop that line of inquiry if you know what's good for you. He's dead."

And now I knew. Carla hadn't been given a forget by the police. Rather it appeared that Kumar had either helped her find her past, or she had found it on her own.

"Good-bye, Benny," Hero said over his shoulder as he turned away. He walked out, but he had his head down. He was thinking hard. His headache had gotten much worse, and I was pleased to know that his headache's new name was Benny.

Chapter 26

It was hard to think of Arno's house as Denise's house now, and as I walked up the driveway, I imagined that Arno still lived there, that we would continue to sit outside on summer nights and argue about politics and my lack of motivation, or that I would again be brought over for dinner and a girl on Sundays. That sort of thing didn't actually happen very often, but the better times rose up to obscure the more traumatic aspects of my relationship with Arno. I still didn't think of him as dead, even though it was I who had killed him.

A homeless person would have been summarily arrested anywhere within five blocks of Arno's, that is, Denise's address. Not wanting to show myself without my disguise anywhere near Carbide's apartment, I took along a bag into which I stuffed my disguise while in a restaurant bathroom.

When I walked up to the door and pressed the button, I was struck by how much everything looked the same. The imposing and sophisticated aspect of the house and the pristine and carefully tended grounds were unchanged by Arno's departure. Unconsciously, I'd expected the edges to have softened, the grass to be less perfectly flat, the hedges to show a missed sprout here and there, even though I knew he hired the work done.

Denise opened the door only as far as the security wire allowed. She peered at me and sighed, then closed the door, released the safety and opened the door again. I expected a faltering smile or perhaps a weary dull look. Instead, she looked tense and wary. I'd always thought she reserved that demeanor for Arno.

"I told you when you called, Benny, I don't want you here. You killed my husband. You killed your own brother. Even if it was self-defense, you could have run away. You could have not come at all. You could have let it all drop. Instead, you had to see everything through to the end. To Arno's death. I lied for you, Benny, but I won't do it again." She tried to close the door, but I stuck my arm in. It hurt, but I just kept up a steady solid pressure until she relented with a huff and released the door. She walked away from me toward the back of the house.

I followed her back into the solarium. Denise was an attractive woman from any angle, and I couldn't help but think she wouldn't have any trouble finding a more companionable husband than Arno. OK, it was a sort of awful thing to think about so soon after Arno's death, but Arno had been mean and condescending toward her.

She sat down facing the other direction, looking out into the yard. The remains of the garage had been cleared away and all that was left was a blackened and cracked concrete pad. With the right light, it would look like a hole. The tree limbs around the garage were dying back and the grass was brown where it had been too near the heat.

"I'm sorry I had to kill Arno. I even miss him, but there wasn't anything I could do. He and Kumar would have killed me."

Denise didn't respond. She wasn't listening and the excuses were sounding hollow and pathetic, so I tried a different strategy. "Did you know he used to hire me to kill people?"

She whipped her head around and glared nails at me. It hurt. I'd thought she hadn't loved Arno. That he'd made her stay with him somehow. "Why are you telling me this?" she said. "You already killed him, why poison my memory of him as well? Just go away." She looked out the window again and crossed her arms.

"There's something I need to know first. Did you start Up Your News before or after you met Arno?"

"Good grief, Benny, what's that got to do with anything? The children will be back from therapy soon. Therapy to help them deal with their father's death. I want you gone."

"I need to know, Denise. Arno hired me to kill people. Some of them were people he wanted dead, but others don't seem to have anything to do with him. He was subcontracting the jobs out to me, so he wouldn't have to do the killing himself. I need to find out who was the source of the orders. I may have killed people, but someone paid me to do it, and I can't let that person continue to operate that way." I didn't mention that I would be the next victim if I did. Nor did I mention that they would probably pay the woman I loved to do it.

"What is it you want from me, Benny? Are you putting up a pretense of investigating Arno's death, so I'll think better of you, so you can show me who really killed him in some bizarre version of reality where you pulled the trigger, but someone else made you do it? Just look inward, Benny. Just look in the mirror. You'll see the killer."

I sat quietly, thinking about that. Denise didn't believe I would bother to actually investigate anything. She didn't think I would work that hard. OK, maybe she was right, which annoyed me. I had to admit that had my life not been threatened, I might have left well enough alone.

Denise was crying quietly now, her face in her hands. She looked up. "Arno wasn't a nice man, I know that. He had his tender moments though. He loved me, and he was such a good father. He never hit them, you know. Sometimes he would have a temper, sometimes he would get so stressed."

"When did you start Up Your News, Denise?"

"Arno bought me Up Your News as a wedding present. I'd worked at some other agencies, and I knew the business, so he liked the idea of me having an agency of my own. It was a romantic idea. I don't know where he found the money, but he bought it wholly in my name. I went to work there for a while, got it going again, but he decided that he didn't like me working, and when I got pregnant with little Arno, I never went back. They don't even have an office now. I couldn't go back if I wanted to. Arno had me sign some things once in a while."

She seemed about to say more, but then she sobbed and quieted.

"Can I see his office? I want to see if he has any records that might help."

She laughed bitterly. "Sure," she said, "you can see his office, but you're not going to like it." She stood, and I followed her to the front of the house. Arno's office had been stripped even more completely than my apartment.

"They just removed the windows, frames and all, and took everything out that way. I was at the funeral home making arrangements for the body." She cackled, hiccupped, then started crying again. "They didn't even unlock the door. They just backed up a truck to the window and shoveled everything out."

Everything was exactly the right word. It looked as though they had vacuumed. You could still see the imprints on the carpet where the desk had stood, the file cabinets, the bookshelves. They had taken no chances with notes taped under drawers or boxes disguised as books. The ceiling light fixture dangled by wires, and the globe which had covered the bulb was gone. One-way vision plastic imprinted with "Chicago Boardup" had been screwed up over the window holes.

I sagged against the wall. "I'm sorry," I said. "I really am. You're too nice a person for all this to happen to."

She looked for a moment as though she was going to rant or turn hysterical, but instead she said, "I'm sorry too."

She went down the hall to their bedroom, but I didn't follow. I went out the front door and around to the study's windows. There was nothing unusual about the tire tracks in the sod. The neighbors couldn't see into the property well enough to notice the truck. I thought about trying to find the watchful neighbor who noticed me getting into Chen's car, but she might have recognized me and probably wouldn't be able to tell me anymore about the truck anyway.

Whoever stole Arno's study knew him well enough to know where in the house the study was and that he kept all his records there.

I went back to the front door and rang again. Denise opened it after a few minutes. "Please go away, Benny." Her eyes were puffed and watery.

"Only one more question, then I'll leave. Who did Arno take into his study? I don't remember ever having been in there. Who would have known where in the house it was?"

"You were in there lots of times, Benny. You've been having forgets again, haven't you? You need to stop doing that. Every time you come back different. I don't like you this time."

"Who else has been in his study?"

She sighed and closed her eyes for a moment. She seemed to get smaller. "Detective Kumar, of course, JB, that's his accountant, that's about it. He was a bit secretive about his study. He even cleaned it himself. I didn't go in there. He always said he wanted a place where he could be by himself, where he could get away."

"No one else you can think of?"

"Good-bye, Benny."

I started to turn away, then shot one last question through the closing door. "Arno knew Che Chen, didn't he?"

Denise closed the door, then opened it again. "Yes. Chen took over from me at Up Your News after I left to have little Arno. He's also been in Arno's office, several times. In fact, he was here just last week. I heard him talking to Arno about you then they moved to the study." She closed the door again. I heard the deadbolt slide home.

Chapter 27

Chen was like the back of my hand. I thought I knew him, but upon detailed inspection, he turned out to have features I hadn't expected. Finding out that he actually ran the whole news agency had been a surprise. He'd always seemed too strange and wild to do anything so respectable and businesslike. Yet he'd handled the fire efficiently, I'd seen him looking through stacks of papers with careful purpose and, even before the last week's turmoil, he'd always known about international events and important legal decisions. I had thought he was just well read, as in fact he was, but I'd thought he was well read because he wanted to be, not because his job demanded it.

And he had a sinister aspect, or perhaps that was just my newfound perception. Ever since he asked me why the police hadn't arrested me, just as they had arrested Jon Tam, I'd imagined a change in his attitude toward me. I couldn't be sure if his demeanor had actually changed, of course, because I didn't know what I'd had forgotten. Maybe we'd talked at times about him running the news agency or about his knowing Arno or maybe not.

It was possible that Chen held no relevant secrets, but I was beginning to rely on the idea that even after a forget, there is some peripheral memory of the actual events that lets you in on the secret if you probe hard enough and know what to look for. I believed parts of the memory were stored elsewhere, fragments, small islands, peninsulas of remembrance, places where you can fumble around at the crisp edges of the gap made by the forget. Or perhaps your brain fills in the missing spots, builds bridges with false memories which tend to be similar to the actual happenings because they are the most likely to be shaped just right to fit the gouge left by the forget.

In any case, I felt, or perhaps hoped, that my gut feelings about Chen and even about Carla were correct, that I could rely on those feelings, that I could make decisions by them. Each day I noticed things that reassured me of this. My feelings for Carla were foremost in my mind as a gut level reaction which I could trust.

Also, the way I dealt with the two hoodlums who approached

me on the street, and my innate understanding of the tools of the trade which I found in my boxes at Arno's, were based on unconscious knowledge, knowledge not directly accessible by normal means, but that came out when it was needed. The reactions came unbidden. It was as though I heard the echoes without having heard the originating sound.

I wondered too what other echoes I would hear in the future. Where would they lead me? The thought didn't make me happy.

So I allowed my echoes to convince me that I hadn't been aware that Chen had known Arno. They must have kept the fact of their acquaintance from me on purpose, but I wasn't sure why they would do that. Did Chen pay for the killings? That seemed unlikely, but my miscomprehension of Kumar's true character showed how inept I was at judging people.

To find out who had paid Carla and me to murder people, and to find out which persona inhabited Carla now, I had to rely on information from Chen. Relying on Chen for anything other than a laugh or a slap on the back of the head was a bad idea, I knew, but whatever scenario I played out, Chen was right there in the middle. I had to find him before I got myself killed, I just didn't know where to look.

Back at Carbide's apartment, I tried to relax with a beer and watched Up Your News' update channel. Trying to relax is like trying to sleep or trying not to be afraid. The more you try, the harder it is. The big news of the day was a fire that burned the top floors of the Thump building by the north river. Death News had video of people jumping, their screams dopplering to a sudden stop. I turned the PAL to blues harmonica music.

The old guy playing on the street a few days before reminded me how much I used to like listening. Maybe I used to play. How would I know? I would have to buy a harmonica, put it to my lips and see what happened.

The image of me with a harmonica caused a spark of a scene to flare into existence in my mind. I vividly recalled sitting at a stop light in my car while playing the harmonica. I was still in school at the time. The image was accompanied by a memory of a sharp pain caused when a mustache hair caught between the harmonica's comb and the metal cover. When the light changed, the harmonica was dangling from my upper lip by one hair. I'd yanked it off, so I could drive. The car was a Fairchild Seven. It was green as grass and had a huge splotch of bird shit just to the right of the crease that ran down the center of the hood. The harmonica was a Madcat Special. It had a blue comb with a black metal cover.

I rubbed my upper lip, still feeling the pain and feeling giddy at the same time. Chen had asked me if I could even remember the car I once drove. It was a green Fairchild Seven with bird shit on the hood. I shook out my hands to release some of the strangeness of the quirky remembrance. I hopped out of my chair and started pacing. Carbide's apartment was bigger than mine. I could go eight steps before turning around instead of five.

By the time Carbide returned, I was back to myself. No more sparks had manifested themselves into flashes of memory, and I was again doubting my history.

Carbide dropped into the stuffed chair and let out a long sigh. "I haven't worked that hard in years."

"Moving stuff or making deliveries?"

"Moving. The Gnomes are moving around. I guess someone vacated some good space, or died or got kicked out or something, and now everyone's moving to the next more valuable spot. It's like they're all on a ladder and the top one fell off, so they all feel the need to move up one step. What a pain."

"Sounds profitable," I said trying to look on the bright side.

"I guess, but I'm having trouble finding help. No one wants to work under there. They're afraid they'll get killed after they're done, like old-time pirates who were shot by their captain after they helped him bury their gold. What's more, the Gnomes have nothing better to do, so they stand around talking and watching us move their furniture and equipment, all the while complaining about how long it takes and how roughly we're treating their precious junk. Yes, it's profitable, but it's work."

"I'll help you tomorrow," I said.

Carbide's eyes went wide and his eyebrows lifted in disbelief. "You! I doubt it. I need actual help, not just someone to make them think I have more people than I actually have."

"No, I mean I'll actually help." Some physical labor was what I needed to clear my head, and also I thought that whoever intended to kill me was probably a Gnome and lived back behind Under The River where Carbide was working. Perhaps Chen now lived there too.

He looked suspiciously at me. "What's your character's motivation? I don't find him believable."

"OK, so I have an ulterior motive. I'll still help. I'll move boxes. I'll hold up my end of the couches and desks and exercise equipment and armoires."

"I can't afford to have any of them see a member of my crew loafing. You're not lying to me are you?"

"No one will see me loafing."

He still looked at me suspiciously, but he also looked a little relieved. "OK, it will be just you and me. The other two I had helping today already said they couldn't put in two days in a row like that. If you work hard, I'll let you stay here for free for a few more days."

Carbide eyed me, watching for a response to his initial offer. When I didn't respond with a demand for cash, he smiled. "We leave at four-thirty in the morning."

"Four-thirty? Can't we make it more like ten?"

"No, those people have their clocks all messed up. They never see light. Most of them don't keep track of time at all anymore. They go to bed and get up when they feel like it. The next woman we have to move, Ms. Poynting, told me to be there at five, so I'll be there at five. You're not blinking me about this, right?"

"No, I'm not blinking you. It just seems early, that's all. Do you know who vacated the space at the top of the ladder?"

"No, and I don't want to know and you don't want to know either. What is your ulterior motive anyway?"

"I want to get a feel for the Gnome's space. I think the people who are trying to kill me live there, I think they're Gnomes."

"You never said someone was trying to kill you."

"It never came up."

"What else never came up?"

"I used to drive a Fairchild Seven and play the harmonica."

"That's not what I meant."

"There are lots of things that never came up, Carbide. What do you want me to say? The more you know the more likely it is that I'll get you into trouble too."

"What a load of bricks. Are you trying to convince me to throw you out on the street? Well, I just might. I know I owe you a lot. You stuck your neck out pretty far for me in the old days, and I'll help you if I can, but if you keep dumping bricks on my head I might just decide your friendship isn't worth the shoveling."

I guess I gawked at him because he stopped talking and looked at me. So I'd stuck my neck out for him. I couldn't remember. I felt at ease with Carbide, as though we'd know each other for a long time, but I wondered what I'd done for him that made him feel like he had to pay me back. Beyond that, I felt like he wasn't even viewing his help as a payback, but rather as just what friends do. I had the urge to whack myself on the side of the head, hoping the impact might jar some good memories back into the accessible parts of my mind. I wondered if Carbide knew Carla and if he knew what my relationship with her had been, but it didn't seem the time to ask.

"Anyway," Carbide continued, "If the person who wants you dead is down there, then why go inside? If they grab you, I'll say I have no idea who you are, you just offered to help. I won't second you. You're a stranger."

"Don't worry, I've got my disguise." I held my arms out wide and grinned, probably looking like a moron.

Carbide looked worried anyway. I don't think he thought much of my disguise or my chances.

Chapter 28

Before we left Carbide's apartment to go to work, I took all my money and cards, which were contained in the two mismatched socks I'd found in the laundry at my apartment building, and hid them in Carbide's laundry hamper with his dirty underwear.

I'd been in the Warren, which was the Gnomes' hiding place, once before and entering it had been a much more elaborate procedure than getting into the police station. They had sniffers too, of course, right in front of the visitors' entrance, but once past those, they had also searched me, then interrogated me while giving me looks that implied they would kill me if I were lying or if I tried anything untoward.

As it turned out, we didn't go in the usual way and Carbide just nodded to the heavily armed guard at the south entrance to the Warren as we walked in. No doubt they had the sniffers going, but the complacency of the security guard startled me, even at five in the morning. The visitors' entrance in the middle had flashy security. I began to wonder if it wasn't all show. The people who had to work there or who brought in food obviously didn't have to go through all that every time they went in or out.

I followed Carbide down a hall that curved gently to the right. After a few minutes, we turned left, then quickly right and entered into a cul-de-sac with five doors. He pressed the button for the middle one.

We stood staring at the door for a couple minutes before a dark haired, dark skinned woman wearing clunky gold jewelry opened it with a sudden rush. "Good, you're here. And on time too."

We went into her rooms and surveyed the effort. Carbide knew where her new quarters were. We carried a few things together until I had the route down, then we just moved at our own pace. We had a few boxes, but mostly we moved lamps and end tables and chairs which took only one person. We'd break down what we could, taking the drawers out of chests and carrying them individually. I worked more slowly than Carbide, even though I was trying to keep up my end of the bargain. While we shuttled her belongings, sometimes on hand trucks and sometimes by the arm-load, I was watching for anyone I knew. I was trying to learn what I could.

People went by, but no one paid us any attention except the woman whose things we were moving, Ms. Poynting. She watched us closely and pointed to the next item she wanted moved each time I returned. It wasn't clear to me why the order could possibly matter, but she wanted something to do that seemed important, so she continued with her eponymous activity.

The new space looked the same as the old space to me. Based on the lingering aroma, I assumed they'd painted it the night before, but other than that I couldn't see why she wanted to move.

We sat down for a short break at eight. Carbide explained that space further in was more prestigious. The rooms at the front were mostly filled with warehoused personal belongings and storage for some of the commercial tables out Under The River. Then came the apartments for underlings and petty criminals who could afford the rent. Only deep inside were the real Gnomes, and we weren't even close to that part of the Warren.

"Have you moved anything into the warehouse area in the last few days?" I asked on a whim.

"Yeah, I helped them move some office furniture and equipment into the north side. Not valuable space there at all. It's too close to the north entrance. The Gnomes like the south. They were keeping an eye on us though."

"Do you know who owned it?"

"What are you messing with, Benny?"

"Do you know who owned it?" I was thinking that maybe this was Arno's study.

"One of the Pirates. You don't want to mess with them. They're dangerous. They kill people."

The owner came into the room, and we stood up to move a settee, but I wanted to know more.

Around two in the afternoon, I saw Chen and he saw me. Carbide and I were moving a huge stuffed leather rhinoceros. I suspected it was sex furniture, though it wasn't obvious exactly how it was supposed to be used. I was carrying the butt end and when we came around a corner there he was, talking to Rela. Chen turned and looked me right in the eye. My disguise felt tissue thin. I'm sure I swallowed hard.

Rela was carrying a machine pistol, one of those that fired ceramics that shattered into a hundred shards when it hit flesh. I paused, and got a better grip on the rhino's butt. Chen winked at me, the bastard. Carbide began to move again. I kept shuffling along, my legs thumping into the rhino's butt with each step, waiting for Chen to tell Rela who I was and wondering how much protection the rhino could give me from ceramic bullets. I knew if I ran, she would just alert the entrance guards, and I would be trapped, then killed.

But he didn't tell her I was there, and she didn't recognize me from our dinner at Arno's house or from Chen's Fairchild. He nodded to her a few times as part of their conversation, then he turned, looked at me again, and went into a room just down the hall. Rela went back east toward the entrance.

The disguise was getting hot. I grunted "Stop," to Carbide, set down the rhino, then rubbed my hands on the harsh surface of my outer pants and tried to breathe easy, tried to settle my fear and anger.

After we dropped off the rhino, I told Carbide I had a side trip to do. He glared at me, but then told me to be careful.

"I have a rule," I told him. "Always look at your laundry carefully before you wash it. You never know what you might find."

I'd swear his ears flattened back against his head as though I'd blown a great wind in his face. "Tell Ms. Poynting I took a rest room break," I added, then rubbed my palms on my pants once more and followed Chen.

Chapter 29

Chen had ducked through a door and left it ajar. No one was in the hall, so I slipped in after him and closed the door behind me. It was a tiny office, no larger than the cardboard office he'd had Where The Sun Don't Shine. The desk was the same and the soundproofing, which once lined the box, now lined these walls. The same lamp was pointed toward the ceiling, and Chen was standing by the far wall looking at a small video window, which displayed a view of Fate Street dazzled with sunshine and tiny people.

"I thought you were dead," Chen said.

"Why did you send your hounds to kill me, Chen?"

He turned away from the window and pondered me for a moment. "They're not my hounds. They were Arno's hounds, as you call them, and now they work for my new boss."

"They tried to kill me."

"I didn't know he'd sent them until they were already out tracking you down. I hadn't heard anything else, so I thought they'd killed you. There's nothing I can do, though. I run a news agency, Benny. That's all I do. The Pirates use it to their advantage when they want to, but mostly it's just a news agency."

"I thought Denise owned Up Your News."

He raised an eyebrow. "Technically, but the Pirates don't necessarily care. In fact, they prefer someone else to actually own it. It makes the accounting easier and gives their operation a hide of respectability. She'll sign whatever they need her to sign."

"So why kill me? Where do I fit in?"

"You were Arno's enforcer and his brother. They don't know you killed him. They're worried you might come after them thinking they did it, or thinking that you should control Up Your News because your brother did. They expect you to ask for some of the profits, maybe the files."

"Tell them I don't care about that stuff at all. They can have Up Your News and everything that goes with it."

"Why would they believe that you would really stay hands-off? It's easier and cleaner to just kill you. That way there's no one to come back and bite them in the ass. You're a liability they aren't going to risk. You lose no matter how you look at it, Benny."

I started pacing, but at least I resisted biting my nails. If there were only one person who wanted me dead, I could deal with it. If the whole organization wanted me dead, then I worried that Chen was right, I was going to lose. "Did they pay Arno to have me kill people?"

"No, actually, Arno paid you directly. When people got in his way, he used you. You used forgets to avoid your troubles, he used you to avoid his. I guess the Pirates knew he did that once in a while, but he must have had protection from some higher ups or something, because no one ever made a play for his income. Maybe they were just afraid of you. Up Your News made money for him in net protection and in blackmail. We're a respected news agency, but Arno would have us run peculiar stories once in a while. He used those items to show people who hesitated to pay him just what he could do if they didn't pay. He used people like Rela and Mike as spies. They don't usually carry guns. In fact, they used to be pretty good investigative journalists. They would do infiltrations and investigate the gov, you know, the risky stuff. But they liked the danger too much and Arno took advantage of their danger fetish and used them to spy."

"How much money was Up Your News helping Arno make from blackmail?"

"I have no idea. We pay our people better than any other agency, which is one of the reasons we can uncover so many juicy stories, but I don't know how much Arno made on side jobs or what he did with the money."

Some of that money was in a couple socks in Carbide's laundry basket at that moment.

"Who's your boss now? Who took Arno's place?"

"You could just leave Chicago. Hop a train and go to Cleveland."

I could also break Chen's neck, then wait to see if anyone else was interested in me. "Who's your boss, Chen?"

He studied me, then sighed and turned to the door. "You're going to get me killed, Benny. You're going to get me killed. Is that what you want?"

"Who is your boss?"

"I only know him by his initials. Everyone calls him JB. He's not formally my boss yet, though. I think they're still arguing over who should take over Arno's enterprises. I guess JB thinks it'll be him, since he went and stole Arno's office, but he's been hesitant to do any more just yet. He hasn't come and told me I work for him, for instance. I expect he will soon."

They were pressing me and so far I'd played defense, but if I was going to survive, I had to change that. "If they're so worried I'm going to take over at Up Your News, maybe I should."

"You have no idea what you're dealing with." Chen walked past me to the door. "I'm sorry, Benny. I've got to go. If I'm caught in here with you, then we're both dead."

Chen grabbed the doorknob, then turned his head back to look at me. "If you take him out in some dramatic way, a way that impresses people, you might be able to hang onto Up Your News, the power that goes with it, maybe even your life. You need to get a hold of Arno's records. He must have had ways of keeping the rest of the Pirates at bay."

"How can I talk to you again?"

"You can't, you'll be dead. Carla's been given your number."

Chen walked out the door, leaving it partially open. I heard him say, "It's clear," and I walked out after him. He was down the corridor, already distancing himself from me.

Chapter 30

Carbide and I worked the rest of the day moving Anita Poynting's belongings into her new apartment. When we were done, I was still alert, but I felt more physically exhausted than I had when I first went to Carbide's place. Once we were back out Under The River and on the way home I asked him to walk us past the north entrance of the Warren where I hoped Arno's office materials were. We walked by a low, grimy doorway. He Indian-eyed it and told me they had moved the office materials to the room behind the third door on the right as you walk down the hall.

"The door's palm locked and gas locked and has a touch alarm. If you even touch the door, the entrance guard will be right there in ten seconds."

"OK," I said. "What are the walls made of?"

He stopped suddenly. I walked another two steps then turned and looked at him. Carbide just stared at me, then he shook his head and walked on looking at the ground. "I'm not sure of the material. It probably isn't very sound proof, but I know that when we set the desk down, Art let his end down too fast and we punched a hole through with the corner."

"Do you remember the desk, what it looked like?"

"It's dark red or maroon with gold wire embedded in the top. The wire formed a bird design or something, maybe some bamboo plants."

We stopped at a Chinese carry-out place on the way back to the apartment. Carbide paid. Back at his apartment we ate hungrily, then while Carbide was in the shower, I retrieved my socks. I called Denise and convinced her to talk to me long enough for her to affirm that Carbide's description of the desk he had moved matched Arno's desk.

I sat down to think out how I was going to get Arno's records out of the secure area, and fell asleep. I shouldn't have done that, because when I woke up a couple hours later, I ached everywhere except for the tip of my nose and a small area on the top of my head. Even my face hurt. I took a long shower, trying to steam out the wrinkles in my plan and my muscles.

Carbide was up and working at his PAL. "We did all right today, Benny. You worked pretty hard except for a few lapses. Can you work again tomorrow?"

I tried to avoid a loud groan as I eased myself down into the chair, but one escaped anyway. "My character has no motivation any more. I wouldn't be believable in the part."

"Didn't think so. Well, thanks for the one day. It helped. One of the two guys I used yesterday should have recuperated by now."

He made a few phone calls. Both of his helpers were enthusiastic about working the next day. Their enthusiasm made me wonder how much money I'd passed up. Carbide looked satisfied and pulled out a couple of beers.

"So what's your plan?" he asked.

"Plan?"

"Yes, plan. What's your plan for doing whatever it is you have to do."

"Now that's what I call fishing."

"Fishing or not, I think you've involved me. Either you're doing something for profit or your doing something for revenge, or you're doing something to protect yourself. Which is it?"

It was a good question. One I hadn't thought out. Chen was right that I could just leave. Especially since I had enough money and in a different town they wouldn't know who I once was. So why wasn't I on a train? Why was I instead looking for the man who stole Arno's stuff and who, presumably, tried to kill me and was still trying to kill me? In a word, Carla.

"A little revenge, a little protection for myself and for others." If JB needed an enforcer, Carla would fit the bill nicely until, like me, she became unreliable.

"No money in it?"

"No. Well, probably not, at least money is not the objective. I have all the money I need."

"Yeah, you've always lived cheap." He looked pointedly at his couch.

"What's next door to the storage room that you moved the stuff into the other day?"

"You mean as you leave the Warren, closer to the rest of Under The River?"

"Yes."

"There are two rooms between the Warren entrance and that room. They're both used to store inventory for Ray's, the junk store that takes up the space just outside the entrance to the Warren against the west wall of Under The River."

"Are those rooms as well protected?"

"Well, you still need to get past the guard and the sniffers and anyone else who happens to see you go in, but the locks aren't much. They're just standard gas locks. In fact, you can buy auto-pickers right there at Ray's, if you ask him nice, if you have enough money. It's the guard and the reputation of the Warren that keeps his stuff safe."

I already knew Ray would sell me a gas-lock picker. How I knew that, I wasn't sure, but I also knew of a few other shops that would sell me that kind of tech whether I asked nice or not. "Have you been in the one closest to the room with the office stuff?"

"Yes." He seemed interested now. He leaned forward enthusiastically, wanting to be in on the idea part of the operation. Carbide was still at the edge of plausible denial should I be caught, but he obviously hoped I would explain it all when everything was over. If I was still alive, it would be the decent thing to do.

"What's along the common wall?"

"Oh, you're going in through the wall. That's not bad. The door's very well protected, but you could probably just cut right through the wall. Ha. That's good."

"What's along the common wall?" I asked again, ignoring his second guessing.

"If you're looking to hide your entry, there's an old steel safe about halfway back that's been there for years. No one would want it, and it's too heavy to move out. It's on wheels, but I wouldn't want to move it up the stairs and, besides, the lock would be an easy pick."

"Will it still roll?"

"I suppose."

"Try to imagine what would be on the other side of that wall from the safe."

"Let's see, well, empty wall I guess. That's not good, is it?" He looked disappointed with himself, like he was failing me and that failure was important to him. I had a strange feeling then. One that I hadn't felt before. Carbide was acting as though he was impressed by me, as though he wanted me to succeed, as though he was helping without any motive other than helping a friend, or maybe to be part of a joint project. The whole time from when I showed up at his apartment to now, he acted in every way as someone would act toward a friend or maybe as a team member would toward a team captain. Yet, he was a stranger to me in most ways. I knew I had forgotten parts of our history. I only remembered him calling once in a while to ask if I wanted to make some extra money moving or delivering stuff, but we apparently knew each other better than that. I liked having a friend. I hoped I wouldn't get him killed.

"Draw what you remember."

Carbide sat down at his PAL and pulled up a blank screen, sketched out the walls, then drew in the doors and placed the safe. He drew in shelves of lamps and hoses and rope and cement figures along the rest of Ray's side of the wall. The other side of the dividing wall he drew as a clear line for about half the distance back, then he placed the desk, followed by some bookcases and then a few stacks of boxes. There wasn't anywhere, at least based on Carbide's estimation and memory as shown by the drawing, where there was something against both sides of the wall to cover a hole. Also, it had been a few days since they had stolen and moved Arno's office and several weeks since Carbide had helped Ray move a human-sized papier-mâché gargoyle into his back storage room.

"How would you get past the guard anyway, Benny? I mean, it's a nice idea, but you have to get past the guard and have enough time to open the lock. Even with the picker, that would take, say, thirty seconds. That's a long time. Then you have to get out. A distraction might work once, but I don't see it working twice."

Carbide had hit on the biggest problem. Worse, I had to leave with some unknown quantity of records, maybe a PAL or memsticks. I just didn't know.

"Do Ray's people go in and out freely?"

"I think they only go back there when he's with them. Mostly he does business off his tables and out of the closer room. The far room, the one you want to sneak into, contains seasonal things and the stuff he can't sell, but just can't bear to get rid of."

"You think he would sell the space with everything in it?"

"You have the money for that?"

"I'm just wondering"

He looked at me and chewed his lip a bit. "I think he would be suspicious if someone offered."

I tried to remember Ray. I didn't deal with him because he wasn't discreet, that much I remembered. Using him to get into that room seemed like a bad idea from the start.

"Can you get into that part of the hall from the back?"

"I don't know. The corridor continues back some and turns south, but I've never been beyond the third room."

Clearly, I needed a map and I'd never heard of there being one. "I might be wanting to help you move stuff tomorrow after all," I said.

"You can't go sneaking around back there, Benny. They all know each other. Anybody they don't know, they stop, maybe before they shoot them, maybe after. They would have no problem hiding your body in the river mud."

"They didn't stop us when we were moving furniture. I could get lost one day, and found the next, all I need to do is carry a couple lamps or maybe a stuffed badger."

"Benny who? I never met any Benny. I've never seen him before in my life." He said it with a smile, but I also knew he meant he would indeed deny any knowledge of me except that I helped him move stuff.

"When are you leaving in the morning?"

"Five. This guy gets up late."

"Wake me up. I'm going with you."

Carbide looked surprised, but he didn't say anything.

I put my disguise back on. It made me look heavier and slower, but didn't really disguise me that well. The head rag made my ears stick out and made me look a bit stupid, I thought.

I distributed a thousand around my outside pockets and went shopping.

Chapter 31

I was balancing my whole plan on the head of a pin. That pin was the assumption that Arno's office was still stored in that room, that JB hadn't gone through everything yet because he hadn't gotten permission from the people higher up in the River Pirate organization, and that I could spend enough time in the storage rooms to steal what I needed and not get caught.

OK, maybe it wasn't the best plan. I'd never thought of myself as a planner. Actually, I wasn't really a doer either, but I blinked myself with that Benny, Benjamin thing. I recalled Carla's pronunciation of Ben-ja-min and tried to act like a professional.

Egon Mert was a map dealer. I went to him first. Egon made and sold building maps that included alarm systems, guard locations, which doors were locked, and at what times. His maps were expensive, but he kept them up to date and accurate. He liked special orders. Egon sat in a walled-off nook not far from the South Entrance.

It took some talking to get past Egon's assistant, but he finally went behind the wall and told Egon my name, and that I wanted to see him. The assistant returned and waved me in, but once inside stood silently staring at me, ready to handle any problems, while Egon and I talked.

The walls of Egon's shop were lined with waist-high blue cabinets containing wide shallow map drawers. He had a large table at one end of the room and a desk with two comfortable looking guest chairs at the other. The table and the cabinets were well lit with focused lights allowing the desk area to feel more comfortable with an easy, soft light. The room was warm.

"How's business, Egon?" I said, settling down into a cushioned chair.

"Business is fine Benny, and how is your business?"

Sometimes the simplest questions are the hardest. I didn't even try to answer. "I need a map."

Egon looked me over. "Maps aren't inexpensive, Benny. Perhaps you should check the used market."

"I can pay, Egon. I need a map of the Warren."

The assistant let slip a puff of astonished air. Egon didn't change expression at all. "No, Benny. You don't need such a map, and I will forget that you came to me asking for one." He glanced meaningfully at his assistant, who grunted.

"It doesn't have to be up-to-date. An older copy would be fine."

Egon stood up and walked around the desk. "Unless you have some other business, I need to finish a commission job."

As he walked me to the door he whispered, "Carnival," in my ear at a time when the assistant couldn't over hear.

I said, "Thanks anyway," and stalked off toward Carnival's tables, doing my best to appear irritated. I wasn't sure why Egon had pointed me toward Carnival's place, why he was being so helpful. I guessed that he wanted to stay on the killer's good side. That didn't make me feel better about it, but being feared has its advantages.

Carnival sold entertainment toys and immersion disks two aisles in from the north wall. He had a lot of topsider customers who were willing to drop down Under The River once in a while to get the prices he could offer. His stuff was stolen, and he had lower costs for his space than the street stores. I perused the goods awhile until he became impatient and came over to run me off.

"Hi, Carni," I said.

He looked at me for a moment before his eyes gleamed in recognition. "Benny, what do you need?" He said it like he was in a hurry to get rid of me too. It seemed like everyone knew all along that I was a killer except me.

"I need a map of the Gnome's Warren."

He leaned close. "Who would be stupid enough to keep a map of the Warren? Just having such a thing would get you tossed."

"Do you know anyone who might be that stupid?"

"No."

He didn't say he didn't have one, he only said 'no', although it sounded final. "I can pay you well."

"Look, Benny, I'm not saying I have one, but even if I did, it would be my life to sell it to you."

I stepped closer to him, and stared into his eyes. "This is important, Carni. I'll memorize the parts I need, then destroy it if you want, or I'll give it back, but I need to look at a map."

Carni was a dealer, and he couldn't pass up money. Also, I think

I scared him more than the Gnomes scared him. He sighed. "Come into the back. I'll let you look at it for five minutes for a hundred."

"Fifty."

"A hundred. Cash. No swipe cards."

"Give me a gas lock picker too."

"Yeah, OK. I've got one of those"

I followed him back behind the tables and into his warehouse, as he called it, which was actually a structure made up of a combination of tarpaulin, cardboard, wood and some gray metal roofing. Once inside I realized it was more structurally sound than it had looked from the outside.

He gave me the gas-lock picker, and pulled an engineer's diagram out of a black plastic box that had been buried under a stack of older style music disks.

After unfolding the diagram and orienting myself to the entrances, I realized that the drawings were done a very long time ago. The print had faded and the creases were yellowed. Still they showed the entrances as they actually were, and showed that the north corridor turned left, headed back west, then curved slowly south to interconnect with the passages Carbide and I had been working in. I studied the drawing for my full five minutes. I gave Carni his money and left.

I went a few tables down, bought a pad of paper and drew out what I could remember, hoping the layout hadn't changed all that much since the drawings were done.

Rocket's flea market shop had everything else I needed. His store wasn't Under The River. It was over on Fate Street just north of Hackson. Some things I needed were legal, like a couple of accordion bottles and a few bars of People Food which he had in the front, but he had other things I needed too, like slapfaints and ceramic knives, which he kept in a hole he'd dug under the back room of his shop.

Finally, I walked back north to my apartment building. Hattie was sitting there as usual. She was surprised to see me. My muscles still ached from working for Carbide, and it hurt to sit down.

"Hello, Hattie. How are things today?"

"They fixed the lock on the building. I can't use the toilet in the basement anymore. I have to walk over to LaSally to pee."

"That's a pain," I said.

"That's a crime. I live here too don't I?"

I didn't argue the point. "You want to move up to a better place?"

"You mean die?"

I laughed. "No, I meant I need some help, and I'm willing to pay for it. Enough money for you to get an apartment inside for a month or two. It's getting cold."

"If I go inside for a month or two, I won't be able to handle coming back out. It'll kill me. I'd need enough to last till March."

"Maybe I could arrange that." Five months was about four hundred and the dole would pay the rent after the first two if she brought in her receipt. "I need you to provide a distraction Under The River at precisely three-thirty in the morning, not this coming morning, but the next."

She thought about that for a while. "Why are you willing to pay so much for that; for a distraction? You aren't doing anything illegal are you?"

"Yes."

"What do you mean, 'Yes'. You could at least lie about it. You could say, 'I'm saving a damsel in distress,' or 'I'm capturing some bad guys and putting them in jail.' You could say something like that."

"Actually, it is part of a plan to put an especially bad guy in jail. I'm stealing something that belongs to him."

"Well, why didn't you say so. I want five hundred plus expenses."

I laughed, but she didn't. "Expenses?"

"Yes, expenses."

"How much for expenses."

"Give me the five hundred now, and we'll settle accounts when everything works out."

If Hattie was blinking me, she was doing a great job of it, and I had no one else to trust. Carbide was too well known, Hero was a cop, and even if I could find Chen, I wouldn't trust him with my lunch, even accounting for all his protestations that he was just a news man.

She took the five hundred and put it in her shirt. We went over exactly when and where I needed her to provide the distraction. I even explained why, and that the guard might be hard to distract.

"How are you going to distract him, Hattie?"

"I'll think of something, don't worry."

She wouldn't tell me, but she had a gleam in her eye that said she was going to enjoy herself.

I checked to see if my palm print had been reprogrammed into the new lock. It was, so I opened the door and jammed the ceramic knife into the mechanism. They wouldn't notice or fix it again for weeks. Hattie lived there too, after all.

Although Hattie told me not to worry, I worried all the way back to Carbide's place, where I spent an hour sewing pockets inside my bum's coat and loading them with my purchases.

Sleep finally came while I was running my plan through and through, trying to convince myself that I wasn't an idiot and hoping I would run into Carla Under The River, then desperately hoping I wouldn't.

Chapter 32

At five the next morning Carbide and I, and two other guys I didn't know, went to the Warren. The guards nodded us in as before, and we started moving furniture for a Gnome with a really long last name that started with a 'K' and had mostly consonants in it.

A half hour into the move, I decided it was time to look for the back way into the hall where Ray's storage rooms were. I picked up a box loaded with pants that were obviously considerably too small for Mr. K., piled a coat that was also too small on top of it, which partially hid my face, and took a wrong turn on my way to his new apartment. I figured he was keeping the clothes because he thought he would eventually fit into them again. It would be a long time before he missed them.

I walked rapidly, humming "I Gotta Right to Sing the Blues" and trying to act like a bored mover. Three people passed by me in a group and took no notice. After that, I worried less about the Gnomes and more about where I was. When I got to where the corridor should have gone north there was an unbroken wall. I almost stopped, but someone walked down the corridor toward me, so I kept going.

The map was wrong. They'd walled up the connecting hall that ran from the south end to the north end. Finding my way back wasn't a problem, but I might not get another chance. In fact, I couldn't be sure that my chance hadn't already gone by. I kept walking, trying to find my way by heading in the right general direction. I switched my wrist unit to compass and wandered around, humming and moving at a steady pace to make people think I had somewhere to go.

I rounded a corner and suddenly I was right where I wanted to be, but I had walked too far out into the hall to stop and wait for the right time to come out and unlock the door. I could see the entrance guard's back. Walking right up to the door, I placed the autopicker and waited with the box, hoping the guard near the entrance would not take any notice of me even if he did turn away from the crowd to glance back.

The lock popped, an unnaturally loud sound. I didn't look toward the entrance. I just went in and closed the door behind me.

A moment later I heard voices outside the door, but the people didn't come to the room I was in. It must have been Ray going into his other storage room. Had I been a minute later, I would have been caught.

I waited for them to leave the other room, before I turned on my flatlight.

The room was much as Carbide had described it. Up on a shelf I found some space to put the box I had carried in with me, then I found a nook large enough to hide in should someone come into the room. If I had enough time to hide, that is. It was small security since I doubted I would know anyone was coming until the door actually opened. I was relying on Ray not using that room much.

Trash, junk, treasure, I didn't know what exactly to call the accumulated piles of sofa cushions, buckets, chairs without legs, tools without motors, stacks of plates and cups, brass pipe fittings, a concrete Madonna, and of course the papier-mâché gargoyle which was huge and ugly, hollow and light and stared at me with bright eyes. Should Hattie's diversion not work out, I could always stuff myself inside the gargoyle, cut out eyeholes and try to sneak out, stopping every time someone looked, hoping they wouldn't notice me. Gargoyle camouflage.

The safe stood about where Carbide said it would. They'd moved it a bit further away from the door, but it still stood against the wall. I thought I could move it just a little further without anyone noticing.

The wall sheathing was made of a nylon fiber, laminated with glue and sheets of thin plastic. For no obvious reason, the stuff was called woodboard. It was hard and shiny on the surface, but the tungsten drill and ceramic saw I'd purchased were up to the task. I'd decided against power tools because the noise level would keep me from hearing someone at the door until it was too late to hide.

I made a starter hole with a hand drill, then started sawing. After cutting for ten minutes, I measured and calculated that it would take me two hours to cut through this side and another two to cut through the other side, but I had about eighteen hours, until three-thirty the next morning, to do the job.

Sawing low to the ground was hard, uncomfortable work and after a while, I stood up to stretch my legs, pee into the accordion bottle, and look at Ray's accumulation. Here and there, I found something that I thought would be worth money if it were placed in one of the antique shops on the near north side. My favorite item was still the gargoyle, though.

After I'd cut through on the top, bottom and left sides, I scored the right vertical and pulled the piece toward me like a door. It cracked and groaned, but the nylon fibers held it together and acted like a hinge. The studs left a gap of about a hand's width between the wall sheathing on one wall and the other. After I drilled a few small holes to make sure no one was in the other room and to make sure I wasn't sawing into the desk, I used the same procedure on the other side.

People Food was some nutritionist's idea of the perfect human food. It was cheap, compressed, lasted almost forever in its special packaging, and supposedly contained everything the body needed. It tasted halfway between rotten eggs and rancid peanut butter, but I ate a few pieces anyway. It kept me awake. It wasn't supposed to have that effect, but it worked that way on me. The bars probably contained more vitamins than I was used to.

The other room was about the same size as Ray's, but it was split into three separate sections by white lines painted on the floor and half way up the walls. The section nearest the door was taken up by large crates stamped with a skull and crossbones. A bit overdone I thought, but it made it clear who owned them. The second section was Arno's office and the section behind that contained an early century Dodge Challenger disassembled, apparently complete and well stored. Some Gnome apparently hoped to eventually get out from under his legal problems and wanted an investment that would hold its value. You couldn't drive it anymore, of course. Old cars which weren't retrofitted with modern safety gear were considered a menace on the road and unsafe.

They'd moved Arno's office chair along with everything else, so I made myself comfortable and started with the drawers of the desk. I quickly scanned through everything I could find, including the papers taped under the desktop above the right top drawer, the e-plastic under the blotter and the block of cards in the drawer hidden behind the molding on the credenza. I spent eight hours searching and sorting until I had a stack of papers, cards, disks and memsticks as well as a PAL, all of which I wanted to take with me.

Then I searched again, measuring to find any hidden compartments I'd missed the first time. I found two more. One, at the back of a small end table where the depth of the inside was less than the depth of the outside by more than the thickness of the wood, the other was where a drawer was shallower than it should have been. They would have found all of these hiding places, of course. They would dismantle each piece in turn. Now they would find the hiding places, but not the contents.

I found some blank cards and carefully wrote on each one, "What is it worth to you?" Under that I wrote, "Rela & Mike."

I didn't think JB would believe Rela or Mike would be that stupid. Maybe he would, but I put the notes there to confuse and annoy, and hopefully, anger him and maybe them. I wanted JB to be frustrated to the point of stupidity. Strong emotion is always a bad ally in negotiations.

Once everything was back on Ray's side of the wall, I had to cover my tracks. I put everything back as I found it, including Arno's chair. Realizing that I hadn't studied it carefully, I turned the chair over. Underneath was a small hatch in matching black plastic. I opened it slowly, but there was no triggering device, only a micro memstick. It occurred to me then that the chair was probably the best of the hiding places. The micro memstick went into my pocket while I debated how to best hide my intrusion. I couldn't move the desk over because it was too heavy to pull back against the wall after I was through. I settled on a painting of a World War II destroyer I'd found leaning against the far wall. After I went through the opening, I pulled the painting up against the wall and pushed the cutout back up against the painting. Tape around the edges of the panel held it flat to the rest of the wall. It would be pretty obvious when someone moved the painting, but I figured they would hesitate to open the little door. To add to their hesitation, I placed a smoke bomb in the cavity between the studs, rigged to go off when they pushed. I left a card in the cavity also.

Back in Ray's room, I sealed up the other side with tape as well, then pushed the safe against the hole. I took the time to wedge the wheels, so they would have a very difficult time moving it from the other side. Like I said, I wanted JB mad.

I still had four hours. Ray's would be closed for the night, so I didn't worry about being disturbed. Tiredness was fast overcoming me, and I couldn't stand having all that data and not reading some of it, but I also couldn't afford to fall asleep.

The gargoyle stood there staring at me, and I decided it would be an amusing hiding place for the data. I put most of the materials into an empty accordion bottle, sealed it and stuffed it up and into the gargoyle's head, then sealed the bottle in place with some more tape. I shoved the PAL and the memsticks and disks into the hollow feet, securing them the same way.

Just before three-thirty, I hid the accordion bottle that I'd peed in on a top shelf—let them figure that one out in ten years when someone tried to clean the place out.

If Hattie's diversion didn't work out the way I hoped it would, I didn't want to be caught with the evidence of the crime on me. I wanted to be able to claim I'd wandered into the Warren by accident and the guard didn't notice. They wouldn't believe me, but I might be able to escape while they were thinking about it. Anyway, I would need a large box to carry everything, and slipping past the guard would be a bit difficult carrying something like that.

At three-thirty, I shook myself so I would be more alert, then I went to the door. I couldn't hear anything. I opened the door just a crack and listened. Nothing. Hattie's distraction should have started. I had no choice, so I opened the door far enough to poke my head out and look.

Hattie was there all right. And she was distracting.

Chapter 33

Her dress was a lustrous topaz blue and it draped down her body and slid out onto the dusty concrete floor like a morning mist. Around the waist she'd tied a silver colored rope belt, allowing one end to hang lose down her left hip. Her arms were covered by long white gloves, and her black hair was spun high on top of her head, adorned with a breath of tiny white-tipped flowers. She smiled gracefully like a young princess meeting her people for the first time and believing that they would love her because she loved them. She was a fantasy under dim fluorescent lights.

There were perhaps twenty people staring at her. I stared too, not at first realizing it was her and then in dumbfounded astonishment. The distraction almost worked on me, but I stirred and walked out into the main area, sidling to the left to avoid the guard's view, then I too stopped and watched. No one made a move to rob her or even talk to her. She just posed there, a jewel, an almost heartrending apparition standing among the destitute and the dirty. And no one took offence.

Our eyes locked for a second, hers expressing gratitude and the enjoyment of playing a part well, mine expressing thanks and maybe a bit of wow. Few people were up at three-thirty, but the ones who were would have a story to tell. I doubted anyone would believe it except as a fairy tale.

I slipped out the north entrance and hung out on the block so I could make sure she got home, but I didn't see her come out. I went back in a half hour later and everything was quiet. I had no idea where she went.

Back at Carbide's apartment I stripped off my supposed disguise and sat back on the couch, figuring that Carbide would wake up soon when he went to work. I fell asleep.

About two in the afternoon I woke up to a nut-like basmati rice smell. Carbide was in the kitchen whistling something from *The Barber of Seville*. When he saw me sit up and rub my head, he said, "Feeling chipper?" He was grinning happy.

"No," I said with a groan. I stood and wobbled over to the kitchen stool. "You are considerably too happy. What happened?"

"Well, you're still alive." He grinned even wider to let me know that that had nothing to do with his wide grin. "And we moved the last one today, so I'm taking the rest of the week off." It was Friday.

His chipper attitude was getting me down, so I went in the bathroom and wiped off my stubble, took a shower and toweled myself dry with extra vigor.

Feeling a bit more alive, I tried to face Carbide's joy again. "What are you cooking?" I said walking back into the kitchen.

"Shahjahani biryani, it's a favorite."

Carbide didn't seem to have any troubles. He worked hard and felt useful and productive. He was paid well enough to eat chicken once in a while. What more could he want.

"Got enough for two?"

"Well, yes. Enough for me and a lady friend."

Carbide was a bit older than me, perhaps a little over forty. I hadn't thought about him being hooked up with someone.

"So, do I need to find somewhere else to sleep tonight?"

He stopped chopping cilantro. "No, actually she knows you. I made enough for all three of us. You're welcome to stay. I was just being slap."

My hair prickled. "Who did you tell that I was here?"

"Oh! I didn't even think. I mean—I'm sorry."

"What did she look like?" I grabbed my bum's coat and put it on.

"You wouldn't believe me if I told you."

"What did she look like, Carbide? Did she have short black hair, sort of curled around her face? Was she a short blonde, athletic?"

"No. She's tall with black hair all in a twirl. She was wearing this dress. . . ."

"A blue dress, slinky and expensive looking?"

"Yes. That's her. She's a looker."

I sat back down. So that was where Hattie went after the diversion. "How did you meet?"

He chopped and talked at the same time. "I was going to move Mr. Hollner this morning, and when I went down Under The River, there she was, just standing there like an angel. She looked lost. I mean, she sure didn't belong Under The River. I asked her if she was OK. She asked me if I would be so kind as to escort her to the ball. Can you imagine that? She asked me to escort her to the ball. She wasn't drinking either. She just asked that."

He opened a cabinet and pulled out a bag of pistachios. "Anyway, I told her I'd love to be her escort. It was maybe quarter to four and I was a bit early for work anyway, so I walked her by all these staring people and out the south entrance, and all the while she's got her arm through mine and she's leaning on me a little. I felt grubby, you know, because I was dressed for the job and all. I told her I cleaned up OK and, when she got in her cab, I asked her to come to dinner. She should be here soon."

"How did my name come up?"

"Oh, well. She said she didn't usually dress so nice, that it was only a one-time thing. She had a benefactor. I said that he must be rich and that she must like him a lot. I wanted to know if she was already taken, you know? Anyway, she saw through that right away, and she said she would be glad to come to dinner if it was in the next day or so because after that she would be unavailable. I wish I knew what that meant, unavailable. She might be married and not letting on. I'd hate to be thinking this way about another man's wife."

Carbide had stopped working and just stared at the counter. His happiness seemed to be leaking out.

"She's not with anyone."

"Really?"

"No," I said. "She lives by herself." Hattie on vacation, wowing the natives and having a good time with my money. She was thinking she would have to go back to her concrete bed at some point, and she didn't want to get too used to vacation. The longer she was away, the harder it would be to go back. She was spending the money fast.

"We sort of eased into talking about you. We danced around the issue until we realized we were talking about the same person. Then she said you were her benefactor, and I said you were staying with me. Did I give you away?"

"Yes, but in this case it doesn't matter. Hattie knows a lot about what I'm doing. She was my distraction."

"Hattie? I never asked her what her name was. It's hard to think about someone without knowing her name." He was all smiles again.

"Her name's actually Myra, but she seems to prefer Hattie."

"Where did you get the money to be her benefactor?"

The door buzzer buzzed and we both jumped a little. The door video screen showed Hattie and no one else. I let her in. She was wearing gray slacks and a light blue shirt. Light blue was definitely her color. Her face was smudgy from makeup she'd used to cover too much time outdoors without benefit of sunblock or moisturizer, but she was a fine looking woman and she seemed to know it. Cleaned up, she looked to be in her late thirties. "Hello, Benny-Benjamin." She smiled at me, pleased with herself. "Did I do OK?"

"Yes, Hattie, you did fine. You should have been in pictures."

She looked startled for a second. "I was. Did you know, or were you guessing?"

"I thought you were a fashion designer."

"Oh." She said moving into the room and nodding to Carbide who had briefly looked up from his intense food preparation. The nuts were dust now under his chopping knife.

She wasn't going to explain. She wanted to be the mysterious type. She was doing a good job.

"What made you pick Carbide out of the group to be your escort?"

"He looked like he could handle any problems if someone decided I looked too rich. I didn't want to go out the same way as you and draw attention to you. Anyway, I like his face, he looks honest." She gave him a beneficent smile.

Carbide said dinner was ready in a voice that didn't sound like him. I decided to put off asking them both for one more favor.

Chapter 34

We had a delightful dinner, during which I listened and watched while Carbide and Hattie shifted in and out of roles, playacting, flirting, and having a great time. They didn't seem to notice me at all, yet I had a feeling that without me they would have sat there staring at each other, not knowing what to say. They needed an audience.

After dinner, I asked Hattie if she could play another part for me.

"I'm wondering how you ever got along without me," she said, happy to be asked.

"It's been difficult," I admitted. "I need you to buy a gargoyle for me from Ray's. I need you to buy it first thing in the morning, and, Carbide, I need you to bring it here, preferably without anyone following you or knowing that you brought it back to your own apartment."

Hattie looked eager, but Carbide sat back in his chair. "Why do you want the gargoyle? Are you putting Hattie in danger by asking her to buy it?"

Looking at Hattie I said, "Yes, it is dangerous, I suppose. I'd do it myself, but if I dressed like a bum, they would be suspicious of the money, and if I went as myself, my cover would be lost. It's best if they don't know I'm still in Chicago and alive. But if you go looking for something unusual to decorate your front porch for Halloween, Ray's likely to think of the gargoyle himself and try to push it on you. Buy it, then tell him you'll have someone come by and pick it up."

Carbide perked up. "That would be me."

"Yes. Since you do that kind of work all the time, no one will be surprised."

"And how on earth am I going to transport a man-sized gargoyle with ears the size of basketball hoops out from Under The River and walk it all the way here without anyone noticing?"

"Throw a sheet over it?"

Carbide crossed his arms. "I can get a truck, but I want to know why you need the gargoyle."

"You're better off not knowing."

"I want to know." He glanced at Hattie, but she didn't lend him any support.

I pulled two fifties out of my pocket and put one in front of each of them.

Carbide brushed his onto the floor and leaned forward. "I'm not asking to be bought, Benny. Where are you getting all this money, anyway? I want to know what Hattie is risking her life for. We don't want your money, we want to know why."

As if to reject his statement, Hattie grabbed her fifty and stuffed it in her shirt. Carbide turned toward her, wide-eyed. She shrugged with an apologetic smile.

"OK, fine," he said, crossing his arms again. He wasn't happy about it. He was trying to protect Hattie, but if she didn't want to be protected, there wasn't much he could do about it.

Staying up for twenty-four hours had worn me out, and the sleep I'd gotten during the day just made me more tired. After Hattie left for the Cuban—she was living high while she could—I laid down on the couch to think about my plan and promptly fell asleep. Once Hattie had left the apartment, the train was in motion, and I couldn't stop it.

Saturday morning I woke up at nine, a much more rational hour than had been the rule of late. Ray's would open for business around nine. I showered and worried. So many things could go wrong. If JB discovered the theft, he might have searched the room next door. Hattie might ask for the gargoyle specifically and tip her hand. Worse, he might let her buy the thing, then follow it to its destination, leading the mysterious JB from Hattie to Carbide and me. The gargoyle might fall apart in transit. The records could break out right there in front of everyone. I wanted to be there, floating in the background, watching, ready to help if the need arose. Instead, I had to stay put and worry. I didn't know the details of their plan. They were doing it together, Hattie for the money and the chance to play a part, Carbide for the chance to be with Hattie and the chance to be a part.

I paced for twenty minutes, thinking one minute that I should go down there anyway, then deciding the next minute that I would be exactly the wrong person to help if there was trouble. Any plausible deniability they had would vanish if I showed up.

A little after ten, I heard noise outside the door. I flung it open before I considered that it could be someone other than Carbide with the gargoyle. It was Carbide, but he didn't have the papier-mâché beast. Hattie was with him, though.

"What happened?"

Carbide offered Hattie a chair. She sat down and said, "Sorry, Benjamin. I got there at a few minutes before nine. I waited for them to pull the tarps off the tables, you know, to open up properly. Just as I was going to ask about the Halloween decoration, this guy came out from the Warren hopping mad. He grabbed Ray and drug him back past the guard yelling about locks and walls and security. He was quite vulgar about it."

"Did he say anything about the gargoyle? Did you hear that word?"

"No."

"And then you left?"

"No, I hung around to see if anything else happened. I went over to the place two stands down and asked them about Halloween decorations, so if I do get to go back my story will have some extra support."

"You did exactly the right thing, though I wouldn't have blamed you if you'd left immediately. I imagine there were people who did."

"Yes. A lot of topsiders took off when the ruckus started. I waited a few more minutes, then left and went back to the diner where Carbide and I had breakfast."

I must have looked startled. I couldn't imagine when they'd had a chance to set up a meeting for breakfast. Carbide used Hattie's shrugging apologetic smile on me.

I had to think. To think, I needed to walk. "I'm going out for a while," I said. I put on my disguise, which I was less and less impressed with. They asked if they could help, which pleased me for some reason I couldn't quite grasp.

I said no thanks, and left, heading out onto the street in the direction of Under The River and having no idea what I would do when I arrived.

Chapter 35

While I'd been in Ray's storage room waiting for the designated time to leave, I'd had a few hours to read over some of Arno's records. The ones I saw, while useful if I wanted to take over the Up Your News operations, weren't effective blackmail material against anyone other than the marks Arno had already been blackmailing. I'd stored them in the gargoyle to keep JB from using them, but I didn't really have a use myself.

Yet, I knew there had to be more. The number of secret compartments in his office made me think there might have been at least one I'd missed. Some of the disks or memsticks might have had something else on them, but they were labeled and, if the labels were accurate, they weren't useful either. Perhaps the PAL had some things hidden on it, but I doubted that, since it would be an obvious place, and it would need backups and repairs—too much of a data leak. The information in the gargoyle, however, wouldn't be available to me for at least a few days, even if JB didn't think to look in Ray's room for the missing records.

The missing records were leverage only as long as JB didn't find out I'd actually left them in the storage room where he could easily retrieve them. I wanted him to think I'd brought them out.

One thing I did learn from Arno's records was that Sukey was more than just a regular Elf for the Gnomes. He was also a surveillance expert and Arno had used him several times. Specifically, he'd used him to take a look into Kimbanski's private life.

Sukey must have found something that hit home, something dirty in a way that affected Sukey to his core, because he'd killed the judge.

Sukey went to Arno for help afterward, and Arno paid Paulo to give him a forget. Arno had notes about it in his ledger book. He was quite happy and added the comment that he should be able to get my fee back since it was someone else who'd committed the murder.

Sukey must have gone to Paulo and had the forget, then somehow found out later. I figured he got buzzed on derpal with Paulo, trying to get Paulo to tell him what he'd forgotten. Arno's notes didn't specify what the personal discovery was that Sukey had made about Kimbanski, but I already knew from the news articles that Sukey's girlfriend had been taken by the slave traders and then dumped out on the street after they'd used her for a while.

I started thinking about what I could do with the information Arno had accumulated. Not for blackmail, but for the police. I almost walked into a stoplight pole. The police weren't my friends. I had respect for some of them, but the idea of working with them to uncover the slave underworld, or gov workers on the take, or whatever, struck me as wrong—and yet right. It was a messed up thought.

I went down the stairs and into the gloom of Under The River. Ray's was against the west wall not far from the north entrance. I strolled by at speed, going somewhere else. The store was closed. The tarps were back on the tables and strapped down. There were two guards at the north Warren entrance and they were examining with careful eyes anyone who came close.

It was then I saw Carla. Luckily, she didn't see me. She strode into the Warren entrance like she lived there. She didn't nod to the guard, she didn't show any deference to entering a maximum security area at all. I almost shouted out her name. I almost ran after her. I suspect that at that moment, I almost died.

I had been harboring a hope for a while that maybe Carla was being used as a bargaining chip, as a hostage of sorts to keep me from doing something consequential. That wasn't an inherently better scenario than her working for JB or the River Pirates, both possibilities had a downside. At least now, I knew. After some thought, I decided that knowing was worse than not knowing.

I noticed the guards at that entrance staring at me, so I shuffled off.

I went to Carni's booth and hung around until he noticed me. He came over after a while.

"What did you do, Benny?"

Carni was rubbing his palm with his thumb. That was his tell. He always did that when he was nervous. He'd make a lousy poker player. "What makes you think I did something? I was just wondering what happened to Ray's. It's closed."

"Yeah, it's closed all right. They killed him, Benny. They tied his hands behind his back and took him out to the river then tossed him in headfirst. I don't want to see you for a while, OK?"

"Who called that one, Carni?"

"JB that's who. Don't fool with that bastard. He's a killer from way back." Carni blanched white when he realized how I might take that.

I thanked him for filling me in and left. Back up on the street I felt sick. The picture of Ray, head down in the silted river, hands tied behind his back, feet flailing in the air while he sucked in mud gave me stomach cramps. I had to stop and sit down.

JB was larger than life for me because I didn't know him. All I knew were his actions. It was like playing chess with a machine, the game loses all its psychological components. You can't detect the chinks in your opponent's defense because you don't know the man who designed it. Not knowing him didn't mitigate my hatred, though. OK, some of it was guilt displaced. Ray's hideous death was my fault. There was no way around that. Ray wasn't a nice guy and the things he sold got people killed or worse, hooked, but I already felt guilty enough. Ray just added to the weight on my chest, and I vented that guilt as anger toward JB.

Was I in too deep? Out of my depth? Maybe I was, but I was going to play it out to the end and, if I made it, maybe I could start in on some penance for past deeds. Bitter thoughts about myself bubbled up. How was I better than JB? Weren't we much the same? I tried to tell myself that the old Benny was like that, but Benjamin wasn't.

Carla's laugh made me look up. But it wasn't her. It was just a girl laughing at her friend's joke. My ears playing tricks brought me to thinking about Carla. Knowing she was an assassin again, knowing I couldn't be with her, but also knowing that she was not that far away and remembering her face, her ears, her hands, was putting a strain on my moorings. I beat my fists against my knees until they hurt. If I had wanted to look like a homeless mental patient, I couldn't have done a better job.

I stood and shoved my hands in my pockets, resolved to go find Hero Fish. Something hard scratched my hand. It was the memstick I'd pulled from Arno's chair. I'd dropped it into my pocket during the search and forgot to add it to the pile I'd hidden in the gargoyle. I stood and looked at it.

It was unlabeled and the write-tab had been broken off. The library would have readers and at that moment, I didn't want to get Carbide any more involved by leaving ghost images of the stick's contents on his PAL.

I strode south to Incongruous and east to the library. Walking up the library steps, I laughed. I was convinced that the information I needed was on that stick, and I was passing under the library's gargoyles to read it. I've always felt that the fundamental humor of Providence is irony.

But of course, the library wasn't open on weekends. Beandogs! I went over to Mythagain and walked north to a small cafe that had PALs, but they wouldn't let me in. The guy actually kicked me. Providence being ironic again. I tried another cafe, producing pretty much the same result, although I got in the door before the staff escorted me out. I even showed them a ten, showed that I could pay, but it didn't matter.

Hattie had told me, but I hadn't understood. Once you put on the appearance of being homeless, people treated you like a windblown piece of old newspaper. They ignored you unless you disturbed them, then they stepped on you or kicked you aside.

The automat across the street from the cat house had no front employees to throw me out. They also had no PALs. I went there anyway, paid for a cup of chocolate tea from the machine and sat down by the window. Maybe Hero worked on Saturdays. I hoped he worked the same hours. I could go in and ask, but that seemed like a bad idea.

I'd almost given up waiting when he walked out of the police station. He was with the woman detective who had helped Hero take me in to Kumar the first time. I figured she wasn't dirty because Kumar could pay her to go out and bring in the likes of me. Her lack of nice clothes and Kumar's use of her to go arrest me at three in the morning as though she had nothing better to do implied she was a good cop, not that that was a terrifically good reference, but it was all I had.

I walked across the street toward them. They stopped talking and watched me approach. When I was close enough, I said, "Hello, Hero. Nice day for catching crooks."

"Benny. I was wondering if I'd see you again."

The woman detective looked at Hero. "So this is the guy?"

"Yes," said Hero.

She looked at me. Stared at me actually. Studied me. Finally she said, "Let's go inside."

"No thanks," I said. "I'll meet you in twenty minutes where I met Hero last time." I walked away wondering what I was going to tell them.

The bar where I'd met Hero before was called The Bin, but The Pit might have been a better name. It was full of police this time. They glared at me as I walked brazenly past and sat down with Hero and his detective. They went back to drinking then, probably thinking I was a snitch, which, I realized, I was.

I sat down and Hero formally introduced me to Detective Laverick. She asked me what I had for her.

Not being sure of her, I wanted to talk a little before I revealed too much. I ordered a beer then asked, "Do you give a bonus to your police support when you make a big arrest?"

"What's that got to do with it? You looking for a cut of some arrest? There has to be an arrest first. Unless you have something directly useful in an investigation, you get nothing. I might arrange to give you a few bills if you lead me to something big."

"It's not me I asked about, is it?" I looked at Hero. "What's he get out of it?"

Hero perked up. "She's always been fair to us, Benny. Come on. Don't waste our time."

"I need access to a PAL. A private one."

Laverick grunted. "We had those at the station. What are we doing here?"

"No," I said. "It has to be a private one."

Hero said, "I have one at my apartment."

"Is it secure from ghosting?"

"Yes." Hero didn't give any explanations or any references to college degrees to back up his stated ability to set up sophisticated software on his PAL. I took his statement at face value for that reason.

"OK," I said. "Let's go."

Laverick put her hand flat on the table with a smack. "Wait a minute. Why are we doing this? You've given me nothing to make me believe you're doing anything more than wasting my time. I've got better things to do. If you want to take Hero out fishing, fine. But until he says it's worth the trip, I'm going home." She cast Hero a long disgusted look. Hero looked hurt, and I wondered what went on between them. "OK, fine," she sighed. "We'll go to Hero's apartment, it's not that far, but if it's a waste of my time, I'm going to have him beat your ears off."

I smiled, wondering what was on the stick. I hoped it wasn't video of Arno and Denise at the beach.

Chapter 36

Hero lived in a dirty yellow brick building over on Shooter Street. His apartment was on the first floor, near the front door and next to the vator, but he did have a lot of space. He had free-weights and some auto-resistance gear and not much else. The place was clean as a cop's gun.

I handed Hero the stick. "Let's take a look at what's on this," I said. I added a little bravado, hopeful that, if the stick did contain video of Arno and Denise on the beach, I could escape a beating by acting surprised and inventing something I'd expected to see there.

Hero inserted it and waited for it to be scanned. I held my breath. Laverick went to use the bathroom. She didn't expect much.

Hero watched his screen. "It's certified video. Never been touched. The only kind you can use in court."

Laverick came out of the bathroom just as the video started.

We all shrank from the screen when the first image came up. The camera was placed high and in a corner of a small, low room. The room had soundproofing on the walls and ceiling of the same type as Chen's office, gray foam that seemed to suck all the light from the single bulb hanging in the center of the ceiling. To the left was a wall of horizontal metal bars standing away from the wall, like stacked curtain rods about a hand's width apart. Against the far wall were racks of whips and paddles, chains and cuffs. A sofa stood out perpendicular from the right wall like audience seating. In the middle of the otherwise bare room, a woman was bent over a four-legged wire rack, her feet tied to the front legs of the rack, and her hands tied to the rear legs. Her back was striped with red welts. Her butt was covered with purple bruises.

A door under the camera opened, and the girl stirred and moaned. She lifted her head slightly, as far as she was able. Around her head, we could see a rope that was used as a gag.

Two men entered. We couldn't identify them because their backs were toward us. They were laughing at something on the other side of the door. I heard party sounds in the other room that disappeared when the door closed. The men were carrying brown bottles.

The taller of the two took off his pants and raped the woman while she was still strapped down. As he grunted his way to satisfaction, he said she was still a nice tight fit. The other man sat on the sofa and drank and watched. When the rapist finished, he turned around to pick up his bottle.

Hero pushed his chair away from the screen, almost pushing it over as though he were trying to escape the picture. "Shit!" he said. "That's that judge. That's Kimbanski."

I'd stepped back too and was peering nervously over Hero's shoulder.

On the video the other man stood to take his turn at the girl, but turned back to say something to Kimbanski. He had a tattoo on his belly that said, "Wand of Wonder," with an arrow pointing down. I didn't hear what he said because Laverick drew a startled intake of breath. "That's Jackson Yoder," she whispered loudly. "He's had some surgery, but that tattoo gives him away. God, I thought he was dead. I knew he was dead. Kumar killed him last year. No, two years ago. He resisted arrest and Kumar killed him."

I couldn't watch. I went over by the sink. Laverick and Hero continued to make comments about the sadistic meanness of the two men. I tried to tune out them and the video, but the cracking sound of torture punched its way through. I stared at the sink and breathed slowly.

When Hero said they were letting the girl up from the wire rack, I forced myself to go back and look even though I had the dreadful feeling I knew who it was. Jackson Yoder and Judge Kimbanski stood her up and turned her around to guide her out the door. Yoder complained about the blood getting on him. They had to support her, one on each side. Her eyes were taped shut and a red ball had been stuffed in her mouth and her face was swollen and discolored, but I still recognized Sukey's girlfriend.

Nausea welled up from my stomach and I felt dizzy from the realization that Arno had had Sukey install that surveillance gear. Sukey was Arno's Elf. I had to believe that Sukey had seen the disk. My mind touched on Carla, and I would have thrown up if I'd eaten anything at all that day. Instead, my stomach heaved and cramped. I slumped down heavily on the floor.

I didn't know if Arno had planned things to happen that way, knowing who Kimbanski and Yoder had kidnapped for sexual slavery, or if it was just fortuitous circumstance for him. Either way, he achieved Kimbanski's death and had been happy thinking he could get his money back from me for the murder.

Sukey couldn't let it pass, could he? He'd gotten to Kimbanski before I could.

Kimbanski and Arno and Sukey were all dead, but Jackson Yoder, whoever that was, still lived, and that seemed very unfair.

Images kept coming unbidden into my head, Carla and Sukey's girlfriend changing places. It made me dizzy. I felt myself turning into that monster I'd worried about so often in the last week. I couldn't help but believe that "B" had to be Jackson Yoder's middle initial, and I wanted to kill him.

Laverick crossed the room and sat on Hero's auto-resistance machine. She looked drawn and worried.

Hero sat in his chair and stared at the blank screen. "That poor woman," he said.

"Yes," I said. "That was Sukey Mack's girlfriend. She didn't die." I didn't know quite what I meant by the last part. I hadn't heard much about how she fared after that mess, only that she'd been dropped off and lived. "Sukey was a surveillance expert. He must have seen that video when he collected the information from the remote."

Laverick went over to the kitchen sink and splashed water on her face. "Jackson Yoder is alive."

She wasn't talking to anyone, really. She was repeating a litany to herself in an effort to believe what she'd seen. To reinforce the dramatic truth.

"Hero, is that stick genuine?" she asked quietly.

"Hold on, I'll run the verifier, but I think so."

We waited about a half minute. "Yes, it's genuine, including the date stamp. It's properly certified and encoded. The totals match."

We sat in silence for a few more minutes. I stood up and started pacing. "What was Jackson Yoder's middle name?"

"Balner." Laverick watched me walk back and forth.

"Did he ever go by JB?"

Laverick thought about that. "I don't know. Hero, look it up."

Hero worked a few minutes while I continued pacing. I wanted to kill Jackson Yoder, promise to myself or not. Was I feeling what anyone would in my situation? Or was I a murderer who wanted just one more murder? Would there always be one more?

Hero said, "Here it is."

Laverick and I went over and looked over his shoulders. He'd brought up Yoder's police history, something I shouldn't have been allowed to see, but Laverick didn't seem to mind me looking. It had pictures of him and under his name it showed JB as an AKA.

The front page had a list of possible crimes, which included his apparently indiscriminate killing of street people. His picture was prominently displayed. I'd seen him Under The River previously, just around. I couldn't remember any specific time or place.

I asked Hero to find the Death News report of Kumar's killing of Yoder. I figured they would have pictures.

An expert at searching, he found it quickly. We waited while some advertisements flashed around the screen—mature singles, Caribbean vacations, and illegal surveillance gear you could buy direct from Venezuela.

As I suspected, Death News featured a close-up of the fleshy remains. Supposedly, Kumar had shot Yoder at the train station and Yoder had fallen in front of an oncoming train. The body could have been Yoder's, but we knew it wasn't. The article included a small picture of Kumar and a note that as primary detective on the case and "arresting officer" he would get five thousand added to his paycheck that month.

"Yoder's in the Warren Under The River," I said. "He's a Gnome"

Laverick clenched her fists. She wanted to hit something. "I hate that place. They can run down there like rats down a hole and stay there forever and we can't do a thing about it. In two hours with five hundred police we'd net a hundred of Chicago's most wanted, and we can't do a damn thing."

"Why not," I asked. "Why not get your five hundred cops and do it right?"

Laverick laughed bitterly. "Yeah, like the city council or the Mayor are going to let us do that. They would have to admit that there are street people living down there, like everyone doesn't already know. They'd have to admit that they don't have anywhere else to put them. The police would have to evict them. It's like knocking down a wasp's nest. The wasps just find somewhere else to go and the new place might be a lot more of an eyesore."

She started rhythmically beating her hands against her hips. "I heard Champlein say it's cheaper to keep the most wanted down there than to put them in jail or do the psychological testing required to do forgets. The fact is the people who could do something are all scared to be the one to give the order. And anyway, there are so many back doors, and someone would tip them off, and on and on. Excuses."

"OK," I said. And I almost added, "I'll kill him for you," but instead, I said, "I'll bring him out for you."

Laverick studied me. She wasn't sure I was able to do any such thing.

Hero said, "How can we help?"

"If I bring him out, will his conviction stick?"

Laverick responded explosively. "Ha! It'll stick like white on rice, Benny. He was already convicted before Kumar supposedly killed him, even though he wasn't at the trial. Because of the crimes he was convicted of, no one seemed to mind a cop killing him. By the time the courts are through with Yoder, he'll have forgotten his own mother."

That hurt. I still couldn't remember my mother's name, and Laverick's comment made me wonder if I'd been convicted of a slew of things many years before and was wiped clean. It seemed more and more likely. If there were such a forget in my past, it hadn't made me a better member of society, unless killer was better than what I had been before.

"Hero," I said, "I might need your help when I'm inside. I'll send mail signed Gusset with more information when I know exactly how I'm going to extract him from the Warren."

Hero smiled a grim, determined smile and wrote down his computer address. Laverick said she was in too, if I needed anything.

It was time I met J. B. Yoder.

Chapter 37

Laverick wouldn't let me have the stick back. She said it was too valuable to lose. I let the implication drop.

Hero made a copy for me before I left, however. The new memstick wouldn't pass a verifier check, but I could use it as trump should I need it. I wrote down Hero's phone address and told them I'd be in touch, but to give me at least a couple of days. I left them in Hero's apartment. They were quietly staring at the floor.

My walk back to Carbide's was full of unwanted images and the moans and slashes of torture. I couldn't rid myself of them in the usual way of picturing Carla and smiling at her. That had exactly the wrong effect.

And thinking about Carla just brought up my biggest worry: that Carla was by JB's side. That she was his hired killer now, and based on our last interaction at her apartment, she would not be too concerned if I was her target. What would I do if it was her or me to die? I knew the answer to that. It would be me.

As I passed the river, it started to rain. By the time I reached Carbide's apartment, my shoes were sloshing, and I was soaked, but I didn't really care. I was playing out a conversation with JB. The one where I had all the cards. But that was all daydreaming because however good my cards were, I still had to get him to the table.

At the apartment, Carbide was washing a light switch plate and whistling, "Kill Da Wabbit." His natural cheerfulness was somewhat contagious. I took out a beer, quick-frosted it and sagged into a chair. Carbide came in and sat down. "So, what do you have stacked and ready for takeoff?"

"I'm going to give JB to the cops."

Carbide leaned forward, "That's a big plane. How are you going to get that off the ground?"

"I thought I'd call him and tell him he'd won a million, he just needed to come to the police station to collect it because my company didn't want to have all that money somewhere that wasn't safe."

"That plane has no lift."

I wanted to talk about what I'd seen on the video. I thought talking about it would ease my mind, but I'd be giving Carbide a burden he didn't need. He was a happy man. I didn't want to change that. Just then, I needed someone happy around me. "OK, how 'bout I walk up to the Warren guards and tell them I have a bullet, and I would like to deliver it to Jackson Yoder?"

I could almost make out a descending line as the blood drained from Carbide's face. He turned pale, then slowly turned red. "This JB you've been talking about is JB Yoder, Jackson Yoder? I thought he was dead."

"A police detective named Kumar faked Yoder's death a couple years back—and was paid five thousand by gov for it too."

Carbide sat, stood, then sat back down. Then he stood up again and returned to vigorously scrubbing the switch plate. Finally, he said, "Jackson Yoder should be dead. He's an evil man."

"I would agree with you on that. That's why I plan to get him out of the Warren and give him to the police."

"No. I mean he should be dead." I'd never seen Carbide angry before. He scared me. He had the taut, ominous look of impending, irrational violence.

"Don't think that way. If we give him to the cops, he'll be wiped completely or have to be jailed for the rest of his life. He's already been convicted, all we have to do is get him out of the Warren."

"He killed people because he thought they were useless. Not for any other reason, just because he thought they were useless. He was proud of it. He wrote editorials about it. Suggested others do it too. He was a Goddamned evangelist for death. They can wipe his memories, but not his evil soul."

Carbide stomped off to the bathroom. I let him go without comment. He needed the last word. Yet, I couldn't help but wonder what Carbide would say if he knew I had killed for no better reason than money. Did I have an evil soul that could not be fixed with a forget?

I was feeling the effects of drinking the beer, having not eaten in almost a day. The door buzzer went off like an alarm clock.

I carefully walked over to the door and looked through the viewer. It was Hattie carrying two bags. I let her in and stumbled back to the chair. She said hello and went into the kitchen.

Carbide came out of the bathroom. He didn't know Hattie was

there. "I can get in the Warren," he said. "I'll go in there and kill him myself."

Hattie appeared around the counter from the kitchen, walked up to Carbide, kissed him on the cheek and said, "Kill who, dear?"

Carbide looked from her to me and back a couple times. It was his day to be surprised. "Nobody?"

I laughed. He was caught, and he wasn't a good enough liar to get out of it. It seemed very funny to my addled brain. "The name Jackson Yoder have any meaning to you, Hattie?" I asked.

"No. Is that who Carbide's going to kill?" Hattie was treating Carbide as though he were a little boy having a temper tantrum. Her reaction confused him and eased his rage. I wouldn't have guessed that that technique would work, but Hattie had everything under control. "Well," she added. "It will have to wait until after we eat. I brought all the ingredients you asked for, and I expect to have the dinner you promised." She sat down like punctuation.

Carbide stood flustered and, for the moment, successfully distracted from his murderous impulse. He went into the kitchen.

Hattie was watching me. "Don't get him killed, Benny," she said quietly. It was an odd sort of threat. She would be disappointed in me if I let Carbide be killed, and it would hurt her. She knew that would matter to me, even though until that moment, I wouldn't have guessed that it would.

"Hattie, how would you like to run a business Under The River?"

"You mean a place for all the fashionable people to shop for fine dresses to wear to the ball?"

"No, actually, I mean a place where poor people shop for something to make their hovels look a little better or more comfortable." She looked doubtful. "Ray is dead. This JB guy killed him. I'm thinking of buying his antiques store, lock, stock, and gargoyle."

She watched me, glancing at the beer. "How many of those have you had? Maybe I should get you some coffee or bread or something?"

Hattie stood up and went into the kitchen. I was forming a plan. After I owned Ray's place I could get into the Warren when I wanted to. OK, it wasn't a plan, it was a step toward a plan, but it made me feel better and Hattie hadn't said no. She came back with coffee and a roll. I drank the coffee, ate the roll, felt better, and decided that my plan was better than my previous plan, which was just like Carbides plan only I would have been able to pull the trigger. Carbide wouldn't have been able to. He wasn't like me.

During dinner we avoided talking about JB except once when Carbide asked why we didn't just tell everyone that JB was actually Jackson Yoder and let him play the part of the hunted one. While he'd been talking about landfills in Rockford and how nice Hattie looked, he'd actually been thinking about JB.

Telling the inhabitants of Under The River that JB was Jackson Yoder would certainly open a can of worms, but I figured the big worm would get away. There were too many ways for him to escape and have himself altered or for someone to come in and do it. It could be that the Pirates would kill him just to keep the peace, but I wanted something more definitive. I wanted to see him captured. And if I failed, Carbide could still follow through with his revelation.

After dinner, Hattie and Carbide went to see an opera. They were a strange pair. There was a reason why you could get seats at the opera the day before. Operas are painful to listen to. I wondered how much the opera company paid them to go.

I pulled out a twenty and some ones and stuffed the rest of my money down behind the chair cushion, then headed out into the rain.

Under The River was warm and humid. Biting flies caught on to any exposed flesh and removed a chunk. It was time for the Gnomes to fumigate the place again.

I walked past Ray's. It was still closed. At first, I thought the guard at the north Warren entrance was missing, but then I saw that she'd been moved back into the hallway and stood in front of a new set of bars that separated Ray's storage rooms from the rest of the Warren. So much for plan A. The north entrance was sealed and I wouldn't be able to get in unopposed even if I bought Ray's. They would have reinforced the walls by now too.

I went to a fire barrel from which I could see the south Warren entrance and the south entrance to Under The River from the street above. I gave the woman a quarter and since she didn't have anyone else trying to get a spot at her rather dim fire, she let me rotate in front of her barrel and dry out. She sat on a stack of bricks and leaned her back against one of the massive posts that held up the buildings above.

After I had dried, I turned toward her. "So I heard Ray was tossed in the river."

"Yes," she said warily. "It's a shame."

"Any idea if someone else will open up the tables?" Her wariness dropped away since I wasn't trying to get her into a discussion about his death.

"I heard the Pirates own it now, but I doubt they'll run it. Probably sell off the stuff, then rent out the space to someone new. Don't matter. They only sell stuff near the entrances that you and I can't afford anyway."

She was right about that. The places near the street were prime space because people with money were willing to come that far in for the deals, but they wouldn't want to go any further than Ray's or maybe the next shop in.

Rela walked out of the south Warren entrance just then. She wasn't wearing her gun, at least not that I could see. Wearing weapons was frowned upon, even when the wearer was a Gnome or, as in this case, a Gnome's lackey. Rela walked close past me and on through the crowded aisles to a team of Elves who were finishing the installation of a new light fixture to my left. She talked to them for a moment then headed back toward the Warren again.

I'm prone to stupid impulsive actions. I have a way of making a sudden decision and convincing myself that I've thought it out. I ran around to the dark side of the post, the side away from the fire, and in the shadow I quickly removed my coat, outer pants and my head rag, turned the coat inside out and wrapped the whole bundle in it.

Rela was striding by as I came out from behind the post. I walked toward her and fell into step beside her. She walked on for a moment then turned to tell me to shove off, but stopped suddenly instead. She reached for the gun she wasn't carrying. "Oh, damn."

"It's not so bad Rela. I'm not going to kill you, even though I thought your trying to kill me in my own apartment was a bit tawdry." I smiled and reached into my pocket. She stepped back glancing from side to side, but keeping most of her focus on the pocket. I extracted the memstick and held it out to her. "Would you give this to JB? I think he might be interested in talking to me after he sees it. I'll wait here by the fire." My stomach started doing flip-flops. What on earth was I trying to do? But in the back of my mind, I knew what I wanted to do. I wanted to meet JB. I wanted to talk to him, to understand him well enough to win, well enough to beat him. I never liked plans anyway. Plan B was to not use a plan. I'd gotten the plane off the ground, and I was winging it.

Chapter 38

I offered my bundle of grubby clothes to the fire-barrel woman and told her that if she kept it safe, I would buy it back from her within a couple hours.

She set it behind her and leaned back with a smile. "Feels pretty comfortable. It might cost you more than a quarter to get these back and for me not to tell anyone about the guy who disguises himself as a bum. You a cop?"

"No, I'm not a cop. A cop would have a better disguise." She already knew that, of course, or she wouldn't have asked. The price for getting my bundle back was going up, and she was just letting me know.

Rela trotted out of the Warren. She wore a thigh-length coat this time, which I was sure concealed the gun that shot ceramic bullets.

She didn't say anything. She just motioned me toward the entrance. Once past the guards and the sniffers, she frisked me thoroughly. She found the bit of money I'd brought with me, but didn't take it. She didn't frisk my hair. They never do. Even though I keep my hair fairly short, I still had a slapfaint tucked above my right ear.

We walked past Chen's office. I was ready to wink at him, but he wasn't in the halls. We threaded our way back into the Warren.

It was possible that JB would just kill me. That had already been on his mind when he sent Rela and Mike to my apartment, but I hoped he'd looked at the video on the memstick and would decide to negotiate. I thought I might leave his office alive if I could get past the first few minutes of conversation.

At the door to JB's rooms, Rela said, "You're already dead," but she was trying to blink me. She poked the buzzer.

Mike answered. He stuck his head out into the hall, looked both ways, then let us in.

JB had his front office decorated in a masculine, professorial style with bookshelves of unread leather-bound books and dark wood furniture with red leather upholstery. It looked genuine. JB had money and good taste. It would be a good place to study Milton or Cicero.

Rela took off her coat, exposing her gun. It was nice of her to carry in the weapon I would need should my meeting with JB go badly. She stood close to intimidate me, but it just put her weapon within tactical reach.

Mike rushed out to the back room, and then walked slowly back in behind JB, who entered the room at a leisurely pace. JB was wearing a suit coat with shoulder pads and shoes with lifts. If he hadn't been stuck in the Warren, a criminal, he probably would have had his legs lengthened and maybe his back too. Now that he had the money, he couldn't use it. "Mr. Khan. It's good of you to come to see me. It saves me so much trouble tracking you down to kill you. What made you come to see me? Luck?"

"I certainly think so," I said.

"Any particular reason I shouldn't kill you now and throw you in the mud?"

"You mean like you did to Ray?" JB hadn't actually killed Ray first. He'd just tossed him in the mud to slowly suffocate.

His eyes narrowed. "You don't seem to understand. There's no reason for you to be alive. No one would care if I killed you."

"I didn't come here to listen to bluffs and threats. Did you watch the video on the stick?"

He nodded, still watching me carefully.

"I have the original, certified file which will be sent to one of four news organizations in the morning along with a note that states you're living in the Warren under the name JB. The other news organizations will get a copy. There are enough people who know what you look like to identify you to the people out there Under The River. Street people don't like your old persona, do they? Someone will kill you when that information gets out. Eventually, someone will kill you."

JB considered that. He'd been modified since the photos I'd seen were taken. Even though the differences were considerable, I could still tell it was him. However, according to Carbide, the street people who were around a few years earlier knew who Jackson Yoder was, and once they connected JB and the hated Jackson Yoder, he would have to leave or someone who lost a friend or relative would kill him somehow. No one Under The River would admit to witnessing it happen either. At least that's the way I pictured it. I hoped he saw it that way too.

"I also have Arno's materials, which I believe you would like to have."

He sat down and crossed his legs comfortably. He was putting on a show for Rela and Mike who were looking at him a bit differently. I hadn't yet said who he really was, but Rela in particular was watching him, trying to figure it out. I could have grabbed her gun and shot all three of them at that moment, but I wouldn't have made it out past the guards alive.

"Those records are of some value to me. Why did you steal them? What made you think I would deal with someone who steals my goods then tries to sell them back to me? I don't see that I have to deal with you at all."

If he didn't have to deal with me, he wouldn't still be talking, so I continued. "Look. It's not clear that I stole anything from you. They were Arno's records, so to me, you're the thief here."

He stood and took a step toward me. I almost went for Rela's gun, but he stopped.

"I want ten thousand," I said. "And I'll leave Chicago. We'll both be happier that way."

"I'll give you two and throw you in the river. You can use the two to buy your way into a better brazier in hell." He was smiling now. He'd made up his mind to take the satisfaction of killing me over the profit and peace of mind.

"There's information in those records about you. Other sticks, and it's all going to the news if I fail to stop it." He didn't seem too worried about that.

"Arno didn't have anything on me that matters."

"You mean other than the video of you and Judge Kimbanski in a soundproof room with Sukey Mack's girlfriend bent over a wire rack? Torture and rape aren't on your list of things that matter? It's certified video, JB. And the news will love to play it. It will ride the sites for years, maybe forever. Do you think your bosses are going to like that? Pirates don't like that kind of attention. They don't mind pushers, but they don't like having the users around. You can capture and sell the girls, but you're not supposed to be weak enough to get hooked on them yourself."

"What I do with my own time is my own business."

"Do they even know who you really are? Do they know about your other idiosyncrasies, your other aberrations?" Killing street people was the one I knew of. I suspected there were others.

JB walked over to Rela. "Give me your gun and go." He looked at Mike. "Both of you."

Rela was reluctant to hand over her gun and JB noticed. His eyes hardened. She was no killer. I could see that. But she knew he was. I could see that too. She handed him the gun and left, with Mike following close behind her.

Holding the gun, JB turned to me. "Ten thousand is too much. I'll give you three. Bring everything here and, if I think it's worth it, I'll give you the money."

"Uh, huh," I said, meaning that I'd heard him, but that I wasn't a chump. "We meet in a public place. I tell you where the stash is and you give me the money. I leave. Eight thousand isn't much to you, but I can live on that a long time. I've got no reason to cheat you, but I could see why you might not want me alive after you have the evidence."

"I don't even know if you have Arno's records at all. You might just have found the stick somewhere else in his house, the bedroom maybe."

I let the taunt drop. "OK, I can understand that. Were Mike and Rela unhappy that I signed all the cards with their names?"

"They weren't happy, but you didn't fool anyone, and you missed two secret compartments."

I doubted that, but I let that drop too. "So you agree I have the missing records?"

"I agree you know something about how the records were stolen. Tell me a little about what's in them."

I told him a few bits that I'd read—that Alderman Hadas liked very young boys and Fantastic Voyage, an illegal weekend-long drug and VR game. A few choice items like that. "It's a big box full, JB. I also have his PAL."

We were starting at opposite ends of the field and approaching the center slowly, negotiating each step. In the end, I agreed to provide a small portion of the records in a delivery to be dropped off with the guards the next day as proof and a good faith gesture. JB agreed to meet me at Socko's the day after that at lunch, should the portion prove interesting. He would have five thousand, I would have the box of records. He would have five minutes to look at the rest of the materials and if he decided they weren't worth five thousand, he would take his money back and go. I think we both knew that wouldn't happen.

He opened the door and called Rela. "Take out this trash and come back here."

Carla stood in the hall, waiting. "Hello, Benny. I'm a bit surprised to see you here. Have you been well?"

I looked into Carla's eyes trying to see some special recognition there, perhaps an implied nod, or a hidden smile. "I've been better," I said and tried to act nonchalant. I wanted to appear to be in control. Was I playing a part, using a tactic, or was I trying to impress her like a teenage boy who might do something stupid to impress a girl? I didn't know. Maybe they worked out to be the same thing. "Have you found what you were missing?"

"Yes, I have. I feel much better now." She stood looking at me for just a little too long as though she were measuring my steel, deciding. "Good-bye, Benny," Carla walked into JB's office and he shut the door. Her good-bye sounded so formal, and so final.

Rela led me out. At the entrance, I asked her if she'd ever killed anyone. She glared at me and returned into the Warren. In any other state of mind, I might have enjoyed watching her walk away.

I bought back my roll from the woman at the fire barrel for two, and walked out with it under my arm. I had eighteen hours to find Hero and Laverick and set up for the arrest, and only twelve hours to rescue the gargoyle from Ray's storage room.

Chapter 39

So I had it all set up. Get the gargoyle, select some semi-useful records from the stash I'd put there, give a few to the guard, then talk to Hero and set up an arrest at Socko's. No big deal.

But the more I thought about it while walking back to Carbide's apartment, the less I believed it. If I were JB, I wouldn't have agreed to leave the Warren at all. Going to a public place would invite arrest, or at the very least, a blink. After all, when he showed up, I could just take the money and run out the door, leaving him with an empty box. It's not like he could yell for the police.

He'd asked for evidence to prove that I actually had the stuff, but I still didn't believe he'd show. Asking for the token records was just a way of obtaining some of them and lulling me into a false sense of security.

The CAT station was across the street, so I crossed and angled my way through the crowd, making sure no one was following. No one was. I ducked into a bathroom and put my outer clothes back on.

JB wasn't stupid. He was mean, and evil, certainly self-centered, but not stupid. He wouldn't show up for all the same reasons that I wouldn't show up were I in his shoes.

But if he wasn't going to show up, why did he allow me to leave the Warren alive? Again I tried to put myself in his shoes. All I could think was that he still hoped that he could get his hands on Arno's records. Which meant I needed to look them over more carefully. There was something in there he wanted more than he wanted me.

When I entered the apartment, it was dark. I turned on a light. Carbide and Hattie were curled up together on the sofa. Their privacy didn't concern me. I needed their help again, and I would need it quickly. "I need to get the gargoyle out of Ray's tonight."

They sat up. Hattie pushed her hair around until it looked better.

Carbide pulled himself up out of the cushions and yawned. They'd fallen asleep. "And why do you need to liberate the prisoner at this time of night?"

"Because I just talked to JB and we set up a meet at Socko's tomorrow afternoon to exchange the stolen records for five thousand."

Carbide looked confused for a moment.

"You talked to Yoder?" He looked horrified.

"Yes."

"You mean you're going to sell Arno's records back to him?"

"No. It means I set up a meeting to do that. I plan to have JB arrested while he's at Socko's making the exchange."

"Clever ploy, but I think you'll need to whistle a more intricate tune than that to get the cobra out of his basket."

"Still, I need to have the gargoyle. He wants to see part of the loot, so he knows I can deliver, so he knows I have the records."

"Doesn't he already know you have the records?"

"Yes."

"So why does he need proof?"

"It's part of the negotiations, Carbide. It doesn't matter anyway. I still need to get the gargoyle and tonight is as good a night as any."

"Well, we can't exactly go over the wall with helicopters."

"No. We're going to use the Trojan Horse approach."

Hattie went into the kitchen. From there she said, "You're going to need a very large gargoyle."

"I was thinking of a crate, delivered to Ray's. Something he supposedly bought a few days ago and that you're just now delivering."

"A crate full of you?"

"Among other things."

"How will you get back out?"

"You'll come back a half hour later and say you delivered the wrong crate. You take that one out and replace it with another one."

Carbide considered that for a while. He went to the bathroom.

Hattie came back in the room. "You talked to this guy?"

I said I had.

"Do you think he'll actually show up at the exchange?"

"I don't know. He might. It depends on what's in the gargoyle that he wants."

I didn't tell her what I really had in mind. That I didn't expect to be at the exchange either. JB and I each had our plans. I was hoping I could guess his.

"You aren't going to get Carbide hurt are you?"

"I hope not." Hattie and Carbide were worried about each other more than they were worried about themselves. "I need you to help too. I don't want Carbide to have trouble convincing the guards to allow him to dump the crate in the storage room. If you're there, asking them questions or demanding to talk to the manager or something, maybe they won't want to deal with too much at one time, and they'll open the door for Carbide. Can you do that for me?"

"Well, maybe not for you, but for Carbide." Her smile took some of the sting out of her words.

"How about for a hundred?"

She looked sadly at me. "Benny, I don't need your money for this. Carbide told me about Jackson Yoder."

Carbide came out of the bathroom and they went over and sat down on the sofa.

"I'm going to use your PAL for a moment. I need to line up a couple crates and a van."

"Sure," he said.

I sent Hero instructions for the two crates and the van. He mailed back just a few minutes later, saying it would take about four hours to get everything together.

Four hours of sleep sounded good to me, and I suggested to Hattie and Carbide that they might do the same. They went off to his bedroom. I set the PAL to wake me in three hours, in case Hero pulled things together early, and laid down on the couch.

Three hours later, I rolled off the couch and onto my feet. It was ten o'clock. The PAL was telling me to wake up, using louder and louder shouts. I turned the alarm off and looked for mail. Hero said where to meet and when. Everything was already set. I sent back a yes and went and pounded on Carbide's door. "Let's go."

Ten minutes later, we were out the door and walking fast toward the Hack&Hack Meat Market at the corner of Hacker and Hackson. Behind the store, we found a dark green cargo van and climbed in.

Hero and Laverick were inside. We sat on the crates, which were lying down and looking vaguely like double-deep coffins, then I made introductions. I asked Hero if the crates were made to order.

He said yes and introduced Carbide's temporary assistant, Kim, who would help him move the crates around. She was driving.

"Take us to the north entrance of Under The River," I told her.

She started the engine and pulled out onto Hackson. I explained to everyone my suspicions of JB and why we would be taking extra precautions.

When we pulled up in front of the north stairs, Hero and I climbed into the larger crate, him first, then we installed a divider, then I climbed in. I sealed the crate with a hasp that I could open from the inside and I waited, breathing tube in my mouth and hearing device in my ear, both courtesy of the Chicago Police Department. Hero had the same gear.

They pulled us out onto a stair-capable dolly and thumped us down the stairs, at which point I lost my earpiece into the bottom of the crate. It was too tight to reach down and get it. We slid along the lumpy floor and I felt the right turn as we went into the entrance of the Warren. I could vaguely hear Carbide and a guard arguing. I hoped his repeated deliveries over the years would help him persuade the guard to let him put the crate in the back storage room. Then a door banged open. We turned to the right again, meaning that the guard had let us in.

I waited. Without my earpiece I couldn't know if they'd left the room or not. Finally, Hero pounded on the woodboard behind my head, so I opened the crate slowly and peered out.

It was dark in Ray's storage room. I let out my breath and turned on my flat light. I didn't hear anything strange, so I stepped out of the crate and looked around. The first thing I noticed was that the gargoyle was missing. The second thing I noticed was Rela and JB sitting in comfortable chairs. Both were smiling at me. Rela had a gun. The third thing I noticed was Carla standing to my right near the door. She had a gun too.

Chapter 40

Carla put her hand to the wall and turned on the lights.

JB leisurely picked up his gun from an end table beside his chair. "Ah, Mr. Khan. So you've decided to join us." Three guns, they weren't taking any chances. "I was wondering how you were going to get in here to get your cache. It did take some thinking to realize you must have left the records here. The gargoyle. A very good hiding place."

"Thanks." I couldn't think of anything else to say.

"Would you mind clasping your hands behind your head so Rela can search you? I don't want any surprises."

I did as I was told, hoping that Hero hadn't lost his earpiece too. I also took a small step to the left so I would be farther from Carla and so I no longer stood between them and the crate.

Carla didn't take her eyes from me. She was there because Rela might hesitate to kill, she had never used her weapon except as a threat, and JB wouldn't want to kill anyone if he could pay someone else to do it for him. Carla was focused on the job. Strictly professional. I could have been a sinner or a saint, it wouldn't have mattered. The Carla I was hoping for wasn't there. She would not help me.

Rela gave JB her gun then she frisked me. She found the thatcher and a pocketknife, then went back to stand beside JB. She scowled at me. I think she was hoping to find weapons to prove I was dangerous and should be killed.

JB returned Rela's gun to her. "Benny, Benny, Benny. Did you think I was so stupid? I feel ashamed that you would think so. I've not gotten where I am today by being stupid. I'm Chief Financial Officer for the River Pirates. A person would not reach this high in the business without some intelligence."

"I thought Bonarubi was CFO. Oh yes. That's right. I killed him. Next would have been Arno, right? Oh yes, I killed him too. So you're the new one. I guess you owe your success to me don't you?" Why it was that I thought irritating him would be helpful, I don't know, but for some reason JB just affected me that way. Poking him with pins felt right, even when he was about to kill me.

Oddly, the other advantage of poking at JB this way was that if Carla was the one to kill me, I didn't want her to feel too bad about it. Maybe after she thought about it, she would decide not to forget this one.

JB stood and took a step toward me. "How did you plan to get out of here? Who are your accomplices in this? Did Chen know? Who else knows?"

"You mean who else knows you're really Jackson Yoder? Only Rela and a select few others." I watched Rela, wondering if she'd already known who JB was.

But Rela suddenly looked sick. She hadn't known. The end of her gun drooped a little and wavered. She stared at the back of JB's head, trembling. Even Carla was looking at JB now, but she appeared more curious than anything else.

JB took another step toward me. I decided to egg him on a little more. "Why are you worried about Chen, Yoder? Worried he's interested in your job just like you were interested in Bonarubi's?"

A deep breath can have a calming effect, but it didn't seem to help JB's disposition much. He tried to ignore my taunt. "You thought you had this all figured out, didn't you? But you slipped. You said you had a whole box of stuff. That was a stupid thing to say, Benny. When you said that, I knew you couldn't have gotten out past the guard with it, even with your marvelous distraction. You had to have hidden it in here. I found it the first place I looked."

JB relaxed a little. He enjoyed showing me who was smarter and maybe showing the women who was smarter. I thought he must have had a complex. "If you're so smart," I said, "why are you standing in front of Rela. I think now that she knows who you really are, she's going to shoot you."

The pinpricks were having a diminishing effect. JB didn't even waver, much less turn around. I didn't really expect him to, but it was worth a try. He wasn't concerned about Rela at all. Her leash led to his hand even when he wasn't looking, yet her distress was evident.

"I think I'll just shoot you," he said. "I was going to take you out and throw you headfirst in the mud just like Ray. After all, it should have been you that time. You should have been the one sucking mud into your lungs. Ray was guilty only of being stupid. But you might get away, so I think I'll just shoot you now."

Carla said, "Put him the box first, then we can just close up the box and ship it out without any clean up."

Carla seemed way too helpful. To JB I said, "You'll shoot me? You mean you'll have Carla shoot me."

Yoder smiled a little pleased smile. "That would be fitting, wouldn't it. She would, you know."

I looked at Carla. "Yes," I said. "I know." I sounded sad, but mostly I was disappointed. Maybe she understood, maybe she didn't.

Had he actually just shot me, things would have turned out differently, but, as amateurs are apt to do, he raised the gun instead of shooting from the hip or stepping back. He wanted to intimidate me before he killed me. He wanted me to see down the barrel; see the bullet coming. We were only a bit more than an arm's length apart now. I slid my fingers around the slapfaint I kept over my right ear. I grabbed it, lunged forward, and whacked him on the forehead with it even as he shot me. His aim was off because of the surprise, never getting his arm up all the way. We both went down.

Rela was trying to get a shot at me that wouldn't kill JB too. Her gun was too powerful because the ceramic shatter of the bullet tended to shred anyone in the immediate proximity of the target. When we rolled, I saw Carla had kept her gun up and ready should the opportunity arise to get a good shot. She was patient.

Hero picked that moment to charge out of the back of the crate, gun out. A noisy, but effective entrance. Rela, startled, turned toward him, and he shot her. Carla must have been pulling the trigger to shoot me at the same moment as Hero burst from his hiding place because her shot hit the inside door of the crate which Hero had just opened, and splintered it. Hero turned on Carla and fired. A guard burst through the door a second later and Hero shot him too. Hero wasn't an amateur.

I rolled JB off me and watched Hero run to the door, move the dead guard's legs out of the way and push the door closed. JB had shot me in the left side of the stomach. Oddly, it didn't hurt that much, but I was bleeding a lot. Luckily, it was JB who shot me, not Rela. Her gun would have minced my whole torso.

I raised myself enough to crawl over to Carla. She was breathing, the shot had grazed her gun hand and entered her right shoulder, and apparently clipped a lung, which made a wet sucking sound as she breathed. I put my hand over the hole and looked over at Rela. She was dead, a perfect shot through the heart. Hero was a marksmen. Rela's face was calm, less anxious. Even at Arno's house, where we'd had dinner and talked about saving egrets, she'd seemed nervous. Now her face was more relaxed and she was actually very pretty with her blonde hair loose and splayed out on the floor. Her large green eyes gazed into mine. She hadn't been sure enough or mean enough to be a killer.

Ear against the door, Hero listened for more guards. They'd probably been warned that they might hear a gunshot and not to worry about it, but there had been four shots.

I took the tee shirt off my head and wrapped it around my middle, hoping to keep my insides from coming out and to slow the bleeding, but it wasn't helping much. Hero came over and looked at the wound. "Not too good. Are you going to be able to get back in the crate?"

"No, you'll have to pack us both in, I'm afraid. In fact, I think I'll be passing out soon. I don't like the sight of my own blood."

"We aren't taking her. She's not our objective and we've got no room for her."

I breathed hard for a moment, trying to stem the nausea. That made me light-headed instead. "Move the bodies away from the door. Throw something over the blood. The next guard is going to want to know what happened to the previous one and might take a quick glance in here."

Hero wadded up my tee shirt bandage and used half of JB's shirt as a wrap to increase the pressure. Now the wound hurt and my fingertips began to tingle. When he twisted the bandage hard to tighten it, I felt woozy for a moment. He let me lay back down. "We've got to call someone once we're out so they know to come get Carla. She'll die if we don't."

"Don't worry, Benny."

"I am worried," I said, then I passed out.

I woke up inside the crate when it was moving. I almost cried out, but didn't have the energy. Hero had scrunched me up on some padding. I felt the crate thump up the stairs and passed out again when we were dumped into the van.

When I opened my eyes, it was bright. The room smelled of antiseptic. I was in the hospital, somewhat surprised that I was alive and wondering if Carla was.

Chapter 41

Hero came to visit me in the hospital. He even brought some Cajun lemon drops. "You feeling any better?"

"I think I felt better when I was out cold."

"Maybe. You look bad."

"Thanks. At least *I'll* look better in a few days."

Hero smiled. We'd been through something together. I think that made me OK with him. He wasn't treating me as though I were a criminal anymore, even though he must have heard me say that I'd killed Bonarubi and Arno.

"How did you get us out?"

"Well, I had to fold Yoder up a little. He made a nice soft cushion for you. Carbide and Kim didn't expect the extra weight so the dolly wasn't really made for it. One of the bounces we took broke his shoulder, but everything else went just as you wanted it to." Hero didn't seem too concerned about Yoder's shoulder.

"What about Carla?" I whispered.

"Don't know. I imagine they found her, but I don't know. I'm sorry. There just wasn't any way to take her too. You understand."

I sucked on a lemon drop and nodded my head. We didn't really have much to say to each other. His life was separate from mine and we had no history before a week ago, forgotten or otherwise.

When Hero left, I sighed back into the bed, letting my muscles relax. No, not everything had gone as I'd planned. I'd been shot, for one thing.

Carbide showed up later, after visiting hours. "Well, Chum. Looks like you found a way to take an all expense paid holiday at sunny Municipal Hospital. You need any sunlamps? No? I guess you don't want the tan lines around the bandages." He didn't say how he'd gotten in. Everyone seemed to ignore his comings and goings. Oh, it's just the delivery man.

"Anything new, Carbide, or are you just here to disturb my vacation?"

"You stirred up the hornet's nest." He grabbed a lemon drop, then made a squinty face when the Cajun spice hit him. "The Gnomes were stinging everything that moved for a few days. They still don't know who snagged Yoder, and your police friends admitted they had help, but wouldn't say who it was. The Warren is to be renamed Paranoia Park. Some bold soul already zapped the concrete over the south entrance with that name." He smiled proudly. Carbide had a mischievous side.

"You surviving?" I wasn't sure that his part in my operation was unknown.

"They installed doors with palm locks at the entrances and guards inside and outside the doors. It is a real pain getting in and out right now, at least until everything settles down. But, just about everyone below JB in the Warren is moving again, so I'll be making money."

Carbide spit his lemon drop into the trash can then told me that the street people who lived Under The River were upset with the River Pirates. They were happy Jackson Yoder was taken care of, but they weren't happy at all that the River Pirates had employed him. The Pirates' claims that they didn't know who he was, fell on disbelieving ears. Carbide was proud of our success and seemed to like the idea that the street people, and the Pirates and the other Gnomes wouldn't be quite so cozy for a while.

Carbide looked tired for a moment, "I still kind of wish you would have let me kill him."

"How do you think you'd feel about that now, Carbide? Don't you think it would bother you if you'd pulled the trigger?"

He stared at me. "No. Yes. Still, I wish he'd actually paid for what he did. Being wiped just doesn't seem sufficient."

Revenge was what Carbide wanted, but society had deemed revenge a poor reason to kill someone. I could think of poorer reasons.

Carbide also said Mike was nowhere to be found and that Hattie had left that night. He'd not seen her since. "She said she could only be around for a while, but I hoped she would find a way to stay. I liked her."

"She might be back," I said. "Maybe she just went to take care of some unfinished business." I knew where she was. She'd be sitting on her old piece of real estate.

Carbide didn't respond to that for a minute. He just looked dejected and soulful, then finally, he looked out the window and said,

"She'd make a fine leading lady, don't you think?"

"Yes, she would." I didn't know how things were going to work out, so I didn't tell him where she was. Hattie had the right to disappear if she wanted to.

Laverick also came to see me the next day. She asked me if I wanted to go after any other criminals who lived as Gnomes. "Maybe later," I said. "But I might come by asking for a favor sometime. Just remember."

She didn't seem to like the idea, but she nodded anyway, then she said, "Maybe I won't mention your comment about killing Bonarubi to anyone else."

"OK, I guess we're pretty even," I said.

She actually smiled. "We arrested Carla Shoen when she stumbled into a hospital this morning and passed out on the floor. And I got more than the arrests out of this, Benny, more than just the money. Everyone thinks I have a mole in the River Pirates. They think I planned this for months. You've made me the start of a reputation."

"Is that something you wanted?"

Even in the bright lights of the hospital room, Laverick's face softened. She was troubled and putting on a show of bravado. "I knew if we succeeded that I might take on a new role. The press have named me. They're calling me Bird Dog. They're expecting more arrests like Yoder's in the future."

"You can do that, Detective." I knew she could, if she didn't let her good intentions get too much in the way.

"Can I? I guess we'll find out." She slid on her coat. "My first name's Pallas, by the way. Let me know when you're up to flushing another bird and we'll see if I can retrieve it."

I was released from the hospital two days later. Carbide took me back to his place where he said I could use the bed for the next week while I was recuperating, but that he was really used to living alone and wouldn't I like to move back to my place after that? Carbide was a bit big to sleep comfortably on the couch, but I didn't point that out.

The doctors told me to walk when I could. It would help the healing process. I walked to Under The River the first day and no one came out of the Warren and shot me. Carni gave me a warning look and pointedly ignored me. He had his suspicions, but he wasn't sure I was involved with JB's capture. I figured if Carni wasn't sure, than no one else was either.

On the second day, I walked up to Obyeo. Hattie was in her usual spot, looking somber. I eased down beside her.

She stared at me for moment. "You feeling any better?"

"I expected a visit from you."

"They won't let the likes of me into a hospital. Didn't wearing those clothes teach you anything?"

"What about your other clothes?"

"Sold 'em"

"I asked you once if you would be interested in running Ray's tables, but you never answered me."

"I don't answer silly questions."

The couple that lived next door and played Russian piano music walked toward us hand-in-hand up the street. When they saw it was me sitting by the door with the doorman, they broke their grip and edged their way along the opposite wall and through the doorway staying as far as possible from us. I expected them to make the sign of the cross over their hearts, but they just looked worried. "I'm moving out," I yelled to them, but they shot through the door as though I were a terrier about to hop up and chase them. I turned back to Hattie.

"I don't think they trust me."

"Neither do I."

"It wasn't a silly question."

She kicked me, though not very hard. "What? Are you buying Ray's?" she said sarcastically.

"I already did."

She looked startled. "Where do you get your money?"

"You might say I inherited it."

"What else might I say?"

"Yes?"

"Why do you want me to run it? Why don't you hire someone else?"

"You've run a business before, right?"

"Yes, but I never told you that."

"Didn't you?" I shifted to ease my pain, but the movement just made the bullet wound hurt more. "The other reason is that I trust you. I can't say that about very many people. I want someone there when I need them. I figured you and Carbide would make a good team. Maybe you could sell some of the stuff to other shops up on Mythagain or someplace. You've got the personal presence to do that. You can act like one of them if you want to."

She leaned her head back and let the sunshine fall on her face. "It's hard to give up giving up," she said. "Life's so easy when you have nothing."

"I know the feeling, Hattie."

"Yes, I believe you do."

We sat there for a while. Two children played in the street, kicking a ball to each other. A woman walked into the building, carefully ignoring us both.

Hattie stood. "How much are you going to pay us, Carbide and me?"

I stood up too. I handed her a hundred. "You can buy your clothes back. I'll give you one of those each month and ten percent of the profit."

Her eyes narrowed. "You still owe me for 'expenses' remember? And twenty-five percent seems fair to me."

"OK," I said. I would have been willing to go up to fifty-fifty. They wouldn't get rich, but they would do OK, especially if Carbide continued to do deliveries and moves on the side. "How much were expenses."

"Expenses were another two hundred."

"You know, Hattie," I said while I counted out her money, "Carbide's been thinking his movie was going to have a sad ending, that the girl would turn out to be married or have some terminal disease or something."

She watched me handle the money then said, "No, I don't have any terminal diseases." She stuffed the money down her shirt then walked off south at a pace I could not keep up with.

Finally, when I was feeling up to it, I walked out to Denise's house. She greeted me at the door with a frown. Some wounds take a long time to heal.

I offered her a small fortune to buy Up Your News from her.

She declined. "I plan to start managing it myself again." She didn't think I had the money, which I could understand. "Chen called me and told me he's quitting. He's found other employment."

She paused, considering, then she asked, "Did you know Arno didn't have any other business?"

I said I thought he did.

"I can't find any public record of it. He went to work every day. He talked about the people there and everything, but there is no business."

"I didn't know that," I said. I didn't follow up with the obvious question about where and how he acquired his money. She'd already told me she didn't want to know.

"I need to make UYN work. It's got to pay the bills."

I told her to call if she needed any help and walked back to Carbide's. I could afford a cab, but I still liked walking. It helped me to think.

A week later, I found a studio apartment in Carbide's building. I'd acquired a taste for the Cantonese restaurant next door and Carbide was as close a friend as I had. Hattie moved in with Carbide. Neither she nor I brought anything with us.

Chen moved back out of the Warren a few weeks later. The police had only wanted him as a material witness, and the crime he was a witness to was solved without him. Hero and Laverick may not have even told anyone that Chen was still alive.

I tracked down Chen's new place in the Unapartments by bribing the manager and saying I wanted to talk to him because I wanted to buy his carsicord. He'd moved out of the apartment where Sukey and Paulo were killed and up to a high-priced penthouse suite. He didn't seem surprised to see me. The people-fish had died, but he still had Lena. He said he was going to try taking carsicord lessons again.

When he went into the kitchen to frost a derpal for himself and to get me a beer, I walked over to his chair and opened the drawer in the side table next to it. I pulled out his ridiculous yellow gun, dropped it in my pocket, then went back to my chair and sat down. He'd shown me that gun once when he was woozy. He'd wanted to impress on me how smart he was about security.

Chen walked in carrying two frosted bottles. He handed me mine, then took a long swig of his before he sat down.

I considered him, trying to convince myself that I shouldn't just kill him. What's one more, I wondered. Would it really matter.

"Chen, when we were in the Fairchild, coming back from Arno's after, well, after I killed him, what did you mean when you said you knew more about me than I thought you did?"

"I was just blinking you, Benny. I wanted you to quit killing people for money. You're my friend, you know."

"Why didn't you ever tell me you not only knew Arno, but you visited his house regularly? It seems to me that would have come up in conversation somewhere along the way."

He leaned back in his chair in an exaggerated attempt to show how relaxed he was. He put his arms carefully on the arms of his chair, I believe to avoid crossing them over his chest. I'd made Chen nervous. "We talked about that lots of times, Benny. You just lost it when you had one of your forgets, that's all. You knew at one time. I can't go back through everything and update you every time you go erase your troubles."

That was possible. It could have been lost in a forget, but there were other things. "So you're the new CFO for the River Pirates. When did you start angling for that job, Chen? Was it before Arno had me kill Bonarubi? Or was it you who paid me for that particular kill? You had to remove Bonarubi, Arno and JB. Bonarubi you presumably paid for."

Chen stared at me. His mouth moved a few times, but nothing came out. I continued. "You must have been joyous in the back of the Fairchild when you found out that I'd killed both Arno and Kumar. After all, Kumar could have gotten in the way if he'd figured out that CFOs were falling all around him. He might have figured out it was you behind it and told the other River Pirates."

Was I guessing? Yes, a little, but as I laid out the scenario, it sounded right, and Chen's changing expression confirmed my suspicions.

He reached for the drawer. I didn't move, I just smiled slightly. Chen's fingers scrabbled in the drawer while he kept his eyes on the target; me. When he realized he was coming up empty, he looked in the drawer. Then he looked back at me. I went on. "I wondered why you gave me that shove toward killing or bringing down JB when you and I met in the Warren. I wondered why you didn't tell

Rela who I was and just let her kill me. But you needed me to do your work for you, didn't you? Then Denise said you'd quit Up Your News, that you'd moved up, gotten another job. I'm just a newsman, you'd said to me. But you were lying, weren't you?. You're a lot more than that."

Chen didn't say anything.

"And poor Paulo. He was an incidental loser in your games too, wasn't he? Because you asked him, he helped Sukey get a forget, which Sukey couldn't afford. You were always using him that way, weren't you Chen? Just like you used him to get me my transcript. But Sukey came to your apartment and wanted to know what he'd forgotten. Sometimes, after a forget, you get images, you get little teasers about forgotten times. He was remembering a video he'd seen, and you left Paulo there alone to deal with Sukey's slowly deteriorating mind. I figure you loved Paulo, but you loved other things more."

Chen reached into his pocket. I pulled out his gun and pointed it at him. Two shots, I thought, one in the heart, and one in the head.

"Don't try to thatch me, Chen. The bullet would hurt a lot more. Believe me, I know."

"Are you going to kill me? Are you back to being a murderer?"

I had the temptation, as I was convinced any sane person would, but I decided that Benjamin wasn't a killer. I shot him in the leg. The space-blaster gun had more kick than I expected, but it was quiet.

"You shot me!" He was stunned into stating the obvious.

"It's just a nick," I said.

While he was screaming at me and calling me a bastard, I continued, "I'll let the Pirates know what you did. I'll give them your address. I imagine they'll be by."

"But that's the same as killing me. You can't just kill me."

"No, I can't just kill you. I'm giving you the same chance you gave Bonarubi when you sent me after him, the same chance you gave me when you sent me after JB. So you see, you might make it, if you can get out of town fast enough and if you never come back. You're a good newsman, Chen. If you survive you can go to another town, maybe Cleveland, get another job. I think Death News is based there, isn't it? That would seem like a good match."

"Benny, look, I can make a lot of money with the Pirates. I could cut you in. Put you on the payroll, no one would know."

I went to the door, resisting the urge to shoot his other leg. "Good-bye Chen. I hope I don't see you again."

I heard him yell my name a time or two as I walked down the hall. Watching Chen in pain had made my side hurt again.

Chapter 42

I watched the main entrance of the Unapartments for a day and a half before I saw Carla leave a little before noon. I followed her past Carla Alley and to the grocery around the corner. She'd gotten her old job back, maybe as part of the forget the gov did on her. They didn't have her for murder, just her part in the attempted murder of one Benjamin Kahn.

I picked up some CoolBars, broccoli doodles, peanut butter, and some bananas. Her lane was the longest, but I waited there anyway. She was wearing a brown and yellow employee's smock with "CG" painted over her left breast. Her hair was pulled back in a tiny ponytail, making her look energetic and carefree. When I began putting my stuff on the checker in front of her, her big gray eyes turned up toward me.

I have no way of knowing how pretty she really was. I was in love and saw starlight and roses. She smiled at me. An, "I know you," greeting, of some passable enjoyment. I'd take that.

"Cold today," I said, feeling a bit moronic for not having thought of something more delightful to say while I waited in line.

"If you're planning on stealing those bananas you should at least hide them in your pants." She looked pointedly at the bunch of bananas still in my hand, then raised one eyebrow with mock suspicion.

I placed the bananas on the counter. Her smile went on like a light bulb and caught me by surprise again, just as it had at the Beef Tucuman. More than anything, I wanted to reach out over the counter and touch her cheek. I took a deep breath and shoved my hands in my pockets to keep them from betraying me. "Couldn't hide them in my pants," I said. "That's where I hid the frozen cauliflower."

She tilted her head and with a devilish little smile she said, "I can see why you'd say it was cold today.

I paid cash and left, still holding the change in my hand. Carla didn't recognize me. She would be fine. Like Chen said, what did she see in me anyway?

I had a lot to straighten out. I needed to get used to a new life and do it without forgetting the previous one. Carla needed to get used to a new life too, and I figured she would be better able to start that new life without me.

Walking home, I again thought of what Wilde had said, "No man is rich enough to buy back his past," but I was looking forward now. Everything was out in front of me. My future was as a "Purveyor of Fine Antiquities."

I also thought about Laverick's suggestion. She wanted me to find other Gnomes from the most wanted list and bring them out into the light of day, but in some ways, working with the police was no different from working with the River Pirates. They don't let you quit, and they can enforce that rule because, after you've worked with them for a while, they know what you've done. So I decided to stay in between, and maybe I'd stir the pot a little once in a while to keep life from getting too stale.

As I crossed the river, a buzzcar slammed past at twice the speed limit, leaving a roaring echo in my ears. I realized with a smile that I had the money now to go to Jolie's Teckbay and buy a buzzcar buzzer that would bring buzzcars down to earth. Everyone needs a hobby.

Clifford Royal Johns lives in the Chicago area, and designs integrated circuits. His stories have been published in science fiction, mystery, and mainstream magazines and anthologies. WALKING SHADOW is his first novel.

ALSO FROM GRAND MAL PRESS

Animal Kingdom

by Iain Rob Wright

Aside from being freakishly tall, Joe is just an ordinary divorcee taking his son, Danny, to the zoo for his weekend of custody. Everything is going great until a bizarre snake attack sends everybody in the zoo running for cover. It isn't long before Joe realizes that there is a lot more going on than a simple snake attack. And if the hungry lions and monkeys outside the door have anything to say about it, there is more bloodshed to come. All of the world's animals are attacking, and man is now on the bottom of the food chain.

Available in paperback and all ebook formats.
ISBN: 978-1937727048

"Cuddle up to this novel and it might rip your throat out. A fun, thrilling read!" — David T. Wilbanks, Co-author of Dead Earth: The Vengeance Road

ALSO FROM GRAND MAL PRESS

Last Stand In A Dead Land

by Eric S. Brown

A small band of survivors is on the run during the zombie apocalypse. Led by a mysterious man with an arsenal of deadly military weapons, they must work together to stay alive. In a desperate attempt to locate other survivors, they find sanctuary in a lone farmhouse, only to discover the surrounding woods hold more dangers than just bloodthirsty undead. Featuring Sasquatch, roving rotters, and even more surprises, Last Stand in a Dead Land is an explosion of cross genre action that will leave you wanting more.

Available in paperback and all ebook formats.
ISBN: 9780982945971

"Last Stand in a Dead Land throws everything at you at a non-stop pace. Eric S. Brown's latest monster-mash is one of his best yet!" - The Horror Fiction Review

"Brown delivers exactly what he promises, with a storyteller's heart--unless some creature ate it first."
- Scott Nicholson, author of They Hunger.

ALSO FROM GRAND MAL PRESS

DARKER THAN NOIR

When a mundane mystery needs solving, you call a private detective. But when the mystery involves ghosts, demons, zombies, monsters, mystical serial killers, and other supernatural elements, you call the detectives in this collection. They'll venture into the darkness and hopefully come back out alive. Just remember, they get paid expenses up front, and what they uncover, you might not like. Featuring tales from seasoned vets and up-and-coming talent, the game is afoot in a world that is Darker Than Noir.

ISBN: 9780982945957

Available in paperback and all ebook formats.

"Gritty crime stories just the way I like them: supernatural!" -David T. Wilbanks, co-author of Dead Earth: The Vengeance Road

ALSO FROM GRAND MAL PRESS

DEAD THINGS

by Matt Darst

Nearly two decades have passed since the fall of the United States. And the rise of the church to fill the void. Nearly twenty years since Ian Sumner lost his father. And the dead took to the streets to dine on the living. Now Ian and a lost band of survivors are trapped in the wilderness, miles from safety. Pursued by madmen and monsters, they unravel the secrets of the plague...and walk the line of heresy. Ian and this troop need to do more than just survive. More than ever, they must learn to live.

Dead Things has been called “an amalgam of Clerks and everything Crichton and Zombieland.”

ISBN: 978-1-937727-10-9

Available in paperback and all ebook formats.

“Dead Things a first-rate triumph. Darst is taking the zombie novel in a really cool new direction.”
-Joe McKinney, author of *Dead City* and *Apocalypse of the Dead*

“A first-class zombie story which takes place in a beautifully realized post-apocalyptic world. Highly recommended!” - David Moody, author of *Autumn*

ALSO FROM GRAND MAL PRESS

THE FLESH OF FALLEN ANGELS

BY R. THOMAS RILEY & ROY C. BOOTH

It's the eve of The Ripening as Gibson Blount discovers the secret history of an ancient race and the true outcome of Lucifer's fall. Now, the fallen angel, Azazel, has horrific plans for Blount's town...and the world. With the help of a local priest, a prostitute, an orphan, historical figure William Quantrill, and one of God's chief angels, Blount must dig for truth and unearth secrets woven deeply within Time itself to uncover a supernatural plot put into motion by the Church to punish the Roanoke Puritans. The War in Heaven has been lost and the flesh of fallen angels hangs in the balance. An alternative 1860's history Weird Western, The Flesh of Fallen Angels is filled with fast-paced action, intrigue, and good-versus-evil what-ifs.

ISBN: 978-1937727130

Available in paperback and all ebook formats.

"Booth and Riley drag us kicking and screaming into a world of nightmares. A thrilling read!"
- Iain Rob Wright, author of Animal Kingdom

GRAND MAL
PRESS